Blue
Roses

Sharon C.
Cooper

Book Cover Design: By-Dezine, Venisha Simpson

Editor: E. Claudette Freeman

Published in the United States by: Amaris Publishing LLC

ISBN: 0-9855254-4-6
ISBN-13: 978-0-9855254-4-6

Dear Reader,

Where most women would welcome love from a wealthy, good-looking man, Chicago-based investment manager, Dallas Marcel, is not one of them. She will never let a man control her life again. That includes handsome entrepreneur, Tyler Hollister. Dallas is on track to making partner and she's not letting anything or anyone get in her way. But when her life is put in danger, and a Ponzi scheme ignites a SEC investigation of her firm, she realizes the one man she'd banned from her heart, might be the only one who can save her career and her life.

Tall, dark, and handsome, Tyler Hollister can have any woman he wants, but he only wants one - Dallas. When he starts talking marriage, she breaks things off between them, claiming she doesn't want a romantic entanglement to hinder her plight to making partner. A chance meeting, six months later, brings them face to face and Tyler soon realizes the intense sexual attraction they once shared is stronger than ever. But he swore he was done with her. Except he finds out her life is in danger, and his protective instincts take over. Can he save her life without losing his heart … again?

I have a passion for reading books that are a part of a series, and now I find that I enjoy writing them as well. Join me as I introduce you to Tyler, Dallas, Quinn, Skylar and Harmony in the first book of the Reunited Series.

Enjoy!

Sharon C. Cooper

Chapter One

"Man, where are you?"

"I'm on my way." Tyler Hollister pinned his cell phone between his shoulder and his ear as he fumbled for his keys on his way out of the dentist office.

"You were supposed to be here a half-an-hour ago."

"Q, I'm sorry. Is the meeting over?"

"Nah, but I don't know how much longer I can stall for you."

Tyler glanced at his Breguet watch and hurried to his truck. He knew how much Quinn, his best friend and business partner hated meetings. "Okay, give me ten minutes. My appointment took longer than I thought, but I'm ... *damn*, I'd know that sexy walk anywhere." He stopped in his tracks when his eyes zoned in on the beautiful woman on the other side of the street.

"What? Ty, dude what's up?"

He continued to observe as she made her way to the middle of the semi-crowded block in downtown Milwaukee weaving around people along the way. True to form, she caught the eye of a few guys passing. Tyler chuckled when they turned and enjoyed one more view once she'd passed. She always did have that effect on men. It wasn't until she stopped to throw something in the trash, that he knew for sure it was her. Dallas Marcel, his ex-girlfriend.

"Q, I'll call you back." He disconnected not giving Quinn a chance to respond, and shoved the phone into his pocket. Tyler moved in her direction, stepping around a broken orange and white road barrier sign that was lying in the center of the sidewalk.

He stole a quick glance at Dallas as she came to a stop at the corner to wait for the light to change. Not wanting to miss the opportunity to say hello, he leaned against the brick building to his right, ensuring that she would have to walk past him once the light turned green.

Still gorgeous. Tall, fierce, and dressed to the nines. He loved it when she wore her long, thick hair piled high on top of her head, the way she had it now, with a few curly tendrils hanging down. The look complimented her perfectly sculpted face and revealed her long, sexy neck.

He cursed under his breath and looked away. He didn't want to still be attracted to the most bullheaded woman he'd ever met. Too independent for her own good, but one of the best investment managers in Chicago, she was a woman on a mission. Her goal in life, or as he saw it, obsession, was to make partner at her firm – which was why she turned down his marriage proposal. According to her, she didn't have room in her life for a *serious* relationship, despite the fact that they were perfect together, in every way.

"She threw what we had away, so why am I standing here just to say hello?" He mumbled and slipped a piece of gum into his mouth, not understanding his need to see her again.

His cell phone chirped twice signaling a text message, and he pulled it out of his pocket, and scanned the screen. *No need to come - postponed the rest of the meeting until next week. Headed to Bradley Rd. to check on the guys. Q*

Good. One less meeting. Tyler deposited his cell into the inside pocket of his suit jacket and adjusted his tie. As a real estate developer, it seemed most of his days were spent in meetings, reading over contracts, or dealing with building inspectors.

He pushed away from the building and rolled his shoulders just as the light turned green, and Dallas stepped off the curb. Finally, he'd be face-to-face with the woman he'd tried hard to forget, but couldn't stop thinking about. He took a few steps when suddenly their eyes met, and a sensuous light passed between them. All of the sexual energy, passion and love he once felt for her came rushing back to the surface, and his heart hammered double-time in response. *Damn.*

Dallas's pace slowed, but she continued across the street, her magnetic brown eyes held his attention, immobilizing him. Less than twenty feet from him and it was as if he were seeing her for the first time. A raging fire grew in the pit of his stomach, his hands ached to touch her, and all it had taken was that one look. *This is not cool.* He quickly pulled his eyes away and looked everywhere but at her, feeling the need to regroup. *I'm supposed to be over her.*

After a long cleansing breath, he looked up again just in time to see a car barreling toward her.

"Oh shit. Watch out!" he shouted, and then sprinted in her direction.

Screeeeechhhhhh! Boom!

"Nooo!" He yelled as her body bounced off the hood of the car. He slid to a stop before he reached the corner, shock kept him from moving forward. It wasn't until the four-door dark sedan sped away in the opposite direction that he moved into action.

"Excuse me, excuse me." He pushed his way through the swarm of people. An icy fear crawled up his spine when he saw her lifeless body on the hard pavement, a puddle of blood   painted the ground near her head. "Oh my God," he whispered and fell to his knees. "Dallas. Baby…" He caressed her cheek, afraid to move her. His heart pounded against his chest, and beads of sweat surfaced on his forehead as panic rioted within him. "Get some help over here!"

Time ceased as a haunting sense of foreboding wrapped around him when he checked and found her pulse was weak. He needed to do something, but thankfully, in the far distance he could hear the sirens. "Hold on, baby, hold on."

****

Tyler paced the length of the waiting room battling the emotions wreaking havoc throughout his body. It all seemed so unreal - seeing Dallas in Milwaukee for the first time in six months, and then having to lie about being her husband in order to ride in the ambulance with her. And if that weren't enough, he had to relive it all just moments ago when he was questioned by the police. *God, I can't believe this happened.* He ran a nervous hand down his face, and then jammed it into his front pants pocket. One minute he was admiring Dallas from a distance and in the next moment he witnessed her being run down by an idiot driver.

He dropped down hard onto a nearby paisley printed chair and rested his head against the cold, dingy wall. Through half-opened lids, he glanced around the sparsely furnished room. With small groups of people scattered about, he sat trying to tune out the chatter going on around him.

Mixed feelings rattled in his chest knowing he'd have to face Dallas soon. Sure he was glad to have spotted her hours ago, but when their eyes connected, and all of the old feelings returned, he knew he wasn't over her. Despite that fact, he couldn't go back. She'd been the only woman to reject him, and the night she walked out of his life, a part of him left with her. Now here he was, pretending to be her husband in order to get word on her condition. He grunted at the irony of it all.

"Mr. Marcel?" A doctor called out several times before it dawned on Tyler that it was he the doctor was calling. Tyler jumped up from his seat.

"It's Hollister. Tyler Hollister. My wife uses her maiden name."

"Oh, okay. Well, I'm Doctor Malone," he said as they shook hands.

"How is she?"

"She's a very lucky lady." The doctor, short enough for Tyler to see the bald spot on top of his head, glanced at the chart in his hand. He pushed up the glasses that were perched on the end of his nose. "Your wife has a mild concussion and a broken leg. She had a collapsed lung which we were able to repair. And though her left shoulder and ribs are seriously bruised, there's no permanent damage. You're going to notice a few cuts on her face and neck, but they should heal without much scarring. It'll take a few weeks, but I have no reason to doubt that she'll make a full recovery."

Tyler blew out a shaky breath and wiped his forehead with his shirt sleeve. Part of him wanted to turn and leave the building now that he knew Dallas would be okay, but the other part of him wouldn't let him move.

"Mr. Hollister," the doctor continued, "your wife is very dehydrated and her blood pressure is dangerously low. Has she ever had a problem with her blood pressure?" He removed his glasses and stuck them into his jacket pocket.

"Not as far as I know."

"Well, we're going to continue to monitor her over the next couple of days, get some fluids into her, and see how it goes."

"So what would cause those things?"

"Exhaustion and malnutrition would be my first guess."

4

Her workaholic lifestyle must have caught up with her. "Uh, can I see her?"

"Well, she's still—"

"Please. I need to see her."

Moments later, Tyler pushed the door open to Dallas's hospital room. He eased in and stood just inside the entrance while the nurse finished checking the monitors. "You can move closer," she said on her way out.

"Thank you." Tyler watched the door close, and then let his gaze travel around the sterile space. The small window donned with only horizontal blinds across the room didn't seem large enough to bring in a sufficient amount of sunlight, while out of four pale yellow walls, only one held a painting - a boring landscape painting at that. He had never been a fan of hospitals, and looking around he wondered how patients recovered in such a dreary space. He made a mental note to get some flowers and balloons in there.

Tyler shifted his attention to Dallas and moved closer to her bedside. He assessed her motionless body covered with a pristine white sheet and hated the sight of the machines and all of the tubes connected to her. His heart was beating so fast and loud, he was sure the people in the next room could hear it. Why was he so anxious? On second thought, he knew why. He prided himself on being a man of action and being able to fix just about anything or any situation, but this ... this he couldn't fix.

Standing by her side, he noticed the dark bruise near her right temple and an uneasy frisson flooded through him with thoughts of how this could have turned out. *She's a very lucky lady.* He remembered the doctor saying.

He had noted earlier how thin she'd gotten. No surprise there since she was known to go an entire day without eating in the name of closing a deal. He looked at her intently. Despite the small bandage covering the right side of her cinnamon brown cheek, she was still a beauty. Her long eyelashes rested on her high cheekbones as she slept, and he allowed his hand to travel lightly over her forehead, moving thick, dark hair away from her face. "Girl, you scared me to death," he whispered.

Dallas's monitors beeped erratically as her distressed moans filled the space. Tyler straightened. She thrashed against the pillows struggling against the light hold he now had on her arm. "My baby!" she cried. "Please save my baby!"

What the hell?

A nurse rushed in, pushed a few buttons on the machine, and laid a reassuring hand on Dallas's shoulder as she soothed her with her words. Tyler watched as Dallas gradually settled down.

"Is she okay?" He wanted to know once he got his own breathing under control. He wasn't sure what shook him the most - Dallas's screams or her words.

"It's not uncommon for patients to have bad dreams after a traumatic accident," the nurse said, and wrote a few things on Dallas's chart.

Save my baby. He repeated the words in his mind. *Is she pregnant? Why hadn't the doctor said anything about a baby?* He slowly backed away from the bed as shock turned into resentment. Pain squeezed his heart. She had shot him down claiming not to want any romantic entanglements. Yet, she goes and gets pregnant?

"Sir, are you okay?" The nurse stood next to him. "You don't look so good. Maybe you should sit down." She directed him to the chair closest to the bed.

"I can't believe she's pregnant." His voice faded into a hushed stillness.

"Uh, sir. She isn't pregnant."

"What?"

"It was a dream. She's not pregnant."

The knot in his chest loosened. Relief flooded through him like a faucet on full blast.

"Are you going to be alright? You still don't look so good. Maybe I should get a doctor to look you over?"

"No." He shook his head. "I'm fine. It's just ... that caught me off guard."

She patted his shoulder. "I understand. But if you need anything, let me know," she said and left the room.

He couldn't believe how worked up he'd gotten. The thought of Dallas having another man's baby felt like someone had reached into his chest and snatched out his heart. He didn't even want to think about her being with another man.

Tyler slumped over. Resting his elbows on his knees, he put his face in his hands, and took a few deep breaths. *She is not my woman. She is not my woman. I need to remember, she is not my woman.*

Chapter Two

Several hours later, Dallas opened her eyes to a cool, dimly lit room, and constant beeping from the monitor at the head of the bed. She knew she was in the hospital and bits and pieces of being hit by a car were starting to come back to her as she stared up at the ceiling. *Tyler.* Had she really seen him?

Her eyes drifted shut as she attempted to fight the drowsiness that suddenly surrounded her. Never in her life had she felt so weak. *Why now? Why did this accident have to happen now?* On track to make partner at her investment firm, she had too much going on in her life to be laid up in a hospital bed staring at walls. She had worked too damn hard to let a stupid car accident keep her from accomplishing the one thing she wanted more than anything - a partnership.

Her eyes fluttered open again. This was the first time she'd noticed the colorful balloons floating above her, attached to something at the head of the bed. It was thoughtful of the nurses, assuming they were the ones who left them, but Dallas preferred to be home...in her own bed, and in her own room. If only she had the strength to move. Between whatever crap they were giving her for pain and the tight bandages around her midsection she felt like a mummy lying in an open tomb. And the thought of sneaking out was out of the question. She glanced at her elevated leg and cursed under her breath at the cast. It was only then did her gaze zone in on the lone figure sitting in the chair near the window, his eyes closed.

What's he doing here?

Tyler. The moonlight gleamed through the open blinds, casting a stunning glow around him. He looked like an angel, but Dallas knew he was far from that. He was charming, generous and the sweetest man she'd ever met, but a force to be reckoned with when it came to his business and protecting those he loved. It was his possessiveness that reminded her of a time in her past; a time when she had vowed never to let another man control her life.

Dallas fixed her eyes on his attractive face - still as *fine* as she remembered. Smooth brown skin stretched over strong cheekbones, and a neatly trimmed mustache and goatee framed his inviting mouth. With lips so irresistibly kissable, she had to steady her breathing to keep the heart rate monitor from going crazy.

As if sensing her watching him, Tyler opened his eyes. When his gentle gaze met hers, her breath caught and her heart slammed against her chest. *Oh, God. Give me strength.* Those dark, sexy eyes would forever be her weakness.

"Hey there." He rose to his full six-four height and walked to the bed. Towering over her, he swept a few strands of hair away from her face, which was something he used to do often. That small gesture alone made her feel warmth she hadn't felt in months. "How are you feeling?" His smooth, velvety voice made her body tremble. She wished she had energy and a fan, because she was pretty sure her temperature had shot up to 120 degrees in just those few short seconds.

She gazed into his eyes. After they'd broken up, there were many days she wanted to call and tell him she loved him and wanted him back, but it would've been a mistake. He wanted marriage and a family. She couldn't give him that.

Tyler leaned closer, affording her the pleasure of his fresh, masculine scent. She might've had a slight headache, but there was definitely nothing wrong with her sense of smell.

"Can I do anything for you?"

Yeah, you can move away from the bed, is what she wanted to say, his nearness wreaking havoc on her willpower – her desire to touch and kiss him was overwhelming. Instead she asked, "Can I have some water?"

"Of course." He poured her a cup from the pitcher sitting on the bedside table and brought the straw to her lips. "Anything else?"

"When can I leave?"

Tyler chuckled and stared down at her with eyes filled with compassion. "Girl, do you know what kind of condition you're in?" He communicated everything that the doctor had shared, and told her about the surgery, which she didn't remember. Within minutes, she'd fallen back to sleep.

The next day Dallas awakened, again surprised to see Tyler sitting in a nearby corner. This time he was hunched over a small table with files spread out, talking quietly on his cell phone. She could watch him all day. His self-confidence, commanding presence, and take charge attitude were just a few of many things that had attracted her to him. After several moments, he looked over and saw that she was awake and quickly ended his call.

"Ah, so sleeping beauty awakens." He ambled over and sat in the chair next to the bed.

"You didn't have to stop what you were doing," Dallas rasped.

Tyler shrugged. "Just taking care of business, but it can wait. How do you feel or are you tired of everyone asking you that?"

She grunted and gave a slight shrug, vaguely remembering much of anything from the past couple of days.

"I talked with Tim and Simone yesterday," he said, leaning on the bed. "Simone of course wanted to get on the next plane out here, but her doctor has threatened to put her on bed rest in light of a few concerns. And before you ask, she's okay. I can't believe she's five months pregnant, seems like just yesterday they announced they were having a baby."

"Yes it does," Dallas said, thinking about her best friend and happy she was living the life she'd always dreamed of.

Tim Hollister, Tyler's brother, married Simone, Dallas's best friend over a year ago and moved to San Diego. Closer than most sisters, Dallas missed her like crazy and at the moment, wished Simone was the one sitting next to her instead of Tyler. Being near him made everything within Dallas come alive, and she hated it. They'd been apart for months, and she couldn't understand why the sexual energy was just as strong as when they parted.

Her thoughts were interupted when the door swung open.

"Well, I see you're awake," the doctor said to Dallas when he walked in. He nodded at Tyler, and then turned back to Dallas. "How do you feel?"

"Like I've been hit by a truck."

He smiled. "Almost."

"When can I leave?" She couldn't tell which was worse, the shortness of breath or the pounding in her head, but she knew she didn't want to be there. "I guess I should be thankful ... I'm alive, but I don't know how ... much more of this I can take. Everything hurts."

"I'll have the nurse bring you something for the pain," the doctor said. "As far as you leaving - not just yet. But, since your husband agreed to take good care of you, I guess I can release you in about two days. Right now, try to get some rest. I'll check on you a little later."

The doctor was barely out of the room before Dallas cut her eyes at Tyler and said, "Husband?" Each time she spoke she felt like her chest would explode.

He stood over her. Noticing her discomfort, he caressed her cheek, immediately making her feel better. But she wanted to know what was going on.

"We can talk about this when you're feeling better."

"Now."

He released a loud sigh. "Okay. If you stop talking and relax, I'll tell you everything."

She nodded.

"Dallas, the only way they would give me any information on your condition, is if I were a relative. So I said the first thing that came to mind."

She squinted at him, trying hard not to snap, her voice raspy. "You couldn't tell them... you were my brother?"

"Baby, I didn't think of that."

She stared at him until a soft knock at the door drew their attention.

"Hi. I'm Officer Logan, may I come in?"

Tyler moved forward. "Sure, I'm Tyler Hollister." He shook the officer's extended hand. "May I help you?"

"I was hoping to ask Ms. Marcel a few questions about the accident." He walked further into the room. His deep set eyes and strong facial features made him look authoritarian. At least six-three, with wide shoulders that tapered down to a narrow waist and 200 plus pounds of leanness, Dallas was sure criminals submitted to whatever he commanded.

"I'm not sure now is a good time. Besides, we both have already talked to cops."

"It's okay." Dallas gingerly eased the covers up over her chest. "What do you ... want to know?" The officer, who questioned her the day before, told her that although witnesses were consistent with the color and make of the car that hit her, none could remember seeing plates on the vehicle.

"I promise this won't take long." The officer pulled out his notepad. "But first, I have some conflicting information so let me ask you. What's the relationship between you two?"

Good question, Dallas thought. She shared a long look with Tyler before saying, "We're friends." Tyler nodded a confirmation. Despite his good reason for telling the hospital staff they were married, she definitely didn't want to give that information to a cop.

The officer raised an eyebrow, looked at Tyler, and then back at her apparently noticing the silent exchanged between them.

"Alright." He jotted something down on his pad. "Ms. Marcel, I understand you live in Chicago. What are you doing in Milwaukee?"

"I have clients here."

"What type of work do you do?"

"I'm an investment manager. I come here periodically ... to meet with clients, which is where ... I was headed before the accident."

The officer asked questions for nearly ten minutes and Dallas didn't know how much longer she could stay awake. Besides that, she felt like she'd run a marathon with all of the talking.

"I think that's enough for today," Tyler said.

"Last question. Can you think of any reason why someone would want to hurt you?"

"What?" She and Tyler asked in unison.

The officer held up a hand. "Hear me out. Mr. Hollister, I didn't see this in your report, but a witness said the crash looked intentional. And since the accident was a hit and run, I have to ask these questions. You'd be surprised how domestic disputes turn in—"

"What are you implying?" Tyler asked and moved closer to the officer. "Is there something you're not telling us?"

"I'm not implying anything. I'm just asking questions."

"Go on," Dallas said. She didn't know what the witness saw, but she wasn't currently in a relationship and couldn't imagine anyone ramming a car into her on purpose.

"Did you have an argument with anyone lately?"

"No."

"Is something going on at work? Did a client lose a lot of money?"

She shook her head. "No."

"Are you in a relationship that might not be going well, causing somebody to seek revenge?"

Dallas popped up in bed. "No, of course not!" The quick move made her clutch her aching ribs and she fell back against the pillows.

"All right, that's enough. She's in no condition to be badgered like this."

"Sorry. I'm just doing my job." He closed his notepad and reached into his pocket. "I'll leave my card, in case you think of anything." He backed his way to the door. "I apologize if I upset you, but we have to make sure we check everything out."

When the door swung shut behind him, Tyler turned to her. "Are you okay?"

She nodded. There was no way the accident could've been deliberate, *could it?* As far as she knew, she didn't have any enemies.

"Why don't you try to get some sleep?"

She slid further down under the covers. "I don't know what hurts the most, my head or my ribs," she moaned. Maybe taking it upon herself to decrease her medication wasn't the best idea.

"Let me get the nurse so she can give you something for the pain." He turned to leave, but she reached out and touched his arm.

"No. Don't. I'm tired of ... drug-induced sleep. Just stay with me."

Tyler leaned against the bed and cradled her hand. "I'm not going anywhere. Now close those beautiful eyes and get some rest."

****

The next morning Tyler sat in his home office trying to review the documents that Quinn had sent over for his review. But with his sister-in-law, Simone, on the telephone yapping in his ear about how he should let Dallas move in with him, he wasn't getting very far.

"Simone, I can't," he said for the third time. He placed the unread report on his desk, leaned back in his chair and glanced around his spacious office. His suburban home was his pride and joy, but his office provided a sense of calm that was often needed after willing and dealing all day. He noted the curtains on the wall-to-wall windows had been opened, letting in much needed sunlight for the plants his housekeeper insisted he needed.

"Please, Tyler. Who's going to help her? You know she's not going to agree to come to San Diego and stay with us. And my doctor has already told me no more traveling. Dallas will be all alone in Chicago. Just let her stay with you. You have more than enough space in that mini-mansion. At least let her stay until she gets back on her feet," Simone begged. "It's only for six weeks."

Only six weeks. Tyler loved his sister-in-law, but right now she was asking a lot. He had already spent too much time with Dallas. There were moments he had to remind himself that she was his ex, not his woman. He stood and walked over to the floor-to-ceiling built-in bookcases near the fireplace as he half-listened. Replacing several construction books he'd used days ago he asked, "Why can't she stay with one of her sisters?"

"The only sister Dallas still has in Milwaukee is, Harmony. She can barely take care of herself. And when I talked with her sister that lives in L.A, she said there was no way she could get away right now. And her oldest sister is stationed in Germany, so that rules her out."

Tyler hesitated. "I don't know, Simone." He leaned against the mantle and gave her his full attention. "I don't think her staying here will be a good idea. Besides, you know Dallas. There is no way she'll agree to this type of arrangement."

Sure he was concerned about her well being, but after spending days with her, he knew he wouldn't be able to handle being around her much longer. They had a history. A very passionate history that he didn't want to risk revisiting.

"Well, she doesn't have a choice. With a broken leg, she can't drive, let alone maneuver around her house alone. She needs you!" Simone's voice rose with every word.

She needs me? Yeah right. Tyler thought about the many times Dallas had told him flat out that she didn't need him. She never wanted him to do anything for her.

"Tyler," his brother got on the line, "is there anything you can do? I know Simone is not going to let this go until she knows that Dallas is going to be taken care of."

A moment passed before Tyler spoke. He still remembered the first time he laid eyes on Dallas. She projected a powerful energy that sucked the breath out of him. She could walk into a room and attract attention from both men and women. The men wanted to take her home and the women hated her at first glance. She oozed poise and self-confidence from every pore of her body. If it were up to him, he would've spent every waken hour with her. A frustrated sigh past through his lips before he said, "Tim...I thought I was over her. But I don't think I am. I won't put myself through this again. And I can't believe you're even asking me to consider it. You, more than anyone, know what I've been through with her."

"I know, I know." Tim said. "Ty, will you really be able to let her go back to Chicago, by herself? Aren't you going to worry about her just as much as Simone? Why not just let her stay with you, at least until she can get back on her feet?"

"Why don't I just get her a nurse? I can have someone at her place by the time she's released from the hospital."

"And you wouldn't worry about her?"

He was right. Tyler knew he'd be consumed with thoughts of Dallas, wondering if she was okay, if she was eating, or if she was in any pain. Even though she drove him nuts while they were dating, he missed her like crazy these last six months. But could he live in the same house with her for weeks? "I don't know, Tim," he walked back to his desk and reclaimed his seat.

"Just think about it," his brother said.

"All right." Tyler disconnected, leaned back in his chair and closed his eyes, enjoying the stillness in the room. He had once dreamed of the day when he and Dallas could live under the same roof. This wasn't how he envisioned it. He thought they'd be married and maybe have a child by now. If only she wasn't so stubborn and obsessed with making partner, they'd be together.

Chapter Three

"Tyler, I don't care what you say. I'm not going home with you!" Dallas spat. "I think you're taking this *pretend* husband thing a little too far."

Dressed and ready to leave the hospital, she had every intention of going back to Chicago. But between Simone's call, telling her that going home alone wasn't a good idea, and Tyler's insistence for her to stay with him, she wasn't sure what to do. Her head pounded and she still felt weak, but no way was she going home with him.

"I'm not letting you go back to Chicago in this condition."

She glared at him. "What do you mean you're not letting me? I'm a grown ass woman, capable of taking care of myself. I don't need you or Simone telling me what I can or cannot do."

"Dallas, you can hardly walk and you wince every time you move. How are you going to take care of yourself?"

She hated when he got like this. Thinking he knew what was best for her. It didn't help that he was standing across the room looking confident and gorgeous in that tailored dark brown suit. And he probably intentionally wore her favorite paisley tie today.

She rolled her eyes at him and leaned back against the pillow. Getting around would be hard, but not impossible. She had to get back to work. Besides, moving in with him would be too much of a distraction.

"I'm going to make some other arrangements," she said. "I'll call Harmony to see if I can stay with her for a little while."

"Simone said that your sister can barely take care of herself. Besides, don't you think it would be a little cramped in her studio apartment?"

Dallas didn't respond. What was she thinking? Staying with Harmony wasn't an option. Her self-absorbed sister was probably shacked up with some loser anyway. There had to be some other place she could go or something else she could do. Working and attending meetings weren't going to be a problem; thanks to technology. Walking around on a busted up leg, was another story. She gingerly moved her legs over the edge of the bed. The smallest movement seemed to take all the energy she had.

"Dallas." Tyler sat on the bed next to her and took her hand. "I don't want to argue with you, and I'm not trying to cause you any more stress. Like you, I want you back on your feet and well. That's all."

She studied him, surprised by his kindness through this whole ordeal, considering they hadn't parted on the best of terms. Thankfully he didn't realize how irresistible he was. How would she be able to focus on getting better and getting her work done with him around?

"Tyler, I appreciate the offer, it's just…"

"It's just what?"

"I … I don't think it's a good idea," she said, her words barely audible.

A slow, cocky smile spread across his face. "Ohhh, so now I get it. You're afraid you won't be able to control yourself." He stood facing her and folded his arms across his wide chest.

Dallas waved him off. "Oh, whatever. Don't go getting a big head, 'cause you ain't all that." She lied.

"All right, ready to go?" The nurse interrupted and rolled the wheelchair into the room. "Since your husband signed your release papers and the doctor already talked to you about your follow-up visits, you're free to leave."

Dallas looked up at Tyler. Overwhelmed feelings of gratitude welled up in her chest. What would she have done without him this past week? Maybe she'd stay with him for a few days until she could make other arrangements. They were adults. Surely she could live under the same roof with him.

"Thanks for taking care of everything," she said.

He bent and rested his hands on the bed on each side of her, bringing them face to face. The smile in his eyes contained a sumptuous flame. "My pleasure."

Ugh, you're not helping here, she cringed. *I can't go backwards. We can't go back.*

"I'm going to get the truck. I'll meet you out front."

"Oh, before I forget," the nurse said and held out an envelope to Dallas. "A guy dropped this off for you. I told him he could come in and see you, but he said he didn't want to disturb you."

Dallas opened the envelope and pulled out a beautiful card with blue roses gracing the front. *Sorry to hear you've been in the hospital. Get well soon.*

She frowned. "It's not signed."

"Let me see it," Tyler said, and Dallas handed him the card. "Did this person ask for Dallas, or just give you the card?"

Dallas eyed him suspiciously, noting the concerned look on his face. Ever since the visit from the cop, he'd been glued to her. "It's just a card, Tyler. I doubt if there's anything behind it."

The nurse shrugged. "He asked me if I was going in to see Dallas Marcel. I said, yes. And then he said, 'Can you give this to her?'"

"It's probably someone from the Boys and Girls Club. Some of the other volunteers have sent cards and well wishes." Dallas said. A wave of nausea caused her to slump against the pillows. Though the doctors had cut back on her medication, the pills still wreaked havoc on her system.

"What's wrong?" Tyler stooped in front her. Brushing hair away from her face, he let the back of his hand graze her cheek. Dallas wanted to lean into his caressing touch, but she stopped herself. No matter how sweet he was, they were no longer a couple. She needed to remember that.

"My stomach's a little queasy."

"Do you feel like you have to throw up?" The nurse inquired.

Dallas closed her eyes, only to reopen them again to see Tyler's brows knitted together with worry.

"I'm okay. Give me a minute."

"I don't know. Maybe we should have them check you out one last time before we leave."

"I'm fine. Besides, it's time for me to get out of here." She lifted herself up, but didn't feel a whole lot better.

"Well, if you're sure you're okay." He studied her a minute longer. Then he did something that caught her totally off guard. With the lightest touch, he lifted her chin and his soft lips covered hers. At first the kiss was sweet and gentle but soon there was a possessive hunger behind it that sent shock waves surging through her body. When his tongue found hers and they tangled to a familiar beat, she wrapped her arms around his neck and returned his kiss with uncontrolled abandon. She groaned and didn't care who heard her. She hadn't been kissed this thoroughly since the last time he kissed her, months ago. But seconds later, Tyler pulled back leaving her panting and her lips longing for more.

"I'll meet you guys at the entrance," he said and walked away.

Dallas's eyes followed him out the door, and then locked on the smiling nurse before she looked away. *Damn, this living arrangement is going to be harder than I thought.*

****

Chicago, Illinois

Large windows were the first thing Mark Darley noticed when he stepped into his new office on the 50th floor. He knew the building would offer some spectacular views, but he had no idea he'd experience them first hand from his new corner office.

With his hands in his tailored pants pocket, he ambled over to the windows and exhaled a long sigh. It had taken fifteen long years for his vision to become a reality. He had finally made it. He wanted to live someplace fast paced and prestigious, like New York, Los Angeles, or Chicago. So when the top engineering firm in the country made him an offer he couldn't refuse, he went for it. Now here he was, in downtown Chicago, prepared to start living the life he'd always dreamed of.

"Mr. Darley, I put your schedule for this week on your desk," his new assistant said. "The first few days are full of meetings to get you acclimated to the projects that you'll be responsible for, and the people you'll be working with."

So caught up in his thoughts he had forgotten she was in the room. "Okay. Thanks, Liz. I'll take a look at it. Oh, and please call me, Mark."

She smiled and walked to the door. "Okay, Mark. I'll leave you to get settled. If you have questions or need me for anything else, press one on your telephone."

"Thanks." Mark returned her smile. "I'll do that."

His cell phone rang after the door closed behind his secretary. "Hello."

"Hey, Mark, I've made contact. She was released from the hospital. Did you know she was married?"

"Married?" Nah, I didn't know." He walked over to his large desk and leaned against it. "This definitely puts a wrench in my plans."

Chapter Four

Stupid, stupid, stupid, I can't believe I kissed her. What was I thinking? The moment his lips touched hers, he knew he was in trouble. That brief contact made him want more, but he'd promised himself he wouldn't travel down that road again. Flirting with her was one thing, and helping her at the hospital was another, but anything more than that would be suicidal.

He stood over Dallas and watched her sleep. Having her in his home, he couldn't help but remember what they once shared. How could something so right, go so wrong? They were made for one another. Both were ambitious, they enjoyed the same things, sex was off the charts, and when they weren't arguing, life was great. He never loved a woman the way he had once loved her. Months after they'd parted, he had held out hope that she'd be back. He'd longed to hear her say she'd made a mistake and that they belonged together, but nothing. She never called.

Tyler exhaled an exhausted sigh and left the room. It would be hard as hell to stay away from her while living together, but whatever it took.... *Aw hell, I shouldn't have let Simone and Tim talk me into this setup.*

He walked downstairs to his office and took a seat at his desk. Now really wasn't a good time for a houseguest, especially since he'd let his live-in housekeeper have the next two months off to spend time in Florida with her new grandchild. He needed a plan. Not only did he need someone who could keep Dallas company while he was working or traveling, he also needed a voice of reason nearby. Dallas in his home was a temptation he planned to fight.

Tyler grabbed his phone and dialed. He knew the perfect person for the job, his twin sister, Skylar. A month ago her husband, Hadrian, was deployed to Afghanistan, prompting her and their daughter to move back to Milwaukee to be closer to family. Since their daughter was spending the summer with her husband's parents in Tennessee, Skylar was the perfect person for what Tyler had in mind.

After several rings her voice mail picked up. "Sky, I need a favor."

****

Dallas opened her eyes slowly to the irritating sounds of a bird chirping just outside the window. *God, please make it stop.* Her body ached, and her head throbbed. The last thing she needed was a chipper bird singing at the top of its lungs. *I'd give up a month's salary to have something to throw at that damn window.*

A hint of daylight filtered in through the blinds, alerting her that it was morning. It had been three days since she'd left the hospital, and though she felt better, she was anxious to get back to feeling like her old self. She didn't know what she would've done without Tyler and Skylar catering to her every need - especially Skylar. Thanks to her, Dallas and Tyler rarely had a moment alone, which was fine with Dallas. She wanted nothing more than to stay clear of the one man who'd been the reoccurring star of her nightly dreams.

Dallas struggled to get off of the bed, grunting with every move thanks to sore ribs and a stupid cast on her leg. It wasn't until she reached for her crutches that she screamed out in pain. She grabbed her side willing herself not to cry. The sting from her ribs shot through the rest of her body causing her to collapse back onto the bed. *Okay, don't cry. Don't cry.*

The bedroom door swung opened, and her body jolted in surprise, causing more pain.

"Girl, are you okay?" Skylar rushed in, pulling the belt on her long satin robe tighter.

Tyler's twin looked wide awake considering it was still fairly early; and in spite of her tousled hair, and disheveled appearance. Dallas still marveled at how Skylar's oval-shaped face with cocoa-brown skin, dark intense eyes and full lips were identical to Tyler's.

"What's going on? I heard you scream."

Dallas held her side and tried to bare the discomfort. She was glad to see Skylar, but right now she needed to get to the bathroom. "I moved too quickly and my body reminded me that I'm not healed yet. I didn't mean to wake you."

"No problem. I wasn't asleep. What can I do to help?"

"Can you hand me my crutches? I need to get to the bathroom, like now."

"Mother Nature calls, huh?" Skylar grabbed the crutches and helped Dallas to the bathroom, closing the door behind her. "I'm going down to the kitchen. Do you want anything?"

"No thanks."

"Okay, be right back."

A short while later Dallas exited the bathroom, surprised to see a tray of breakfast items at the foot of the bed. "Skylar, you didn't have to do this."

"Yes I did. I was starving." She smirked and bit into a slice of toast smeared with grape jelly. "There's enough here for both of us. I'm sure you're hungry since you slept most of the day yesterday."

"No, I'm okay. A little thirsty, but I ... don't feel like eating." Winded from moving around, Dallas realized her breathing wasn't back to normal. This whole laid up and barely able to move around mess was driving her nuts.

Skylar helped her onto the bed and handed her a glass of orange juice. With her hands on her hips, she stood back and smiled. "Even under these circumstances, it's really good to see you again."

"Yeah, you too. I've missed our talks and our laughs. Are you still crazy?"

Skylar laughed out loud. "Only when I have to be." She winked and moved the breakfast tray closer to Dallas. "Maybe you should eat something, especially since that bossy brother of mine will be in here soon and wonder why you haven't eaten."

Dallas knew she spoke the truth. Tyler practically force fed her at the hospital, telling her that it was the only way she'd regain some of her strength. "So where is that brother of yours?"

"Downstairs in his office where he's been practically all night working." She handed Dallas a bowl of fruit from the tray, grabbed the other for herself, and sat on the edge of the bed. "He said he'd be up before he leaves."

"Okay." They talked and caught up with one another while eating their light breakfast. Where Tyler was more serious, Skylar was the opposite. Dallas found herself laughing and holding her side throughout the conversation.

"Do you mind handing me my laptop? Tyler put it over there in the sitting area."

"Is it a good idea for you to start back working so soon?" Skylar asked. She put their empty bowls on the tray, before getting the computer case and handing it to Dallas. "You still look a little tired."

"I am, but I've been out of commission long enough."

Skylar grabbed the prescription bottles sitting on top of the nightstand.

"Is it time for you to take any of these?"

"Probably, but that stuff puts me to sleep, and at this rate I'll never get any work done," Dallas said as her fingers flew across the keys on her laptop. It would take her forever to get through all of her emails.

"What the hell do you think you're doing?" Tyler's deep voice roared from the doorway.

Dallas jerked her head toward the door, and took a deep breath. *It should be against the law for anyone to look that good this early in the morning.* Tyler dressed in a dark blue suit, looked like the successful businessman he was. And those eyes, his dark sexy eyes were as clear and brilliant as usual. He didn't look like he'd been up all night.

She returned her attention back to the computer screen. "Working. What are you doing this morning?" *Man he smells good,* she thought when he walked farther into the room.

"Dallas, it's too soon. You've only been out of the hospital a few days. Your body is still trying to get back to normal."

"I'm okay," she said, not looking up from her screen.

"I'm sure for the past six months you've deprived yourself of sleep and food. All I'm asking is that you take care of yourself first for a change."

"Tyler, I appreciate your concern," she finally looked at him, "but I have to get some work done."

"It's too soon."

"Shouldn't I be the one to decide that?" she asked, anger lacing each word. This was one of those times when his take-charge attitude got on her nerves.

"Oh, here we go. I'm outta here." Skylar stood, grabbed the tray and hurried toward the door, but said over her shoulder, "I guess some things haven't changed between you two."

"I thought one of the partners, William, was overseeing your accounts while you're recuperating."

"He's not me," she said. "I have clients counting on me, and though I might not be able to get around well, I can still think." She stifled a yawn, and was sure Tyler noticed. *Damn these drugs.*

He shook his head and probably would've said more, but her cell phone rang.

"I have to take this," she said glancing at her cell phone screen. "It's Bianca." Tyler glared at her for a second, and then walked out without saying another word.

"Hello."

"Hey Dallas, I'm so sorry to call you when you're still recovering"

"It's okay, Bianca. What's going on?" Dallas knew her assistant wouldn't call unless it was important.

"David is requesting that the presentation for the Nervona Group be ready by Monday."

"What?" She sat up straighter in bed, still leaning against the headboard. "We're not scheduled to meet with them for another month. What's the hurry?"

"I'm not sure, but Lydia and Carol met with David this morning and he told them to have everything ready by Monday."

Darnit, David Weisman, one of the partners and a pain in Dallas's ass, was good at demanding things despite their already hectic workload. She had just been in contact with the potential client a couple of weeks ago, and they were the ones who had requested the presentation be done next month. Her team had started pulling information together, but four days wasn't much time to get everything done.

"This is definitely going to be tight, but I should be able to pull my portion together in the next day or so. There are a few files that I'm going to need you to overnight me. Also, set up a conference call so that I can meet with the team tomorrow evening."

"No problem."

"And Bianca - thanks for the heads up. I don't know what David is up to, but I'll be calling William soon. I'll keep you posted on anything else I need."

Dallas disconnected and before she could get back to work, her cell phone rang again. Seeing that the screen read "unknown" she answered, "Dallas Marcel."

There was no response, but Dallas heard someone breathing. After several hellos, she started to hang up, but then they finally spoke.

"Keep your nose out of business that doesn't concern you."

She placed the laptop on the side of her. "What? Who is this?"

"Someone who will stop at nothing to protect what's his."

****

Tyler swiveled in his office chair and stared out the bay window behind his desk, still thinking about his conversation with Dallas. The multi-million dollar real estate deals he handled were nothing compared to dealing with her and her independence. But if he didn't look out for her wellbeing, who would? Her health sure didn't seem to be a top priority for her.

"Oh good, I'm glad you're still here," Skylar rushed into his office, interrupting his moment of peace.

He turned and looked at her.

"I forgot to tell you. Quinn called about twenty minutes ago and said he's in Milwaukee and for you to sit tight. Instead of meeting you at the Bradley site, he'll meet you here. Something about you guys needing to revisit the plans for the Chicago project."

"Okay thanks. I'm glad you told me I was getting ready to head out." He stood and removed his suit jacket. "What do you have planned for today?"

"Not too much. Since you're going to be here awhile, you can keep an ear out for Dallas. I'm going to run to the store." Skylar moved to the door but stopped and turned. "Ty, don't you and Dallas get sick of arguing about everything?"

He chuckled. "We don't argue about *everything*."

Skylar lifted an eyebrow. "Then what would you call screaming at each other at the top of your lungs all the time?"

"Communication. We're passionate people who raise our voices occasionally."

Tyler smiled when she walked out of the room shaking her head. Unfortunately, she was right. He needed to find a way to communicate with Dallas without the conversation always ending in a shouting match, especially while she recuperated.

****

"Hey Dallas, I'm on my way to the store. Do..." Skylar started, but stopped when she walked into the room. "What's wrong? You look upset."

"I just had the strangest call." She tossed her cell phone to the other side of the bed and ran her hands down her face. "Someone just threatened me."

"What?" Skylar moved closer and sat on the side of the bed. "What did they say?"

Dallas told her about the call, wondering if someone was just playing around. Now that she thought about it, she'd received a couple of hang-ups over the past few weeks.

"I think you should tell Tyler, or better yet, contact the police."

Dallas waved her off. "It's probably nothing, just some kids playing around. And the last thing I want to do is give your brother any more reasons to hover over me."

Chapter Five

Chicago, Illinois

"Thank you for coming on such short notice. I'm sure you're all wondering what this meeting is about, especially since we just met on Friday." David Weisman paced across the front of the large board room, running his fingers through his dark thinning hair.

"First, let me say that here at the Weisman and Cohen Group, we couldn't ask for a better team. We appreciate all the long hours and work you've put in, as well as your commitment to our clients. With that said, it makes it even harder to tell you about the upcoming changes. As you know, the investment industry has taken a few hits over the last couple of years. After numerous meetings and very careful consideration, we have determined that cutbacks are needed. This afternoon, we'll meet with each of you, individually, to discuss our plans for the future and the role we see you playing."

William Cohen, senior partner, looked on as managers and staff exchanged confused looks, and murmurs floated around the room. He, too, had been surprised when David suggested cutbacks, and decided then that he needed to be more involved in the day-to-day operations. On paper, their company seemed solid. Apparently, that wasn't the case since David recommended cuts.

"Again, thank you for your hard work and commitment to the firm." Everyone stood and exited the room.

William followed David back to his office and shut the door. "Dave, I'm not comfortable with letting people go at this point. I need more information about why you feel we have to make these changes."

"Bill, years ago we agreed I would oversee employees and managers. So I would think after thirty years you would trust my judgment," David said, with a dangerous calm in his eyes. "I have given my all to this company. And yes, I'm just as disappointed, but so that we don't get any deeper into debt, I feel we need to make these cuts."

William stood in front of David's desk with his hands in his pockets. "I definitely respect your opinion and your recommendations. All I'm saying is I don't want to be too hasty in letting people go. Even if it's temporary, I don't like the idea of disrupting these folks' lives if we don't have to. Besides, if we let them go, how will all of the accounts be covered?"

David stood and walked over to his file cabinet. "I have that all worked out. Just until we get back on our feet, I have divided up the work load among our investment managers."

David handed the folder to his partner, and William leafed through the thin file. "At first glance this looks fine, but I'm concerned about piling more work on Dallas," he said, removing a sheet from the file. "She already has a full load, and with her accident, I'm just not comfortable adding more to her plate."

"Yeah, that did cross my mind. But knowing Dallas, I'm sure she'll be able to handle it. Besides, she knows she's in line to make partner, so this is a good opportunity for her to show us her commitment."

William dropped the file on David's desk. "She should've made partner years ago. We both know she's more committed to this firm than anyone. Why keep stalling? She has proven her abilities over and over again. I have no doubt she'd make an amazing partner."

"Well, I disagree." A shadow of irritation crossed David's face. "I think she still has some growing to do. Once I see how well she handles these additional accounts, then I'll be able to determine if I'm ready to cast my vote."

****

Dallas closed her laptop and threw her pen across the room, watching it ricochet off the far wall. *How many more hoops am I going to have to jump through?* She'd been killing herself to prove her worthiness and David was still holding out in giving her the partnership. And he had the nerve to add ten additional clients to her already full load.

She'd just met with the partners virtually via video, hoping that they'd say something about the pending partnership. William had been hinting around about it for weeks, but Dallas had a feeling David was the hold up. In the past three days she'd gone back to working long hours, be it remotely, she was still at the top of her game. But, was it worth it?

She released a long sigh and laid her head against the back of the chair. A glance around the intimate sitting area, attached to her bedroom, brought a slight smile to her face. It was perfectly decorated in blues and browns, with formal curtains tied back separating it from the sleeping area. Two high-back upholstered chairs, divided by a small table and lamp faced the fireplace, with a flat screened television hanging above it. She wasn't much of a TV watcher, but it added to the look and feel of the cozy space.

Dallas closed her eyes to the dull ache in her head as she thought back on when Tyler first purchased the five bedroom five bathroom house. This was the room she'd immediately fell in love with, which was probably the reason he had put her in it, verses one of the bedrooms on the first floor. The thought brought with it guilt that they hadn't been able to see eye to eye regarding her hectic work schedule. Some days, like today, she felt he might've been right. It might've been too soon to go back to work.

"It's nice to see you relaxing," she heard Tyler say from behind her.

She opened her eyes and turned to him. "Hey."

"Hey, yourself." He strolled into the sitting area and handed her one of two bottled waters he carried. He sat in the other overstuffed chair, separated from her by a round, wood table. "So, how did your meeting go?" He took a swig of his water and placed it on a coaster near the reading lamp.

His deep-timbered voice caressed her like a gentle feather against her skin. Aware of the attraction between them, she willed her mind to focus on anything but him. She was a woman facing the harsh possibility of not making partner this year – or maybe never. She should be concentrating on how to attain her dream, not on the sexy way Tyler's lip moved or how he ignited sexual feelings she hadn't felt in a long time.

"It went all right. Not exactly what I expected though," she said looking down at her hands, folded in her lap.

"What did you expect?"

Considering making partner was all she had talked about while they were dating, she knew he didn't want to hear anything else about it. She chanced a glance at him. "They've made some cuts and asked managers to take on more accounts."

Tyler leaned forward. "Dallas, you're still recovering. What's wrong with those people? I hope you said no."

"I've decided I'm going to show them I can handle whatever they give me."

"Sweetheart." His large hands clenched the arms of the chair. "The doctor told you to take it easy. You're making decisions that are detrimental to your health. These folks apparently don't care."

"I know what's best for me and how much I can handle. I take care of myself just fine. I don't need you trying to control what I do." She folded her arms across her stomach, but winced when they made contact with her ribs. Tyler's angry gaze would've caused a weaker woman to wither, but not Dallas. She enjoyed some of their verbal battles. They awarded her the opportunity to see him fired up, his dark, piercing eyes even sexier than usual.

"Look at you. You can't even go a couple of minutes without pain, yet you're willing to take on more work. When are you going to stop putting *all* your energies into your career?" He stood and grabbed his water bottle.

"When I accomplish my number one goal."

"Despite what you think, there is more to life than making partner at a firm that clearly doesn't care anything about you. What about family, your health and … and love, Dallas? When are you going to start putting those things first and stop being so obsessed with this stupid job?"

"Stupid job?" She pushed forward and sat on the edge of her seat. Her mood swerved sharply to anger. "Why do you even care, Tyler? Why do you care anything about me or my *stupid* job?"

His jaw tightened and his eyes narrowed, but he didn't respond.

"And as for having love in my life, who says I don't have *love* in my life? Just because I'm not getting it on with you doesn't mean I'm not getting any. So before you start telling me what I need, or need to be doing, get your facts straight. 'Cause I got this." She tapped her hand against her chest. "I *can* take care of myself!"

"You know what? Since you *got this*, take care of yourself. I don't need this drama." He walked out and slammed the door behind him.

"And my job is not stupid!" she yelled.

****

Tyler stopped midway down the staircase when he saw his sister near the bottom step. He continued down, with all intentions of ignoring her.

"Sounded like another *passionate* conversation going on up there."

Tyler glared at her. "Not now Sky," he said going to the kitchen with her hot on his heels. He snatched his keys from the top of the refrigerator and opened the door.

"Where are you going?"

"Out."

Two hours later Tyler had done everything from playing basketball to running on the track at the gym. Nothing eased his anger.

Sure, maybe he had crossed the line calling Dallas's job stupid, but did she have to throw her love life in his face? The thought of another man's hands on her made him want to punch something. He hadn't expected her to live as a nun, but he didn't want to hear about her *getting it on* with someone else.

Already breathing heavy, he dropped down on the mat and did fifty more push-ups. *So much for showing concern for her health.* To her, he was being controlling. She was right about one thing. Why should he be concerned? It was her life.

"Hey, handsome. Where you been hidin'?"

Tyler lifted his head to the sultry voice. Desiree Thomas sat on the weight bench next to him, looking as if she'd just stepped off the cover of *Shape* magazine. Her fire engine red sports bra showed off the flattest abs he'd ever seen on a woman. She stretched her finely-toned legs out in front of her and crossed them at the ankles.

"What's up, Desiree?" He rose to his knees and wiped his face and neck with his towel. "I'm surprised you're here so late." He threw the towel across his left shoulder and stood.

"Yeah, you know, I have to make sure I keep my girlish figure in check," she said, standing and drawing more attention to her short shorts and skimpy top.

Tyler gave her a quick once over. "Yep, and I see you're doing a fine job." There was no denying it. Desiree had a body that other women would kill for. Had that body been attached to another woman, he would've made a play for her years ago. Too bad for Desiree he wanted more than a pretty face in his life. He needed someone who could also stimulate him intellectually and Dallas immediately came to mind.

He grabbed his water bottle from the floor. "Well, I'm done here. I'll check you later."

"Wait." Desiree hustled to catch up to him. "I've been planning to call you. I want to know if you'll be my date at an awards banquet in a couple of weeks. I'm being honored for my charity work."

"Congratulations," he said and continued to the locker room.

"Thanks. So, will you go with me?" She grabbed his arm and jumped in front of him, forcing him to stop. She was one of few women who came close to matching his height, therefore able to look him in the eyes.

He shook his head. "Desiree, I don't—"

"Ty, don't say no. Think about it," she whined. "We go way back, and we'll be going as friends. Nothing else, I promise."

He swiped at the beads of sweat on his forehead. He wasn't sure if he was wiping away perspiration brought on by his rigorous workout, or if it was from Desiree being close enough for him to smell her minty fresh breath. "Uh, give me a call with the details, and I'll check my schedule."

"Great! I'll be in touch." She made a move to turn and walk away, but dropped her towel. Before Tyler could pick it up for her, she did a slow bend over move that would've put a professional stripper to shame. He wasn't the only brother who had noticed. Every man within ten feet slowed to watch the show. She gave them an eye full of well-rounded hips attached to long shapely legs. With little or no effort, she straightened with the poise of a dancer, looked over her shoulder at him and said, "Okay then. I'll talk to you soon." Seduction dripped from every word as she sashayed to the women's locker room.

Damn. Its women like her who make it hard for a brother to stay focused. Tyler shook his head and continued into the men's locker room.

****

Dallas glanced at the clock on the bedside table. *One o'clock in the morning. Where is he?* She wanted to apologize.

She'd been downright nasty to him. He'd called her job stupid, but she'd overreacted and said things she didn't mean. Most women would've been flattered that he cared enough to voice his concerns, but no, instead she verbally attacked him, rubbing her so-called love life in his face.

Why did most of their conversations have to end in an argument? She knew why. *Sexual tension.* She felt it every time he came within two feet of her, and she'd bet all the money in her bank account he felt it too. Whenever he looked at her with those gorgeous eyes, her stomach tightened and her heart did somersaults.

"Now he's probably at some woman's house licking his wounds," she mumbled as her tired eyes drifted closed and she fell into a deep sleep.

Dallas didn't wake up until ten o'clock the next morning when Skylar came into her room with a breakfast tray and to inform her that Tyler had left town for a couple of days.

How could he leave without saying goodbye? He must be really mad. Dallas couldn't believe she hadn't heard him come home, and if it weren't for Skylar, she wouldn't have known he had gone.

Fine. If he wants to have an attitude, so be it. I have enough work to keep me busy for weeks. She pulled the documents from the box her assistant, Bianca, had sent. Times like this, she wished she was in the office, because having Bianca send everything made extra work for both of them.

For the next hour, she took notes and divided her attention between the data on her computer screen with the paperwork in front of her. Throughout the morning she called Bianca to discuss information over the telephone.

What's this? She read over a form she hadn't seen before, then several pages with figures and various notations. *Hmm ... some type of ledger. I never made these investments.* Dallas picked up her cell phone to call Bianca, but it rang before she started dialing.

"Dallas Marcel."

"What's up girlfriend? Seems like I haven't talked to you all week," Simone said.

Dallas laughed and put the documents back into the file. "Yeah, it's been three days. I'm sitting here all broken while you're probably walking along one of those beautiful beaches there in San Diego."

Simone chuckled. "I wish. Girl, life has been crazy busy. I've barely had a chance to breathe. I have a meeting at work this evening, so figured I'd dash home for a couple hours and try to scratch a few things off my 'To Do' list."

"Oh, so I'm one of the things on your list."

"Weelll …." They both laughed. "No, but seriously, how are you doing?"

"I'm okay. I'm tired of being cooped up in the house, but I'm not too keen on walking around in public with crutches."

"Yeah, I can understand that. How are things going with you and Ty living under the same roof?"

Seconds passed before Dallas answered. "I don't know, Simone. I can't take much more of this."

"Why, what has he done?"

Dallas bit her bottom lip, debating on how much to tell her best friend. Simone knew the history between her and Tyler and wouldn't be surprised about anything.

"Based on your silence, I guess I should be asking what did *you* do. Please don't tell me your smart mouth started some mess."

"Something like that."

"Aw, Dallas, why do you always do that?"

"Hold up. Why do I always do what? You're acting like I always start arguments or something."

"You do when it comes to Tyler. At some point you're going to have to stop pushing him away and face the fact that you're still in love with him."

"He and I are *just* friends, and that's all we'll ever be."

"Tell it to someone who doesn't know you both. You start arguments to keep him from getting close. Dallas he's not—"

"Please don't say the name I think you were about to say." Mark Darley had made Dallas's life a living hell, and thinking about him made her skin crawl.

"That's what I'm talking about. You're making Tyler suffer because of your ex. At some point you're going to have to leave the past in the past and grab hold of your future."

"My future is about making partner at the most prestigious investment firm in Chicago. I don't have time for Tyler or a relationship with anyone for that matter. Just because you found happily-ever-after, doesn't mean it's in the cards for me," Dallas said, frustration rising in her chest.

Silence stretched between them. "Dallas, honey, I'm sorry. I didn't call to upset you or to bring up bad memories. You're such an amazing woman and I want to see you with someone who can love you the way you deserve to be loved."

Ten years ago, Mark had practically destroyed her financially and emotionally. Dallas couldn't do the love thing again. With a lot of hard work and some serious sacrifices, she'd climbed higher in the investment world than most people could dream of. She was almost where she wanted to be in her life, and would never let a man put her in a vulnerable position again.

****

Mark Darley sat at his drafting table looking over the plans for the current project he was working on. He jotted down notes as he thumbed through several pages. Kevin Philips, the previous engineer, was out on medical leave for an indefinite amount of time, but his boss didn't want the project on hold. Mark knew he'd enjoy the assignment since it involved a condo rehab in one of the areas he wanted to live. Top floors overlooked Lake Michigan, Navy Pier and a botanical park. If things worked out, maybe the owner would give him a good deal on one of the units.

He went to his desk and looked through the file his secretary had left containing some of Kevin's notes. The project ideas were impressive. The four penthouse units needed the least amount of work, but the owner had given some good input on changes he wanted for the unit he'd occupy. It appeared Kevin had only met with the owner twice regarding this project, but over the years, they'd worked on numerous other projects together.

"Names, names, I need names here." Mark rummaged through several other documents in search of the client's name. "Okay, here we go," he said, finding the page he'd been looking for.

Hollister. He closed his eyes and shook his head as if he were seeing things. *Tyler Hollister. No way! Could I be this lucky?*

Mark picked up the packet of paper his private investigator had dropped off earlier. He placed both sets of documents on his desk and leaned back in his office chair; his hands formed a steeple under his chin. A menacing grin spread across his face as a plan unfolded in his mind. If Hollister was involved in this project, he'd finally get to meet the man who had stolen Dallas's heart.

Chapter Six

"What's up man? Thanks for picking me up," Tyler said when he tossed his carry-on bag in the back seat, and climbed into Quinn's Escalade truck.

"Not a problem. How was your flight?" He pulled away from Chicago's Midway Airport and onto Cicero Avenue, heading to I-55.

"Nice and short, just the way I like it." Tyler glanced over his shoulder to the back seat. "Did you remember to bring the blueprints?"

"Got 'em. They're all the way in the back. Who are we meeting with again?"

"Mark Darley. He's the new architectural engineer overseeing Kevin's projects."

Quinn shook his head. "I can't believe Kevin had a stroke. What is he like, forty-five or something?"

"Something like that. Just goes to show, it can happen to anyone."

"Yeah, you're right about that." Quinn merged onto I-55. "I hope this new guy can guarantee the condos will be completed on time. I want several models ready before *A Taste of Chicago* kicks off in June. I've already set up open houses during that time, and have several realtors excited about the project."

"I hope so too."

On the ride downtown they discussed the Chicago project, a few changes and challenges, as well as the new timeline for completion. Traffic, known to look like early morning rush hour at any given time, was surprisingly light. Twenty minutes later they stepped off the elevator onto the 50th floor of the newly renovated space of Dartsworth Engineering Firm. The plush office impressed Tyler with its high ceilings, top of the line lighting and fixtures, and he liked that they spared no expense on the furnishings. Housed on the top three floors, the firm occupied 50,000 square feet of space.

"Hi, may I help you?" A receptionist Tyler hadn't seen before came around the corner and approached them.

"Hi. Tyler Hollister and Quinn Hamilton to see Mark Darley."

She walked around her immaculately kept desk and typed something into the computer. Seconds later she picked up the telephone and dialed. "Hi Liz, Mark's 10 o'clock is here," she paused then said, "Okay, will do."

"Sorry to keep you gentlemen waiting. It looks like he's on a conference call that should be ending shortly."

"No problem," Tyler said. "We're a little early anyway."

She stood and walked around her desk. "Here let me show you to the conference room."

"Thanks," Tyler and Quinn said in unison.

As they made their way down several short hallways, Quinn made conversation with the young lady. Tyler only heard bits and pieces of the conversation since his mind had again returned to thoughts of Dallas. He definitely had a problem if he couldn't even go minutes without thinking of her.

"All right, here we are." They walked in and took a seat where she directed. "Can I get you gentlemen a cup of coffee or water while you wait?" she posed the question to Quinn, and Tyler shook his head and smiled.

"How about you on a silver platter?" Quinn flirted, his long jean clad legs stretched out in front of him and crossed at the ankles. He exuded confidence with his white linen shirt hung loose and the top two buttons unfastened like a model gracing the cover of *GQ* magazine. His dreadlocks were pulled back and bound at the nape of his neck making it easy to see the African bone necklace he had hanging around his neck. He was dressed more like a man hanging out with the guys, than one attending a business meeting.

The receptionist blushed. "Sorry. I'm not on the menu, but I am free tonight," she whispered, though loud enough for Tyler to hear her. She ripped a sheet of paper from a nearby tablet, jotted down her number, and slipped it to Quinn. He glanced at it, folded the paper, and put it in his pocket.

"I'll be in touch," he said, allowing his eyes to follow her until she'd left the room.

"Man, I can't take you anywhere. You have this girl risking her job trying to flirt with you."

Quinn shrugged and leaned back in his chair. Rubbing a hand down his goatee, he said, "Hey, what can I say, women love me. Besides, you should talk. Don't get me started on that woman at the hotel in North Carolina a few weeks ago who practically fell over the counter trying to get next to you. 'Oh, you have the most incredible eyes I've ever seen,'" Quinn imitated in a high pitched voice, batting his own eyes. "Heck, I'm surprised she didn't show up at your hotel door that night."

Tyler laughed and removed his notepad from his briefcase. "I hope *she* didn't lose her job giving me the Presidential Suite for the same price of a king size room." *Too bad I don't have that affect on Dallas.* He shouldn't have left without saying something, but Dallas's presence in his life was wreaking havoc on his control. Even with her smart mouth, and fierce independence, he still wanted to pull her into his arms and get reacquainted with her gorgeous lips. Oh yeah, they needed this time apart. No. *He* needed this time apart.

"Tyler Hollister?" A tall, fair skinned, well dressed man walked in carrying several blueprints.

Tyler stood and extended his hand. "Hi, I'm Tyler and this is my business partner, Quinn Hamilton."

"Mark Darley." He shook their hands and laid the prints down at the end of the table. "I'm glad you guys could meet."

"I understand you're new to the city. Where you from?" Tyler asked reclaiming his seat.

"I'm originally from Arkansas, but have lived in Louisiana for the past 14 years. I moved here about a month ago, but I'm still trying to get acclimated. I can't believe Chicago's traffic and how crazy people drive around here."

Quinn chuckled. "Don't worry you'll get used to it."

"Yeah, in a few months, I'll probably be one of them." They laughed and participated in small talk for the next fifteen minutes.

Halfway through the conversation, Tyler found himself mentally drifting in and out. Mark's high opinion of himself was getting old. It wasn't often he met someone who dominated the conversation by talking about himself, and who claimed to have single handedly kept a Fortune 500 company out of bankruptcy. He stole a quick glance at Quinn. His doubtful, thin-lipped expression let him know they were thinking the same thing.

Tyler peeked at his watch waiting for the perfect opportunity to interrupt. There was something about this guy that unnerved him, but he couldn't put his finger on it. He'd met plenty of people who loved to hear themselves talk, but this was different. Finally, he'd had enough.

"Well, we probably better get started. Quinn and I have several meetings scheduled today."

"Oh, I'm sorry. Here I am going on and on."

Tyler and Quinn filled Mark in on some of the ideas they'd talked about on the ride there, the history of the building that was being renovated, as well as time expectations. Standing over the blue prints, Tyler pointed out some of the issues they'd been facing in some of the units and decisions that had been made regarding them.

"I see you also made a few changes to the penthouse units," Mark said studying the second set of prints.

"Only the one I plan to occupy," Tyler said.

Mark glanced at him. "You're leaving Milwaukee?"

"My time is split between Milwaukee and Chicago, so I figured I'd get a place here."

"I see."

"This is what I'm thinking." Tyler drew their attention back to the prints. "I want to get rid of the wall between the living and dining room to open up the space more. And here, I want to add a walk-in closet in the master bedroom. There's already one in there, but another one won't hurt."

Mark grinned. "I understand. There can never be too many closets for our women. I'm sure your lady has enough clothes and shoes to fill up both closets."

"Actually, that closet is to increase the resale value of this unit," Tyler continued. "I'd also like to push out this bathroom wall. I'm a little surprised they had such a small bathroom in there considering the size of the bedroom."

Mark nodded and took notes.

"Outside of that, I'm impressed with the suggestions you sent. Your ideas definitely take full advantage of the downtown views."

"I'm glad you think so." Mark unrolled the prints he'd brought with him to propose additional changes and alternatives. "I know things are underway in your unit. Did you want your wife in on the next meeting to discuss the decorating details?"

"Actually, Kevin set me up with an interior decorator."

"I know I'd let my woman do all of that," Mark said as if not hearing Tyler. "You're probably the same with your wife, huh?"

Quinn's eyes bore into Mark. "Man, what's up with all of the wife questions?"

Mark shrugged. "Just making conversation. Most people like to talk about their family." He turned his attention to Tyler. "So, is she going to be a part of any of the decision-making?"

Tyler frowned. "She who?"

"Your wife. You know how women like to—"

"I am so sorry to interrupt Mark," his assistant said from the door, "but you have an urgent call that requires your attention."

"Okay thanks," he said and returned his attention to Tyler and Quinn. "My apologies for the interruption. Let me see what the call is all about and then—"

"Hey you know what? We can stop here," Tyler said. "We need to be going anyway. Besides, we've gone over the most important changes. Everything else is pretty self-explanatory, and you can always call if you have additional questions."

"All right, will do," Mark said and shook their hands before making a quick exit.

"What the hell was that all about?" Quinn seethed when the door closed behind Mark. "Why does he think you're married?"

Tyler shrugged and began rolling up the prints. "I have no idea. I've only talked to him a couple of times and never about my personal life."

"I don't like him."

Tyler glanced at Quinn and took in his clenched jaw, rigid back, and his arms folded across his wide chest. The conviction on his face made him look dangerous. Rarely did he see this side of his friend. Normally he was the laid back one, keeping things light. So when he said he didn't like someone, which was unusual, Tyler took it seriously.

****

Knowing she'd hurt Tyler and that he was avoiding her, was driving Dallas crazy. *This is why I don't do relationships.* The amount of time she'd spent thinking about him was distracting her from what she needed to be doing - generating money for her clients. If she was serious about making partner this year, she needed to step up her game. This was not the time to daydream about Tyler...or his incredibly sexy eyes, or how good he always smelled - like sandalwood mixed with some delicious spice.

A frustrated sigh slipped through her lips. "Stop it, stop it, stop it," she scolded herself and slid her arms into the sleeves of her shirt. She didn't have time for a relationship, especially with Tyler. But on the other hand, she couldn't stand the thought of him being mad at her. *I have to fix this.*

Dallas had just finished buttoning her top when the house phone rang. It wasn't until after the third ring that she moved to get it.

"Hello," she answered out of breath. Even with the short distance from the closet to the side table, moving with a cast slowed her down.

Silence greeted her on the other end. "Hello," she repeated. Her stomach churned with anxiety at the thought of the caller being the same person behind the threatening calls she'd received on her cell phone. "Hello," she said one last time.

"Is Tyler there?"

Dallas released a sigh of relief. "No he's not. Would you like to leave a message," she asked. She sat on the edge of the bed and grabbed her notepad.

"Who is this?" the caller demanded.

Dallas frowned, surprised at the woman's attitude. "This is a friend of his. Would you like to leave a message?"

"What friend?" the lady shouted.

Dallas pulled the phone away from her ear. *No she ain't tryin' to get loud with me.* "It doesn't matter who I am. Do you want to leave a message, or not?"

"I've left several messages, and he hasn't returned my calls. Are you even telling him I've called?"

"Hey, I have no idea what you're talking about, because I haven't taken any calls from you, but if you want to leave him a message, I'll make sure he gets it."

Skylar walked in with a laundry basket and caught that part of the conversation. "It's probably Desiree. Just hang up." Dallas snickered at the face Skylar made.

"As a matter of fact I do want to leave a message. Tell him Desiree called and that it was good seeing him the other night. He left a couple of things at my house, and I also want to confirm our date." Her silky voice held a challenge.

"Okay, I'll tell him." Dallas disconnected the phone. Who was Desiree? She wrote down the message and removed the sheet from the pad of paper.

"Give me that." Skylar gestured for the note. Dallas handed it to her, and watched as Skylar, balled up the yellow piece of paper and walked it over to the trash can.

Dallas sat opened-mouthed. "I can't believe you did that. I know never to leave a message with you if that's how you handle them."

"Girl, that child has called about a hundred times, and apparently my brother doesn't want to talk to her."

"Are you even giving him the messages? They might be important," Dallas said, not believing it herself.

"Yeah, sure, and I'm the queen of Sheba. That girl wants Tyler to escort her to some awards banquet. I don't know why he won't say no and be done with it."

"Maybe he wants to go." Dallas secretly hoped he didn't, but with the way she'd treated him days ago, he deserved to be with someone who wants to be with him.

Skylar put her hands on her hips. "I doubt that. Besides, do you mean to tell me you would let him take that witch on a date?"

Dallas stared at her. "Your brother is a grown, *single* man. He can do whatever he wants. Who am I to tell him who he can and cannot go out with?"

"Well, I thought you two were getting back together."

"Why would you think that?"

"What? Are you kidding me?" She shook her head and unloaded the clothes basket. "Whether he admits it or not, that man is crazy about you. Yet, you're going to push him into the arms of another woman."

"Sky—"

"You gon' mess around and lose him. Desiree has been after my brother since they were in high school."

"Ty is not mine." Dallas said and shuffled into the sitting area and eased herself into one of the chairs, Skylar standing next to her. "I can't very well tell him not to go. I don't have any papers on him. Besides, once I can move around a little better, I'm outta here."

"I can't believe you want to leave. What about Tyler?"

"What about him?"

"Any blind person can see that you guys are crazy about each other."

Dallas snorted. "Oh, you mean by the way we argue all the time?" She cared deeply for Tyler, but nothing could ever come of it. No way would she put a man before her career again. Doing so would mean starting over, and she'd eventually end up with a broken heart. *Been there, done that. I've worked too hard to go backwards.*

"You know I appreciate you hanging out here with me, fluffing my pillows, fixing amazing meals, and doing laundry. But Tyler and I are just friends."

Skylar sighed. "Okay, but I think you're making a big mistake."

****

After two days in Chicago, Tyler couldn't wait to get home. He and Quinn were riding in the back seat of a town car on their way to the airport. When his traveling had increased last year, instead of purchasing a plane, Tyler started chartering a plane making it more convenient to get a flight whenever he needed.

"I'm surprised you're flying back with me. For a person who loves Chicago, you've been spending a lot of time in Milwaukee."

"Yeah, I know. I need to do some work on one of my rental properties and figured this weekend is as good a time as any. And since you've already reserved the plane, why drive?"

Tyler laughed. "Oh sure, just use me," he joked, knowing that he'd do anything for Quinn. His friend had his back more times than he could remember.

Tyler glanced at his cell phone for the second time in ten minutes, debating on whether or not to call Dallas. He had wanted to call and check on her since he'd left Milwaukee, but he waited, hoping she'd call. But why would she? He'd said her job was stupid, despite knowing her work meant everything to her. For as long as he'd known her, she'd had tunnel vision when it came to making partner.

What she told him about her love life still stung. What did he expect, for her to shrivel up in a corner and never date?

Tyler felt his friend's eyes on him. "Whatever it is, just say it."

"For the past couple of weeks, you've been looking for more reasons to do business in Chicago. It wouldn't have anything to do with that gorgeous fireball living with you would it?"

Tyler angled his head at Quinn. "What would Skylar have to do with my business decisions?" he said straight faced.

"Ha, I see you got jokes. But I'm serious. Ty, man, you haven't been this interested in what Chicago has to offer in quite awhile. Why now?"

"What do you mean why now? I've done plenty of business in Chicago over the years. It's just that now more lucrative opportunities have come our way."

"Nah, I think it has to do with that doe-eyed beauty."

"Yeah right."

"Hear me out. Something has changed. You're different - distracted, not sleeping."

Tyler frowned.

"Oh, yeah, I've noticed. Your red-rimmed eyes and constant yawning gave you away."

"I have a lot on my mind," Tyler grumbled and stared out the passenger side window watching cars and buildings pass in a blur. "With the huge project in North Carolina and this one in Chicago, man, I'm tired." He turned to face Quinn. "And don't get me started on the three in Milwaukee."

Quinn shook his head. "It's more than that and you know it. If you don't want to talk about it, fine. But don't try to bullshit me."

Tyler didn't respond. Had he really been that consumed with Dallas? He had to get a grip. No way could he fall for her again.

Minutes later they had arrived and were walking through the airport terminal when Tyler's cell phone rang. He fished it out of his jacket pocket and was disappointed when he glanced at the screen and it wasn't Dallas, but he answered anyway.

"Good afternoon, Tyler Hollister."

"The car accident was just a warning. I suggest you tell that *wife* of yours to stay out of business that doesn't concern her." Tyler froze.

"Who the hell is this?" he growled into the phone.

"Someone who will make her wish she'd never been born."

Chapter Seven

"Where the hell are they?" Tyler yelled and slammed down the telephone. If anything had happened to them, he'd never forgive himself. As he paced in front of his black walnut desk a stab of guilt lay buried in his chest. Why had he let a stupid disagreement keep him away from home ... and from Dallas?

He picked up the phone to dial again but replaced the receiver when Quinn walked in. For a big man, standing at six-five and over 240 pounds of solid muscle, Quinn's moves were smooth and confident as he crossed the room.

"I grabbed your mail out of the box," Quinn said and dropped it on Tyler's desk. "How are you holding up?"

"I don't know man. I've called everyone I can think of and no one has seen them."

"Is the detective still here?"

"He's here. He went into the guestroom down the hall to take a call. I'm surprised he came instead of Officer Logan."

"Yeah, probably because it's turning into more than *just* a car accident. So what did he have to say?"

"For the most part, he stated the same thing you said. I can't file a missing person report; it doesn't look like Dallas and Skylar were forced to leave and it could be they stepped out for some fresh air. I'm starting to wonder why I even bothered to call the cops." He dropped down into his chair.

Quinn shoved his hands into the front pockets of his blue jeans and studied Tyler. "So, are the car accident and that phone call the reason you've been on edge? Or is something else going on?"

Tyler reared back in his seat and dragged his palms down his face. How could he tell Quinn that not once in the past two days had he thought about Dallas's accident? He'd been too busy thinking about her, the woman.

Without responding, he shot out of his chair and turned to the window behind his desk. *Why can't I let her go?* He sighed heavily and let his gaze fall on the dogwood trees. They lined the walkway leading to the park-like sitting area fifty yards from the house. Dallas loved the space, especially when the trees were blooming, like they were now.

It seemed like a lifetime ago when they'd sit out there and talk. Well, actually, he did most of the talking, while she listened. It was during one of those talks he first realized she was everything he didn't know he wanted. Never one for dating exclusively, he knew early on Dallas was the one for him. If he had one complaint about her, though, it would be she didn't open up and trust him enough.

Quinn stepped around the desk and stood next to him. Moments passed as they both stared out at the lush side yard. "I need you to do some checking into all of this for me," Tyler said. "I'm not sure where you should start, but I want to know what she's been up to; if she's been involved with anyone, and whatever else you can find out."

Quinn had more contacts and access to information than Milwaukee's finest could ever dream of. He was ex-special ops for the government. He'd never been forthcoming with what exactly he did back then, but Tyler knew when Quinn walked away from that life and came back home, he was different. Hard and dangerous, he trusted no one. He had battled with sleepless nights littered with traumatic dreams of a life he wanted to forget. It had been years, but this was the first time Tyler dared to ask him to tap into that life again.

Quinn shook his head. "Ty ..."

"Q, I gotta to know what's up with her. Maybe she's being straight with me, but maybe there's something going on that she doesn't know about." Tyler felt Quinn's eyes on him, but kept his gaze on the dogwood trees.

"All right," he said after a long silence. "I know you wouldn't ask me to do this, unless you thought your gir—"

"She's not my—"

Quinn threw him a lethal look. "You can keep lying to yourself, but spare me." He shook his head and turned to walk away. "I can't believe you're still in love with her."

"I didn't say I—"

"Save it!" He shot over his shoulder and moved to the mini bar to pull out a beer. "So what are you going to do about it?"

Tyler knew he still loved Dallas, but no way would he act on it. She'd ripped his heart out once. He wouldn't let her do it again. "Absolutely nothing," he said, turning back to his desk. "All I want is to figure out what's going on with her and make sure she's safe. Then I'm sending her on her way."

Quinn laughed, strode back over and sat in one of the chairs in front of the desk. He took a swig of his beer and said, "Apparently, your lack of sleep has affected your mind, my brotha. You're still in love with this woman and no amount of denying it will make it go away."

"Yeah, whatever. For now, all I want is her back here safe." He picked up the mail that Quinn had laid on his desk. Standing near the waste basket, he tossed several pieces of mail into the trash. *I get more junk mail than…* His hand stilled on an envelope that read *Dallas* in big, bold, cut-out letters from a magazine. "Oh my God."

Quinn stood slowly. "What is it?"

Tyler ripped it open and a small sheet of paper slipped out.

This is just the beginning.

"What's going on?" Dallas asked, easing into the room on her crutches with Skylar close behind.

Tyler's head jerked toward the door, and there she stood, the person responsible for his sleepless nights and his accelerated heart rate. He stared at her as she looked back at him. It seemed longer than two days since he'd last seen her. Her long dark hair hung loosely over her shoulders with a few strands framing her cinnamon brown face.

Though she still didn't look like her old self, he could tell she was getting better. The bruises were barely noticeable, but her face was still thin and her gorgeous brown eyes not as vibrant as usual. His gaze traveled down the rest of her body. She always did look gorgeous in red, and the red fitted blouse didn't disappoint. Even with a cast on her leg, she exuded sexiness in her straight black skirt which stopped several inches above her knees and revealed legs that went on forever. Damn his body for reacting.

Growling within, anger replaced desire when he moved across the room. "Where have you been?"

Dallas frowned and shuffled back. "Tyler, what's wrong with you?" She looked at Quinn, then back at Tyler. She studied him a bit longer. "I'm not trying to be funny, but you look awful ... and you're sweating. It's not even hot in here. Are you sick?" She placed her hand against his forehead.

"Yeah, you are acting kinda weird," Skylar said, holding several shopping bags.

He yanked away from Dallas's gentle touch. "How do you expect me to act? I've been trying to reach you for hours. I thought something..." Overcome with emotion, he reached out and pulled Dallas into his arms, a possessive desperation in his voice. "I thought something had happened to you," he mumbled into her hair, kissing her forehead.

Dallas wiggled out of his arms and glared at him. "Wait a minute! If you were so worried, why haven't I heard from you? You couldn't have been too concerned."

Skylar's eyes narrowed. "Why would you think something had happened? We went to her doctor's appointment and then to the mall. What's the big deal?"

Tyler, already missing Dallas's softness and the heat she generated, shot an icy look at his sister. "The big deal is I didn't know where you were!"

"We were out." His sister challenged.

"I've been calling all afternoon. Why didn't either of you answer your phones? What's the point of having a cell phone if you're not going to answer it?" he shouted, his words harsher than he intended. Tyler walked to the mantle, as a war of emotions raged through him.

"I forgot and left my phone here and Dallas's battery died," Skylar said.

Dallas glared at him. "Are you serious? I haven't heard from you in days, and now all of a sudden you're worried? Why do you care now?"

Yeah, why do I care? He had asked himself that question too many times to count since she'd reappeared in his life. She was the most exasperating woman he'd ever known, but he cared. That was his problem. He cared too much.

"Are you even listening to me?" Dallas grabbed his arm and forced him to look at her. Apparently, she saw the weariness in his eyes, because her tone immediately softened. "Tyler, what's really going on here?"

"Okay, ya'll, let's calm down." Quinn spoke for the first time since Dallas and Skylar's arrival. "I'm sure the detective will fill you in."

"Detective?" Dallas and Skylar said.

As if on cue, Detective Davenport walked into the office. Placing his note pad in the inside pocket of his sports jacket, he said, "Ms. Marcel, I'm Detective Davenport and I'll be taking over your case."

****

Dallas leaned heavily on her crutches and stared at the plump man, who appeared to be in no condition to chase down criminals.

"Okay, will someone please tell me what's going on?" She sat on the sofa, while the detective opted for one of the upholstered chairs across from her. Skylar took the chair next to him, and Quinn leaned against Tyler's desk.

Dallas stole a glance at Tyler who stood near the fireplace watching her. She'd never seen him so freaked out. Not even the time when his oldest brother, Kenny, physically attacked Simone, and he had to keep Tim from killing him.

Tyler finally sat next to her, hunched over with his elbows resting on his knees. Tension vibrated off of him like steam from a radiator, and Dallas's anxiety multiplied the longer he sat without speaking. Minutes crept by while he stared at the floor, his fingers interlocked in front of him. When he finally raised his head and looked at her, the expression in his midnight-black eyes caused an uneasy sensation to slither down her spine.

"Tyler, you're scaring me."

He reached for her hand and held it within his. "On my way back from Chicago, I received a call, actually a warning." As he repeated the words of the call tears sprung to Dallas's eyes and her heart rate tripled. The call she received days ago was bad enough, but a second call scared her to death.

"I haven't even showed the detective this," Tyler said handing her a slip of paper, "but this was with the mail."

"This is just the beginning." Her eyes darted nervously between Tyler, and the detective. "What does this mean?"

Detective Davenport shifted his bulky body in the chair and reached for the small sheet of paper. "I'm not sure, and unfortunately that's not all. I just received a call regarding the car that hit you."

"And?" Tyler asked. Dallas felt him tense beside her.

"It was stolen from a Milwaukee couple while they were on vacation. We found it in Detroit along with something that leads us to believe the accident was intentional."

"And what's that?" Quinn asked from across the room.

"A picture of Dallas balled up between the seats, with the make and model of her car scribbled on the back."

"Oh, my God." Dallas's hands flew to her chest, shocked by what she was hearing. Tyler put his arm around her shoulder.

"She received another call a few days ago," Dallas heard Skylar say. "The threat was similar but Dallas thought it might've been some kids playing on the phone."

Tyler kissed the top of Dallas's head. "Aw, baby, you should've told me. We could have jumped on this sooner."

Unable to respond, Dallas listened as the four of them talked back and forth. Her mind raced and fear rioted within her as the reality of the situation engulfed her. Someone was trying to kill her.

"Ms. Marcel, we're going to do everything we can to put the pieces together and find who's behind this," Davenport said. "Can you think of anyone who would want to harm you?"

She did a mental run through of conversations and incidents over the past few weeks and came up with nothing that would cause someone to come after her. "No," she said swiping at tears she wasn't use to shedding. "I have no idea."

Skylar handed her some Kleenex, sat on the opposite side of her, and rubbed her back.

"So what happens now?" Tyler asked.

"We're going to keep searching for information. In the meantime, Ms. Marcel, I'd recommend you not go anywhere alone."

Tyler squeezed her shoulder. "She won't. I'll be following her like a shadow."

He stood and Dallas immediately felt the loss of his warmth. Her eyes followed his movements as he made his way across the room. He ran a hand over his head and down the back of his neck when he walked over to Quinn. *But wait, what was that look between them? Do they know something?*

"We'll walk you out," Tyler said to the detective, and he and Quinn followed him out of the room.

"Are you okay?" Skylar asked.

Dallas shook her head. "I … this … I can't believe this is happening to me."

"Yeah, it's like something out of a movie or the Twilight Zone. And you can't think of anyone who could be behind this?"

"No, no one. I think that's the worse part. At least if I had an idea, I'd know who to look out for, but I don't have a clue."

Tyler walked back in the room still rubbing the back of his neck. He looked exhausted. The worry lines across his forehead were more pronounced and his face was clouded with uneasiness.

"Quinn left?" Skylar asked him. She stood and grabbed the shopping bags that were sitting next to the chair she'd vacated.

"Yeah, he had to take care of some business."

"Oh. Well, if you two need me, I'll be in the kitchen cooking dinner."

Tyler reclaimed his seat next to Dallas. "I'm not even going to ask if you're okay."

"I could've been killed by that car and now I find out it was intentional." A few tears crept down her cheeks.

Tyler lifted her chin toward him and put his large hands on each side of her face, the pads of his thumbs wiping tears. "As long as there's breath in my body, I won't let anyone hurt you."

He said it with such fierce conviction that Dallas almost burst into a full-blown cry. But then his mouth covered hers, and lips so soft and unbelievably intoxicating sent a flare through her body, causing all thoughts to temporarily flee her mind. God she missed him and wanted nothing more than to stay wrapped in his arms, but she couldn't. One of them had to be strong and stop this before it went too far. She knew it had to be her when he pulled her closer and her breast pushed against his strong chest, and he deepened the kiss.

"We can't," she whimpered against his mouth and slowly pushed away. "I can't."

He studied her for a second and blew out a breath before nodding. "I know."

When he stood and left the room without looking back, Dallas wanted to bang her head against the wall. She wanted him something fierce despite the drama in her life.

An hour later, she sat across from Skylar at the kitchen table picking at her food. They hadn't eaten since lunch and now dined on blackened tilapia, grilled vegetables and brown rice. Though she tried, Dallas couldn't make herself eat.

"Now can you see how much my brother cares for you?" Skylar asked.

Dallas stared down at her plate without responding. She didn't want Tyler to get the wrong idea. Yes, she felt safe with him and knew he'd do whatever he could to protect her. But it didn't change the fact that they could never be more than friends. *Good friends.*

"He probably won't admit it, but he's still in love with you. The man would give his last breath for you."

Dallas's eyebrows knitted together. "I think he cares and is concerned, but that's it. Besides, I haven't been the easiest person to get along with these past couple of weeks. What makes you think he still loves me?"

"Are you kidding me?" Skylar put her fork down. "Did you see the way he looked at you this evening? How worried he was?"

"I think you're reading too much into it. I would've freaked out too if a note had come in the mail like that directed at him and I didn't know where he was. That was a natural reaction. He knows we're just friends."

"Mmm, hmm. If you say so."

****

Tyler walked into his bedroom. Beyond exhausted, he unfastened his belt and slowly pulled the tail of his shirt out of his pants. Removing his shirt he tossed it to a nearby chair and sat on the edge of the bed to take off his shoes.

Too tired to do much else, he climbed further onto the bed and collapsed against the mound of pillows. A sigh of content slipped through his lips as he felt some of the tension leave his body. He'd been through hell worrying about Dallas, and to find out her life could be in serious danger was something he hadn't bargained for. How the hell could he keep her safe without losing his heart to her again? The thought lulled him to sleep.

****

Dallas knocked softly on the door and hoped Tyler was still awake. It was after 10 p.m., but he rarely went to bed before midnight. They needed to talk, and she wouldn't be able to sleep until they had an understanding about their relationship. By nature he was a protector. She wanted to make sure he knew she appreciated him letting her stay there, but they couldn't go back to what they once had.

After waiting outside the door with no response, she turned the doorknob to find it unlocked. Glancing down the long hallway she heard Skylar coming up the stairs so she eased into the room. "Tyler," she called out just above a whisper as she closed the door behind her.

When she walked farther into the room, she saw him stretched out on the bed asleep. Her brain screamed for her to walk back out, but an irresistible pull drew her closer to his side.

His half-naked body looked ethereal, like a sculpted masterpiece under the moonlight that seeped through the window. She studied his sleeping face before she allowed her gaze to travel to his solid muscular chest. No doubt he still worked out faithfully.

She forced her eyes back up to his face and had a sudden urge to touch him; to trace the sharp angles of his jaw like she had often done when they were dating. *We were once so good together.* Sure they'd had their heated disagreements, but making up had always made it worthwhile.

She turned to leave. "Dallas." At first she thought he might've been talking in his sleep, but she turned to find his concerted gaze on her. And she knew slipping into his room hadn't been one of her better decisions.

"Are you okay?" he asked, his voice husky from sleep. He rose up on his elbow. "Did you need something?" He sat all the way up and threw his long legs over the side of the bed.

Momentarily speechless, her gaze dropped from his eyes, to his wide shoulders down to his remarkable chest. Sitting up, he looked even more delicious. She had heard people talk about their mouths going dry, but this might've been the first time she'd experienced it. Her gaze drifted to the tight muscles that made up his six-pack. She appreciated how his narrow waist led to ... *dear God, I have to get out of here.*

Tyler stood and grabbed her by the elbow. "Wait. What's wrong? You look like you're about to pass out. Come and sit down."

She shook her head and gulped. "Uh, I'm fine," she said and readjusted her crutches. "I wanted to talk, but you're tired. I'll go."

"Okay, but first sit down." He helped her to the bed, though she knew it was a bad idea. "Do you want some water or something?" She shook her head no. "Well, if you're worried about some idiot getting to you, don't be. I'm not gonna let that happen. You'll be safe here."

Yeah, but who's going to keep me safe from you. She tried to stifle the strong current that raced through her body. She needed to say what she had to say and get the heck out of there. But each time she tried to open her mouth her eyes helplessly strayed to his flawless body. She ached to run her fingers over his perfectly defined chest. *Goodness, was he this buffed when we were dating? To just touch him—*"

"Dallas?"

"Huh?" She shook her head. "I'm sorry, did you say something?"

"I guess I'm not the only one who's tired," Tyler chuckled. "You said you wanted to talk."

"That's right … I did. I said some things the other day that I didn't mean, and I apologize. Yes, I was mad at you, but I know you only had my best interest in mind."

"I did, but that's no excuse. I'm sorry I called your job stupid. I know how important it is to you, and I didn't mean to hurt you."

Dallas heard the sincerity in his sleep-filled voice and felt her insides melt. But when his finger traveled gently down her cheek, she knew she was a goner.

****

Tyler felt Dallas shiver under his touch but didn't let it stop him from taking what he wanted. He leaned down and placed his lips over hers. Before today, it had been a long time since he held her this close. Shocked by her eager response, their slow, tender kiss quickly turned into one that reminded him of the passion they once shared. No woman had ever gotten him so aroused so fast.

He wanted more. Lifting her, he placed her further onto the bed, and eased her back then covered her body with his. He stared down at her, admiring her doe-like eyes and baby smooth skin. Abruptly, his head lowered and captured her kissable lips again. Divine ecstasy flowed through his veins when she wrapped her arms around his neck, causing him to deepen the connection.

A whimper slipped through her lips as his hand explored the soft path down her taut stomach and over her tempting hips. He loved the way her tantalizing body twisted beneath his touch, revealing her need for more.

He recaptured her lips and a forest fire of desire swept through him. Her mouth was as voracious and as greedy as his, her hands as daring. She shifted and he groaned when she grabbed his butt and pulled him closer, revealing his arousal.

"Ty," she called out breathlessly.

"Yeah, baby," he said, and trailed kisses down her long, graceful neck. He loved it when she called him Ty, which usually only happened during their most passionate moments.

He allowed his hands to move lazily down the front of her body and unbuttoned her nightshirt to reacquaint himself with her generous breasts.

"Tyler?" Skylar knocked and called out on the other side of the door. "Are you in there?"

Chapter Eight

Tyler cursed under his breath but didn't move. Dallas squirmed beneath him.

"Tyler?" Skylar called again.

"Yeah." He looked toward the door and positioned himself in front of Dallas. If Skylar walked in, she wouldn't see much.

"You have a telephone call. Do you want me to take a message?"

"Yes."

"Are you sure? Don't you want to know who it is?"

"I don't care, just take a message," he growled.

"But it's your *mother.*"

Now she was messing with him. "Sky, get away from the door!"

She laughed. "Okay, I'll tell mom you're a little tied up right now. Also, your virtual assistant called. Your nine o'clock meeting in the morning has been canceled. She called and texted you earlier and got concerned when she didn't hear back from you."

"Okay, thanks."

"Oh, and can you let Dallas know her cell phone was ringing?" Skylar let out a mischievous laugh on her way down the hall. He felt like he was back in high school when he'd sneak a girl up to his room. His sister had always been good at running interference.

Dallas pushed against his chest. "Will you move so I can get up?" She punched him in the arm when he didn't shift out of the way.

"Move! What is wrong with me? I can't believe I let things get this far."

There's that fiery attitude he'd grown to love. "What if I'm not ready to stop what we've started?"

"If you don't mo—"

"All right, I'll move. But this isn't over."

"The hell it isn't. We can't go back. I shouldn't have let you kiss me again." She hurried to re-button her nightshirt.

"Please. It's not like you didn't kiss me back." He stood and slid his shirt on but didn't bother to button it. "If I remember correctly your hands were all over me, encouraging me to go further."

Dallas grabbed her crutches from the side of the bed and hobbled to the door.

"So what, you're going to leave without saying anything?" He stepped in front of her. "You wanted that kiss as much as I did. Had Skylar not interrupted, we would've been doing a lot more than kissing."

Dallas shook her head and finally looked at him. "No. You're wrong. That … *all of that,*" she waved her hand over at the bed, "was a mistake. I shouldn't have come in here."

Tyler leaned against the door and folded his arms across his chest. "What are you running from Dallas? You want me as much as I want you. Why fight it? And don't you dare say anything about that partnership."

Her mouth tightened and her anger-filled eyes clawed him like talons. He knew if it weren't for holding onto her crutches, her hands would've been on her hips and she'd be giving him a serious neck roll right about now. It took everything he had not to burst out laughing at the thought.

"This conversation is over," she said through gritted teeth. "Now move out of the way or I won't be responsible for where this crutch ends up!"

"Okay, okay," Tyler put up his hands to block the crutch. "Must you be so violent?"

"Tyler…"

"All right, but seriously, I'm not going to apologize for what just happened. Granted, maybe the timing is not the best, but I want you. And I believe you feel the same way." How many times had he dreamed about having her in his arms again? More times than he cared to remember.

She sighed loudly. "I ... we can't. We're friends and nothing else. That's what I came in here to talk to you about. I appreciate you letting me stay here, and for looking out for me, but we can't go back. *I* can't go back to what we had."

Tyler ran a hand over his head and stared at her before asking. "What did we have Dallas? Was I just one of your many flings?" She gasped at his statement, but he kept going. "When you broke things off between us, I had a feeling that it wasn't just about you needing to focus more on your career. It was something else. What was it?"

She looked everywhere but at him, which surprised him. She was never at a loss for words which confirmed his suspicion. There was another reason she had turned down his proposal.

Tears welled up in her eyes when he lifted her chin to look at him. "Tyler ...."

"Talk to me baby. You know you can tell me anything."

She leaned more on one crutch, and slowly moved his hand away. Swiping at her tears she looked down at the floor, and then back up at him. "I didn't accept your proposal of marriage because ... I have to focus on my career."

She was lying, but why? He opened the door and resisted the urge to touch her. "Sweet dreams," he whispered when she walked past him.

Tyler closed the door behind her and leaned against it. *I'm in trouble. I'm in big trouble. So much for not letting her back into my heart.* He groaned and moved to the bed. What was he going to do? Kissing Dallas made him want her even more. Quinn was right, he might as well quit denying his feelings and deal with them. But he couldn't make someone love him, especially not Dallas.

Several moments passed before a slow smile spread across his face as a plan unfolded in his mind. The way she responded to him tonight was proof she still had feelings for him. There was a chance he could win her back. Now all he had to do was get *her* to realize she wanted him as much as he wanted her. So in addition to keeping her safe, he'd show her they were perfect for one another and meant to be together.

****

Dallas lay in bed still feeling the effects of Tyler's kisses. His soft lips against hers brought back wonderful memories of the times they'd spent together. No man had ever made her feel as alive as he had. And those hands, *Lord.* He always did know how to make her body respond with only a touch. Every stroke set her on fire. Even now, the heat between her thighs spread through her like hot lava. She blew out an annoyed breath and fanned herself with a magazine from the side table.

Frustrated, she tossed the magazine to the other side of the bed and sat up. She had to get a grip. She put her hands over her face and released a low smothered scream. *Tyler and I are just friends – nothing more. We simply got caught up in the moment.* She groaned and fell back against her pillows knowing she was lying to herself. *I am so weak!*

"Okay," she said out loud to the ceiling, "tomorrow is a new day. I'm going to act like nothing happened, because nothing did happen. I'm a grown woman, not some teenager who can't control herself. Tyler is my friend…*a special friend*, but a friend none the less. I will not risk our friendship for a quick lay." She sighed and chanted those words over and over until she drifted off to sleep.

****

Tyler had been awake for hours catching up on some work in his home office. Touching base with his general contractor on the North Carolina project took longer than he expected, but he was glad he could handle some of the issues over the telephone. He also had a chance to talk with Quinn about Dallas's situation, and a workable plan to keep her safe.

He tossed his pen onto the desk and stood. The smell of blueberry pancakes and hot maple syrup permeating throughout the house drew him down the hall and into the kitchen. After missing dinner last night, he felt hungry enough to eat a horse.

"Morning," he said to his sister when he walked into the brightly lit kitchen. He had no doubt she'd give him the business about Dallas being in his room, but he was ready for her. He moved to the coffee maker on the counter and poured himself a cup of coffee.

"Good morning. Sleep well?" Skylar asked between bites.

Tyler glanced at his sister and didn't miss the humor in her eyes. "As a matter of fact I *didn't*, thanks to my irritating sister."

"Hey, don't take your frustrations out on me. You should've put a 'Do Not Disturb' sign outside your door."

He shook his head and smiled. "Sometimes, I can't stand you." Dishes filled with breakfast items were spread across the center island. Skylar enjoyed cooking and always made enough to feed a football team. He grabbed a plate and loaded it with pancakes, sausages, scrambled eggs, and fresh fruit, and then he sat at the table across from her. "So what did Mom want last night?"

"She wants us all, including Dallas, to go to church with her and Daddy next Sunday. It's family day."

"Oh." He hadn't been to church in a few weeks and was surprised his mother hadn't called sooner to inquire about his whereabouts. "I'll check with Dallas. I'm scheduled to be in North Carolina for a few days next week, but I've been thinking about delaying the trip."

Skylar smiled. "So is church the only reason you're delaying your trip? Or could it be that you can't pull yourself away from your bedmate, I mean houseguest?"

Tyler eyed her over his coffee cup. "I don't know why I tell you anything." He put the cup down and cut into his sausage.

"Should I start planning an engagement party?"

"Don't go making a big deal over last night. I'm probably setting myself up again."

"So why do it? Why keep going after her when she apparently doesn't want you?" She grinned mischievously.

Tyler shot her a penetrating look. "I still love her and she *does* want me. She's just fighting it." He shoved the sausage into his mouth.

Skylar threw her head back and laughed. "Yeah. Right."

"I don't know why she's fighting what she feels, but there is no doubt in my mind she loves me."

"Well, she sure has a funny way of showing it. Although, her being closed up in your room last night does suggest otherwise."

She wouldn't have kissed me back if there wasn't anything between us. He felt her hunger and passion bursting to be released, and he was just the man to bring her complete satisfaction. He smiled. *Yep, she wants me.* That little bit of hope was all the encouragement he needed to pour on the charm.

Skylar cleared her dishes and returned to her seat. "So, what about Desiree? Aren't you supposed to escort her to some banquet or something?"

"Yep, this weekend. But that has nothing to do with my feelings for Dallas. I agreed to take Desiree as a *friend.*"

Tyler grinned inwardly. Nothing got a woman's attention like seeing her man, or in this case, future man, with another woman. Oh, yeah, he was going to enjoy seducing Ms. Dallas.

"Speaking of friend, are you aware that Dallas sees you as only a friend?"

"I'm aware of that, but I plan to remind her of how good we once were together. When I finish courting her, she'll be asking for my hand in marriage."

Skylar stared at him for a few seconds and then burst out laughing. "I see you still have a high opinion of yourself. I'm looking forward to watching this courtship unfold."

"Yeah, you laugh now, but wait, you'll see."

Skylar kept him company while he finished his breakfast. They talked and laughed about some of their dating failures back in high school and college. Tyler remembered some of the guys she dated, but was surprised by some of the ones he didn't know about. The conversation eventually went back to Dallas.

"Have you recovered from yesterday's shock?"

He shook his head. "I can't tell you how glad I was to see you guys walk through the door last night."

"It showed. You looked like you were about to faint from relief. So has there been any word this morning?"

"I haven't heard anything, and I doubt that Dallas has. I'm not even sure she's awake yet. One thing I know for sure, though, is that I definitely don't want her going out alone. Quinn and I are going to shadow her until we hear something from the detective. If Q and I aren't around, I have a car and a driver lined up to take her wherever she needs to go. I'm hoping, during those times, you'll be available to hang with her."

"She's going to pitch a fit."

"Maybe, but until we know everything is fine, she's going to have to deal with it."

Several hours later, Tyler knocked on Dallas's door. He wanted them to get reacquainted, and there was no time like the present.

"Come in," she said, her voice groggy.

"Wake up sleepy head."

Dallas opened her eyes slowly and stretched. "What time is it?" She squinted against the sunlight pouring through the opened blinds.

"It's almost one in the afternoon." Tyler sat on the side of the bed and brushed hair out of her face. "Are you planning to sleep the day away?"

"I hadn't planned on it, but I feel like I could," she said, burying her head under the covers.

Tyler pulled the blanket back. Her eyes were red and her hair was all over the place, but she still looked beautiful to him. "Didn't you sleep well?" He smirked. Since thoughts of her kept him awake most of the night, it would serve her right if she experienced the same thing.

She rolled her eyes at him. "I would've slept fine if I hadn't received a call from Harmony."

"Your sister? What did she want?"

"Her usual. *Money*. I wonder what mess she's in now. She only calls when she needs me to bail her out of something."

"So what did she say?"

"We were disconnected before she could answer any of my questions. I tried calling back, but I got her voicemail."

"Oh. Well, I'm sure she'll call you again. But in the meantime, what about spending the day with me?"

Dallas eyed him suspiciously. "If you think there's going to be a repeat of last night, you can think again. You caught me at a weak moment. That's not going to happen a second time."

Tyler threw his head back and laughed. "Dallas, you don't have weak moments. But don't worry I'll keep my lips to myself … for now."

"Forever. I'm not playing, Tyler. We're friends and that's it. Yes, I'll admit there's still a strong attraction between us, but we both know we can't be more than friends."

Tyler frowned. "I know no such thing. You're the one who's fighting her feelings. I'm clear about what I want." He placed a finger under her chin and moved closer as if he'd planned to kiss her. "And I want you."

He felt her go still under his touch and noticed that her lids lowered in anticipation of his kiss, but he needed to exercise some self-control. Until she verbally admitted her feelings for him, any intimate moves from here on out would have to be initiated by her. In the meantime, he'd pour on the charm until she begged to be kissed and loved by him.

He saw the surprise in her eyes when he kissed her cheek then stood and moved to the door. "Be ready in an hour. I'll even let you decide how you'd like for us to spend the day," he said and left the room leaving a stunned Dallas staring after him.

****

"Is your gun license up to date?" Tyler asked Dallas just as she bit into her bacon cheeseburger.

She eyed him and wondered what prompted the question. They were at one of her favorite hamburger joints on Port Washington Road, and the last thing she wanted to talk about were guns. "Yes, why?"

"Because you never know when you might need to pull Foxy Brown out of her case." He took a swig of his drink. "When was the last time you went to the shooting range?"

Dallas put the burger down and wiped her mouth with the napkin she lifted from her lap.

She looked around the outdoor space where the seating was very limited with small bistro tables for two, and noticed the area had filled up quickly. She returned her attention to Tyler. Here they were, having a nice outing with great food on a beautiful afternoon, and he wanted to talk about guns and shooting.

"Tyler, do you know something I don't know?"

"No. I'm asking these questions because I don't know what we're up against, and I want us to take all the necessary precautions to keep you safe."

Dallas didn't want to think about the car accident, the calls, the note, or any of it. The thought of someone trying to harm her freaked her out, but she refused to hide under some rock and stop living a normal life.

"Shouldn't we wait to hear more? I don't want to have to do things differently, especially if this is all some very bad joke."

"And *I* sure as hell don't want to wait until someone puts you back in the damn hospital or kills you before we take this seriously," he growled.

Dallas flinched at his tone. He didn't get angry often, but when he did, he didn't mince words. She should be glad he cared enough to think of these things. It had been a long time since someone showed genuine interest in her well being.

"I don't want you going anywhere by yourself. Quinn or I will take you wherever you need to go. And if we can't, I have a car and driver on standby."

"Tyler, I don't need a bodyguard. We don't even know anything for sure. I think you're overreacting."

"What about the phone calls, Dallas? And have you forgotten about the note? People don't mail threatening notes unless they're trying to get your attention. Now they have mine, and I'm a little surprised they don't have yours."

She didn't want to argue with him. They'd been having a nice time together before this conversation and she wanted to go back to that. Her words earlier were more for her peace of mind than the truth of what she'd been feeling since meeting with the detective. "Okay, whatever you say. Now can we talk about something else?"

He looked at her. Dallas was sure he expected a fight and not for her to give in so easily. "Fine."

She smiled. "Speaking of *fine*, I ran across this the other day." She pulled a local magazine out of her large tote bag and placed it in front of him. "I knew I was keeping company with a *fine* brotha, but I had no idea I was in the presence of the finest man in Milwaukee."

Tyler grinned and shook his head. He briefly looked at the page she had turned to. "I didn't think anyone I knew would see this article."

She lifted the magazine and read from it. "It says not only are you the *finest* specimen who has ever walked the streets of Milwaukee, but you are also the *smartest, wealthiest, and the most charming man* the writer has ever had the pleasure of meeting."

"I guess she doesn't get out much," Tyler said dryly. "So, since you want to talk about making news, let's talk about you Ms. I-can-turn-down-an-offer-from-Wall Street-'cause-I-got-it-like-that."

Dallas's mouth fell open. "How did you hear about that? That was supposed to be kept under the radar." Her hands went to her hips. "Let me guess – Simone. She's the only person I mentioned it to."

Tyler shook his head. "Nope. Let's just say, I have connections in *very* high places. It came up in conversation a few months ago. So why didn't you take the job? You would've been wealthier than Oprah."

"I'm wealthy enough. Besides, I had no interest in relocating to New York. I have unfinished business in Chicago." There was no need to bring up the partnership, since it would guarantee an argument.

"Wait a minute. Are you saying you gave up an opportunity of a lifetime to continue pursuing a partnership at *Weisman and Cohen*?"

Dallas dropped her head. He would never understand the importance of this partnership. How could she explain it to him without revealing too much?

He reached out and touched her hand. "Dallas?"

"Tyler." She gazed at his handsome face. "The partnership is extremely important to me for several reasons. Shortly after my internship, I had an opportunity to make partner at the firm I was with. But due to some unforeseen … circumstances, it was given to someone else."

She looked down at their hands which were now joined. Part of her wanted to tell him the whole ugly truth, but she wasn't ready. Besides, she didn't think she could share the story without breaking down, and there was no way she'd cry in front of him and out in public.

"Ty, where have you been?" A tall, immaculately dressed woman approached their table.

Tyler squeezed Dallas's hand, and looked over his shoulder. "Hey, what's going on, Crystal? I got your message, but I didn't have time to stop by." He stood and hugged her.

"Well, I'm available today." Her face split into a sultry smile, and she batted her long eyelashes as she clutched his arm. "Why don't you stop by this evening? I really need you to take a look at a few things." The double meanings weren't lost on Dallas. She hated it when women threw themselves at men.

Tyler removed himself from her grip and shoved his hands into his pockets. "I can't today, but I … oh, I'm sorry, Dallas, this is an old friend. We grew up in the same neighborhood. Crystal Halden, meet Dallas Marcel."

"Hello," she extended a well manicured hand to Dallas.

"Hi," Dallas said, accepting the limp hand shake, another thing she couldn't stand about some women. Didn't they know a weak handshake meant a weak personality?

"Crystal, I'll have one of my guys come by later to check out the sink."

Her ruby red lips pouted as she ran her hand along Tyler's arm. "Come on, Ty. Why can't you come?"

Tyler shook his head. "Can't. I have other plans, but don't worry, someone will be by later."

A look of defeat covered the woman's attractive features. "Well, okay, make sure they call first." She swung her large Chanel bag over her shoulder, nearly hitting Dallas with it. "I'll talk to you later." She leaned in, placed a lingering kiss on Tyler's cheek, and walked away.

Dallas thought she'd be sick. The woman's childish behavior didn't match her pulled together look. With every word, her hands were somewhere on Tyler's body, and Dallas found herself annoyed by the transparency of the woman's intentions.

"Sorry about that. Occasionally, we help her with her maintenance issues," Tyler said, reclaiming his seat.

Dallas stared at him. "Well, I see you're still Superman, willing to help every damsel in distress." *First Desiree, now Crystal.*

"What? She's a friend who needs some help around the house."

"Yeah, I bet she does. Probably not the type of help you're thinking about. She was all over you."

"Maybe." He leaned forward, his voice low and controlled despite the searing flame in his eyes. "But there is only, and will only be one woman I want all over me. And she'll barely give me the time of day."

Dang, I walked right into that. "Ah, anyway, maybe we should get going. You said we could do anything I wanted to do today, and there's something I've wanted to do for months."

Thirty minutes later, they stood inside of a pool hall.

"Dallas, I'm starting to think this wasn't such a good idea," Tyler said as he grabbed their cue sticks and the balls.

"Come on, Tyler, you promised."

"Yeah, I promised we could do whatever you wanted, but I didn't think you'd want to play pool, especially while you're in a cast."

"I'll be fine." Dallas shuffled with her crutches through the smoke-filled room until she reached their assigned table.

"The moment I see you stumble or wince in pain, we're out of here," Tyler said, close to her ear, his hand around her waist. "I mean it."

Each time he touched her, a sensual charge shot through her body. She shook off the feeling. "Yeah, whatever. You worry too much. I'll be fine. Now break, you loser."

He chalked his cue stick without taking his eyes off of her. "Oh, so you want to start talking trash already? Let me go ahead and beat you real quick so we can get out of here." He broke and several balls sunk into the pockets. "Looks like I have stripes. I'll go ahead and clear the table so we can make our exit." He grinned.

An hour later, Dallas felt the effects of being on her feet for such a long stretch. Tyler had won the first couple of games, but now she was winning. Every muscle in her body screamed for her to stop.

Surely she'd pay in the morning, but for now, she was enjoying his company and was determined to beat him.

Tyler missed his third shot in a row. He rarely missed, especially so obviously. Dallas's brows knitted together. "What are you doing?"

He hunched his shoulders and moved to the other side of the table. "What?"

"You know what! I can't believe you're trying to throw the game. I can beat you without any help, Mr. Hollister. Now stop it."

"Okay, *Mrs.* Hollister." He smirked, reminding her of when everyone thought she was his wife during her hospital stay. "I'm giving you ten minutes to beat me, and then we're leaving. Don't think I haven't noticed you slowing down. We had an agreement, remember? Any pain, we leave."

"No, you had an agreement. I'm alright, but if you're ready to call it quits, fine. Let me sink these last two balls. Then we can leave."

****

The stranger played on the next table, listening to Dallas and Tyler's conversation. His reports to his client had been the same for the last couple of weeks and the guy was starting to get antsy. He took a long drag from his cigarette and leaned over the table. The eight ball bounced off the side rail and into the left corner pocket, just as he watched his target pack up to leave.

Chapter Nine

Chicago, Illinois

The only light illuminated the room from the lamp on his massive desk. For the past two hours, David Weisman had checked every file in his office, searching for the missing documents. If they fell into the wrong hands, he'd be ruined.

"Where are they?" he yelled out loud. A heavy sigh blew through his thin lips as he sat back in his chair. His plan wasn't going the way he had envisioned, and it didn't help that he was getting sloppy. Leaning forward in his chair, he rested his arms on his desk and pressed his index fingers to his temples. It was crucial that he remember where he'd last seen those papers. *Damn, I should've transferred that information to my ledger when I had the chance.*

His private line rang. "Weisman," he answered.

"We're going to need more investors. Otherwise, this little project is going to blow up in our faces."

"I'm working on it," he told the caller. "It's not like I can wave a magic wand to make them appear. You over-extended us on that last payout. Otherwise, we wouldn't be having this conversation."

"Don't try to put all this on me. Until you tell me how you're handling these investments, I'm going to keep doing what I do. And by the way, I've sent five investors your way in the past month, and you haven't been able to close the deals. So I suggest you get it together, otherwise, we're screwed." The caller disconnected.

Weisman replaced the receiver and leaned back in his chair. How would he explain the lost documents? If he didn't find them soon, there was no telling what would happen. "I have to get my hands on those papers."

****

The last few days with Tyler had been fun and exciting, like old times, but Dallas had to get back to work. She glanced around her new workspace and released a satisfied sigh. Tyler had set her up in one of the corners of his home office, giving her more space to spread out than she had upstairs.

The area was a little too masculine for her liking but it had been tastefully decorated. Floor to ceiling wood paneled bookshelves on each side of the fireplace housed thousands of books, making it the focal point of the room. Modern art pieces graced burnt red walls that enclosed several pieces of sturdy, dark furniture. The layout created a functional, yet relaxing space.

Turning her attention to her computer, she pulled up one of her new client's file. The client from hell, she lovingly thought of the older man. He had canceled the last two appointments, yet called every other day with the most ridiculous questions. The meeting they'd scheduled for today had also been canceled, but it didn't stop Dallas from working on a plan that would better diversify his multi-million dollar portfolio. Tomorrow she was meeting with her team, two other investment managers from her firm, and she hoped they all could agree on the suggestions she'd present.

Darn, I can't believe I forgot about these, she thought when she pulled several sheets of loose leaf paper from between a couple of her files. She still didn't know who owned the mysterious documents, or what they pertained to. She initially thought they were David's since some of the papers she'd receive from Bianca were from him, but since he hadn't inquired about them, she figured that maybe they belonged to one of the other managers. They might've been left at the copier and got mixed up with her papers.

"So you plan to work all day?" Tyler asked, strolling into the room with his briefcase and looking finer than any man should be allowed to look. He sported a tailored black suit with a light gray shirt and black and gray tie. His close cut hair and well-trimmed goatee were perfect as usual. *Yep, the article was correct. He definitely is the finest brother in the city.*

"As a matter of fact, I do. I've been goofing off enough these past few days with you. And today I had to get down to business."

Tyler placed his briefcase near his desk and unbuttoned his suit jacket as he strolled over to her worktable. "Well, that's too bad, because you're going to miss out on an irresistible offer." He made a move to turn and go back the way he came but she stopped him.

"Wait a minute. You know I'm an investor, and I don't pass up good deals before hearing all the details." He grinned, and she watched as he shook out of his jacket, and then removed his tie.

God, please don't let him take off anything else. I don't have the will power to control myself today. She couldn't help but notice how his shirt stretched across his wide chest and his large biceps screamed to be free of the garment. She wondered if he'd think she'd totally lost her mind if she acted on what she really wanted to do to him. Which was grab him by the lapels, pull him close, and place soft kisses down his muscular neck until he begged for mercy. She shook her head and tried to focus on what he was saying.

"Okay, so here's the deal." He placed both palms down on the table and looked at her. His woodsy cologne with a hint of vanilla enticed her nostrils. "I have two front row seat tickets to see one of your favorite performers."

Her eyes grew big. "Who?"

"Stevie Wonder."

She squealed. "Are you serious? Those tickets have been sold out for weeks. How in the world did you get front row seats?"

He grinned. "I know people."

She rolled her eyes and laughed. "I'd love to go, but I don't have anything to wear, especially anything that would go with this stupid cast on my leg."

"Well, since I'm taking the rest of the day off I'd be willing to suffer through a little shopping with you."

Her eyebrows shot up. "You … shopping? You hate shopping."

"I know, but for you I'll go. I'll even spring for you to get a little pampering in. So are you interested in my offer?"

"Are you kidding? Where do I sign?"

****

"Wow, look at you," Skylar said when Dallas walked into the house well after midnight, with Tyler following close behind her. "Girl, I love that dress! You look amazing in white. You'll have to let me borrow it next month for the all white party I'm attending."

"Just say when."

"So how was the concert?"

"It was amazing," Dallas gushed and placed her hand over her heart. "I think I'm in love with Stevie Wonder."

"Girl, you and me both," Skylar agreed.

Tyler frowned and held out his arms. "Uh, what about me? Don't I get some love? New dress, some pampering, front row seats and I barely get a thank you."

"Aw, I'm sorry," Dallas said and hobbled into his arms. She reached up to kiss him on the cheek, but he turned his head and the soft kiss landed on his lips. Surprised by his move, but not disappointed she said, "Thank you for the best evening I've had in a very long time." Tyler moved her crutches and pulled her closer.

Skylar cleared her throat. "Okay. On that note, I'm out here. I'm going to bed."

"I thought she'd never leave," Dallas said, and they both laughed.

"What am I going to do with you?" Tyler asked. He stared into her upturned face before placing a kiss on the tip of her nose. "These past few days have been fun. Thanks for hanging out with me."

"My pleasure. It's been like old times," she said, steadying herself. With his large hands around her waist, she took the liberty of wrapping her arms around his neck and caressing the side of his face. He'd been a perfect gentleman all evening and she hated it. It was time she took matters into her own hands. Her speech last week about them being friends worked a little too well. Sure she didn't want a serious relationship, but a little kissing here and there wouldn't hurt, would it?

Her heart hammered against her chest when she stared into his passion-filled eyes. With the way his eyes bore into hers, she wasn't the only one still affected by the attraction between them. Before she lost her nerve, she grabbed him by the collar and pulled him down until her mouth covered his. His reluctance, at first, surprised her until he began teasing her with his delectable tongue and his expert kiss. *Mmm, he tasted delicious.* If she weren't careful, she could get used to this. The way he treated her; the way he caressed her with just a look, and his kisses. *Have mercy.* Shock waves coursed through her body as their tongues played the mating game. How would she ever be able to leave him and return to her life?

To her disappointment, Tyler ended the kiss. He swept her up into his strong arms and said, "I'd better take you to your room before you get too carried away."

"Me?"

"Yeah, you."

"Okay, so what if I don't want to go to *my* room?"

Tyler lifted an eyebrow with a spark of surprise in his eyes. "Well, where do you want to go, *Mrs. Hollister?*" He held her as if she were weightless.

Dallas would never admit it out loud, but she loved it when he called her Mrs. Hollister. If only it were true. If only she could allow herself permission to travel down that road, with a guarantee she wouldn't get hurt. "That depends. Where are you going?"

Tyler gave an unstable chuckle. "Girl, don't play with me, 'cause right now you're playing with fire. I only have just so much control and it's teetering," he said nipping at her ear. "You have me so turned on I'm about ready to take you right here on this kitchen counter."

His expression turned serious. "I'm trying to respect the *friend* title you've given our relationship. So, I can carry you upstairs, to *your* room, or I can take you to some other part of the house. But wherever I take you, I'm leaving you … alone. So what's it going to be?"

Dallas stroked the fine hairs sticking out of the top of his button down shirt. He was right. She was the one who came up with the idea of them keeping their hands and lips to themselves. She needed to behave. Being in the same space with him right now probably wasn't a good idea, especially after that soul-stirring kiss. She wasn't sure how much longer she'd be able to abide by her own rules. "I guess you can take me to my room," she said and rested her head against his muscular chest.

****

"You've been grumpy for the past few days. What's going on?" Skylar asked, finishing up her breakfast of bacon, eggs and hash browns. "You haven't received any more crazy calls or threatening notes have you?"

Dallas shook her head no. She moved her scrambled eggs around on her plate as she thought about the last few days. Apparently, she hadn't done a good job of hiding her funky attitude. *It's all Tyler's fault.* He was avoiding her. Or at least that's the way it felt. She hadn't seen much of him since the night of the concert, and that amazing kiss. She couldn't believe he hadn't taken advantage of the situation. Just last week he had practically ripped her clothes off. She sighed. *It's not his fault. I need to figure out what I want. Either I maintain my stance or we pick up where we left off six months ago.*

Or maybe it's time to go home. Everything she felt for him, before their break up, occupied her mind and filled her heart. It had only been a few weeks, and she was falling for him all over again. And the fact he was attending that stupid banquet with Desiree tonight wasn't helping.

"Oh, so what, you ain't talking today? Well, that's okay, 'cause I know what your problem is. Desiree Thomas. I knew you'd regret pushing Tyler into the arms of that barracuda." Skylar walked over to the sink to rinse out her breakfast dish then load it into the dishwasher. "When are you going to admit you care for him?"

Dallas remained silent. What good would it do to admit her feelings? It wasn't like she'd act on them. He was too much of a distraction. She hadn't been sleeping well, and she wasn't getting her work done, all because of him. He'd sparked a desire in her that she hadn't felt in months and it was taking some serious control to keep her hands … and her lips to herself. He'd been creeping into her every thought, not to mention her nightly dreams.

"Hey, ladies. How are my favorite girls doing this morning?" Tyler asked, strolling into the kitchen and over to the coffee pot.

"I'm fine, but Ms. Sour Puss over there is another story." Skylar fixed him a plate and handed it to him. "I'm going outside for awhile. Maybe you can figure out what her problem is." Skylar dried her hands and left her brother and Dallas in the kitchen.

Tyler carried his plate and cup of coffee over to the table. With one hand on the table and one on the back of Dallas's chair, he leaned over her. "Are you feeling okay?"

She nodded. What could she say? *Don't go out with Desiree tonight. I don't want you with another woman.* She knew she was being selfish, but she didn't care. Tyler was too good for these shallow, superficial, gold digging women. According to Skylar, Desiree only wanted him for his money and his status. Why couldn't he see that? He deserved someone who could love him the way he deserved to be loved.

"Dallas?"

She finally looked at him. *And why does he have to be so damn attractive? And, God he smelled good. Urg,* she growled within. Men like him didn't come along often and here she was pushing him away. *What's wrong with me?* She screamed internally, but answered him calmly. "I'm cool, just a lot on my mind."

Tyler took his seat and bit into his bacon. "You've been kind of quiet for the last couple of days. Is something bothering you?"

"I'm ready to go home," she blurted out. If she left, she wouldn't have to watch loser women vying for his attention. "I've been here long enough. Though you've been absolutely wonderful, it's time for me to go."

Not daunted by her announcement Tyler shook his head. "I don't think that's a good idea," he said, his voice calm, his gaze steady. He wiped his hands and mouth with a napkin. "Until we find out who's threatening you and why, I'll feel better if you were here."

"But there haven't been any threats or any word from the police lately, maybe this has all been a big misunderstanding."

He looked at her doubtful but said, "Maybe, but let's be on the safe side and give it some time. I know being cooped up isn't helping, but I think you should give yourself a little more time to heal. Hopefully in a couple of weeks, they'll be able to take the cast off and put you in a boot. At least then I'll feel a little better about you being by yourself in Chicago."

Dallas hated when he was right. Yes, she was getting around better, but pain still gripped her with certain moves, and the stairs were still her enemy. Hopefully, at her next doctor's appointment they'd give her a clean bill of health and send her on her way. Until then, she'd wait it out. "Maybe you're right."

"I'm glad you agree. You'll be back on your feet soon."

"What's up my people," Quinn greeted as he walked into the kitchen. "Did y'all know the garage door was up?"

Tyler cursed under his breath and leaped from his chair. "I told Skylar about that. I don't want just *anybody* walkin' up in here." He looked pointedly at Quinn, passing him to go and close the garage.

Quinn smirked at his friend. "Man, forget you. So what's going on Ms. Dallas? You're looking beautiful as usual." He rinsed his hands in the sink, grabbed a plate, and then piled it with food.

"Thank you." She'd always liked Quinn. He appeared care-free and laid back, but there was a dangerous, sexy quality about him. It was no wonder women flocked to him like a magnet.

Tyler walked back over to the table and picked up his empty plate. "You finished?" he asked Dallas.

"Yes. I guess I wasn't very hungry." She handed him her plate, still filled with food.

He bent closer to her and spoke only loud enough for her to hear him. "If something else is bothering you, I hope you'd tell me. Quinn and I were headed to a meeting, but I can stick around awhile longer if you need me."

She sighed and met his intense gaze, their lips only inches apart. "Everything's fine. I'm just a little tired."

"Why don't you go and get some rest? If you don't want to go upstairs, you can always camp out in the family room or even the office. The sofa in there is pretty comfortable."

"Yeah, I might do that. My laptop and work files are still in there from yesterday, so maybe I'll work awhile and then take a nap."

****

"Dallas, sweetie, wake up," Tyler shook her. "I didn't want to leave without letting you know. Do you need anything before I go?"

She lifted her heavy lids and focused in on the amazing sight standing before her. *Tyler in a tuxedo.* Her gaze roved over his neat appearance and admiringly assessed him. From his freshly cut hair, to the shawl collared tux that fit perfectly over his broad shoulders and muscular chest, down to his shiny wingtips. The brother looked incredibly sexy. *God, please don't let me attack this man and totally embarrass myself.*

Tyler grinned. "By your appraisal, I'd say I did okay dressing myself."

Dallas rose into a sitting position and looked him over again. "I'd say you did better than okay. You look *good.*" Her voice filled with passion. For the first time since the accident, she was thankful for the heavy cast on her leg, otherwise, she would've jumped into his arms and covered his full sexy lips with her own.

"Thank you," he bowed slightly. "I'm getting ready to leave. Do you want me to carry you upstairs?"

Dallas shook her head. "No, that's okay. Since I slept most of the afternoon, I for real have to get some work done now. I'll be all right down here."

Tyler frowned. "Are you sure? I probably won't be home until late."

Her heart ached with the thought of knowing he'd be with another woman tonight. "Positive. If worse comes to worse, I can lie down here," she said, patting the sofa. "You were right, it is comfortable."

The shrill of the doorbell interrupted them. "Are you expecting someone?"

"No." Dallas snapped her fingers. "Oh, shoot. I forgot about Harmony. She was supposed to be here earlier, and as usual she's late. She wants to borrow some money from me." Dallas rubbed her forehead. "I forgot about her."

"Okay, I'll let her in. Be right back."

Moments later Dallas's sister walked into the room. "What is this place, a mansion or something?" she asked, looking around the massive office. The shady-looking man with her walked around the space as if he was casing the place.

"Hello to you too," Dallas said dryly. "Who's your friend?" She gestured her head towards the tall, dangerous looking guy, now standing near Tyler's album collection. He looked oddly familiar, but she couldn't place him.

"Oh, that's my man, Jerome." Harmony popped her gum and continued her surveillance of the room. "I woulda came earlier, but he didn't get back from Chicago until late. Then he had to get his car detailed."

Dallas studied her sister. For as long as she could remember, Harmony had been slim, but tonight she looked thinner than usual in her pink halter top and skinny jeans. She was beautiful enough to be on the cover of any national magazine, but Harmony had never been one to pursue a worthwhile career.

Dallas attempted to stand and Tyler walked over to assist her. She held onto the hand he extended and pulled him closer. "It's okay if you need to leave," she whispered.

Tyler placed an arm around her waist and spoke close to her ear. "There is no way I'm leaving you with these people. *Especially in my house*. I can wait."

"So who is this?" her sister asked, motioning toward Tyler who had his eyes glued on Jerome. "Daddy Warbucks or something?" She looped her arm through her boyfriend's and walked over to where Tyler and Dallas stood.

Dallas ignored the question. When she and Tyler were dating, she made it a point to keep him away from her blood sucking family. Her mouth tightened into a frown as Harmony's boyfriend looked at Dallas with longing in his dark, beady eyes. It was disrespectful to her sister, as well as Tyler. Where Harmony found these characters was a mystery to her. To be such a smart girl, she seemed to always end up with the scum of the earth.

"Here, let me get your package so you can leave," Dallas said in a chilly tone. She grabbed her crutches and walked over to the desk. After digging through her bag, she pulled out a white envelope. "Here, and in the future, if this is the only reason you're going to contact me, don't bother. This is my last donation to the Harmony Cole fund." She looked at Tyler. "Will you show them out?" Seeing Harmony reminded her of how dysfunctional her family was growing up.

"Oh, so it's like that." Her sister popped her gum and narrowed her eyes at Dallas. "I don't only come to you for money. The last time I was in Chi Town I tried hooking up with you, but you were too busy working. But nah, you don't remember stuff like that. Come on, Jerome, let's go." She shoved the envelope in her pocket and grabbed her boyfriend by the arm.

"Nice place you have here," the boyfriend finally said to Tyler, his voice low and raspy. "Me and my girl gotta come back and visit one day when we have more time." He grinned, showing several gold teeth.

Tyler looked at him, his eyes dark and unfathomable. "That probably won't be a good idea." He stretched out his arm, gesturing them to the door.

Minutes later, Tyler re-entered the room shaking his head. "So that's Harmony?"

"In the flesh." Dallas sat at the desk. "Now you know why I was never in a hurry to introduce you to her. The girl attracts thugs like honey attracts bees. It drives me nuts. She has too much sense to be hooking up with knuckleheads like him." Dallas allowed her eyes to roam the length of Tyler's body before saying, "Thanks for staying. I hope I didn't put you behind schedule."

Tyler sat on the edge of the desk and peeked at his watch. "Nah, I'm cool. But I probably should head out soon, unless of course you want me to stay here and keep you company."

He reached out and moved some hair away from her face, then let the back of his hand trail down her cheek. Dallas closed her eyes and leaned into his gentle touch. She hated to see him leave, but had to face the fact that he'd be hers, if only she'd given them a chance.

Opening her eyes, she moved away from his touch and glanced up at him. "Enjoy your evening," she murmured.

He stood, walked to the door and turned to face her. "Skylar's upstairs, but if you need anything, you know how to reach me."

Chapter Ten

Hours later, Tyler pulled into his garage, and entered the house through the kitchen. He tossed his keys on top of the refrigerator, and shook out of his suit jacket. He should've known he wouldn't have been able to stand Desiree for the whole evening.

"Hey. You're home early," Dallas said as she hobbled in and leaned on the doorframe for support. "How was it?"

"It was all right." He reached into the refrigerator for water. "Can I get you anything? I'm about to cut a slice of pie."

"That sounds good. Can you also grab the milk?" She sat at the kitchen table while he prepared their snack.

"How was your night?"

"It was okay. I didn't get as much work done as I would've liked, but at least I made some progress. So tell me about the banquet."

"Nothing to tell." He took the seat closest to her. "Picked up Desiree, took her to the banquet, hung out for a minute, then left. End of story."

"What's with the attitude and why are you really back so soon?" She glanced at the clock on the microwave. "It's barely eight-thirty." She took a bite of her pie, and her eyes rolled as she savored Skylar's handiwork.

"Tired, so I left early."

No need in telling her what really happened. It wasn't one of his proudest moments, especially the way he'd abandoned Desiree at the event. He knew before going out with her that she wanted more from him. She'd been after him for years, but he really thought he could escort her to the banquet with no drama. She clearly had other things on her mind.

With her fork midair, Dallas's eyebrows shot up. "You were tired? You have more energy than anyone I know. *And* rumor has it you were out with a *very* beautiful woman. So forgive me if I don't believe you." She took another bite and grabbed her milk. "What? Did she try to jump your bones or something?"

Tyler didn't respond.

Dallas stared at him over her glass. Her eyes twinkled with mischief. "Well, I'll be. The strong and sexy, Tyler Hollister, is afraid of a harmless little lady."

He stood, took his plate to the sink and rinsed it. "I wasn't afraid. And there is nothing little or harmless about that woman!"

Dallas laughed. "Is that why you ran? She was too much for you."

"I'm glad you find this amusing. How would you feel if you said *no* to a man and he wouldn't stop but had his hands all over you?"

She wasn't laughing now. As a matter of fact, her downcast eyes caused him to pause. "I'm sorry, I shouldn't have yelled. I—"

"No, no, you're right," she said. "When a woman says no, she expects the man to stop. Men should be given that same respect. I apologize if I made light of an uncomfortable situation."

Tyler reclaimed his seat next to her. "It's not exactly what you think. I told her upfront I wasn't interested in anything but escorting her to the banquet. She didn't attack me." A small smile curved his lips. "She made a few harmless passes, but nothing I couldn't handle. I just wasn't interested."

"I don't know, Tyler. Maybe you shouldn't be so hard on her. I have to be honest with you. There was a moment this evening I wanted to have my hands all over you too. You were looking pretty *hot* tonight. I can understand why she had a hard time controlling herself."

A wide grin spread across his face and he cleared his throat. "Well, anytime *you* can't control yourself, go for it. I won't fight you off." He joked.

"Ha, thanks. I'll keep that in mind."

Tyler grabbed her empty plate and took it to the sink. "How about watching a movie with me tonight?"

"Sure, why not?"

Dallas and Tyler lounged in the theater room after the movie ended. Each caught up in their thoughts as soft jazz flowed through the dimly lit space.

"Dallas." Tyler shifted in the red leather seat to face her. "In the kitchen earlier, when we talked about how no means no, you looked a little uncomfortable. Did something happen in your past?"

Time stood still as he waited, hoping she'd finally trust him enough to share her thoughts and fears.

"In grad school," she finally said, "I got involved with a man who manipulated every aspect of my life. It almost broke me." She stared down at the clenched fist in her lap. Tyler could see how difficult it was for her to share this information, but she continued. "His verbal abuse and … well, anyway, I felt insecure and helpless. I promised myself then, I'd never allow a man to have power over me again."

"Did you love him?"

She forced a smile. "I thought I did. But looking back, I know I didn't. It was like I didn't have a mind of my own. Even with his arrogance and condescending attitude, I let him talk to me any kind of way. It was months before I noticed I didn't control my own thoughts, and did very little without guidance from him."

"I'm surprised. One of the things I love most about you is your strong will and self-confidence. I wouldn't have ever guessed you weren't always like you are now."

"Oh, don't get me wrong. I grew up headstrong to the point of my mother threatening to send me away many times," she chuckled. "But with this guy … I was different. It's hard to explain. Tyler, he had a hold on me, and I don't mean in a good way."

His heart tightened against his chest. "Baby, I hope you know I would never…"

Dallas touched his arm. "What you and I have is special," she said and reached for his hand. "You respect me and treat me like I'm the most important person in the world. With this guy, I'm not even sure he liked me, or if he just got his kicks out of being able to control me."

She bit her bottom lip nervously. Tyler wanted to know more, but didn't push. He lifted her hand and kissed the inside of her wrist. "I didn't mean to bring up bad memories. I'd never intentionally hurt you."

"I know, and that's one of many reasons why I lo…," she stopped and looked away.

A knowing smile spread across his face. "Dallas, look at me." With a finger beneath her chin, he turned her to face him. "I know you have some feelings for me. And now I have a better idea why you've been fighting those feelings. What I don't understand is, why not give us another chance? I'm not the person who hurt you back in grad school." Dallas turned from him then struggled to stand due to the awkwardness of the cast, but Tyler wrapped his arms around her and pulled her into his lap. "Talk to me, sweetie." He kissed her neck below her ear.

"I can't let myself do that again."

"Baby, I'm not him. Don't hold what he did to you against me."

"Tyler, I don't want to get hurt. That time in my life was so horrible I didn't think I'd ever recover. Once I did, I promised myself I would take care of me and accomplish my goals. When you and I dated, I wasn't looking for anything serious. But I got so caught up in us, that I temporarily forgot about me, what I'd been through, and my goals. I can't say when, or if, I'll ever be ready for what you're asking of me. Can you understand that?"

He stared down at her beautiful face and nodded. If only he could get his hands on the bastard who had ruined her for anyone else. He sighed and rested his head against hers. *Well, at least I got her to almost tell me she loved me. Now I need to find a way to get her to trust me with her heart.*

****

Days later, Dallas shuffled into the living room and stopped short. The sight before her took her breath away. Dozens of vases filled with white, yellow, and red roses were scattered around the room. "What in the world?" There were more flowers than she could count.

"I told you it was something you'd have to see to believe. They arrived about two minutes ago." Skylar beamed. "It took three guys to bring them all in."

The sweet, earthy fragrance drew Dallas further into the room. "Oh my goodness these are amazing." She moved first to a vase that held yellow roses with orange edges and inhaled the magnificent scent.

"Here's the card." Skylar scooped it up from on top of the baby grand piano and handed it to her.

Dallas leaned heavily on one of her crutches and pulled the card out of the envelope. *Happy Birthday, baby. Clear your schedule for this evening because you and I have big plans. Tyler.*

"I can't believe your brother remembered," she said softly, still staring down at the card.

"Remembered what?"

Dallas looked up. "My birthday."

Skylar's hands flew to her hips. "Why didn't you tell me? Happy Birthday." She hugged her, and then stepped back and looked at her with all the love of a beloved sister and hugged her again.

Dallas laughed. "Girl, you're crazy, but thank you," she said, steadying herself on her crutches as the doorbell rang.

"Let me see who that is. Be right back." Seconds later, Skylar returned with another vase of roses. "Wow, I didn't know they made blue roses. These are exquisite."

Dallas gasped and stumbled back. An icy fear traveled from the top of her head to the soles of her feet, and her crutches crashed to the floor.

Skylar grabbed her around the waist before she hit the floor. "Girl, the flowers are pretty, but I didn't expect that reaction. You look like you've seen a ghost. Are you okay?" She helped Dallas to the sofa and sat next to her.

Still breathing hard Dallas didn't respond. She couldn't. Small beads of perspiration formed on her forehead and she struggled to catch her breath. It was as if someone had a relentless grip around her neck, cutting off her air supply. She *had* seen blue roses before, and it didn't matter how beautiful they were, she detested them and the person who used to give them to her. *God, please let them be from Tyler.*

As if reading her mind, Skylar said, "Looks like there's another card." She plucked the card from the flowers. "Here."

With a hand on her chest, Dallas shook her head vigorously. "No. You read it. Better yet, don't read it. I don't need to know what it says."

"Dallas, what's wrong? You don't look too good. Here," she grabbed a throw pillow, "lie down for a moment and I'll go get you some water and a hand towel. You're sweating like crazy." She put the card on the table, near the sofa, and rushed out of the room.

Dallas picked up the card. She hesitated, took a few deep breaths and then read it. *I want you back.* "Oh, dear God," she cried. The card trembled in her hands and tears trickled down her cheeks. *Mark. It can't be.* When she heard Skylar returning, she shoved the card into her pants pocket and wiped her face.

"Where are you going?" Skylar asked when Dallas struggled to stand.

"Can you help me upstairs? I need to lay down for awhile."

After Skylar left her alone in her room, Dallas called Simone, who picked up on the first ring.

"Happy birthday, my sister! I would sing to you, but someone once told me that I should stick with my day job and let those who can carry a tune do the singing."

"Simone," Dallas said just above a whisper.

"Dallas, what is it?"

Dallas swiped at the tears that wouldn't stop. "I received blue roses today."

Silence. "Surely you don't think…"

"No one else in this world sends blue roses," she spat out bitterly. On their first date, Mark Darley had given her blue roses and continued to send them for every special occasion throughout their time together.

"I don't understand. Why now? And how could he possibly know you're at Tyler's?"

Dallas massaged her temples. "I don't know." Her tears had stopped, but it felt like a jackhammer was pounding in her head. For a person who rarely had headaches, she'd had quite a few since the accident, which her doctor said was to be expected after having a mild concussion.

"Did you tell Tyler?"

"I can't. He doesn't know about Mark; and I plan to keep it that way. Mark is my past and that's where he's going to stay."

"You have to tell Tyler about the flowers. What are you afraid of?"

"Nothing. I…I…I'm probably overreacting. I don't even know if Mark sent them. They might've been delivered by accident."

"Like you said, no one else sends blue roses. Dallas, what if Mark is the one who left that note in the mailbox a couple of weeks ago, or worse, the person who put you in the hospital? You have to tell Tyler."

Chapter Eleven

"Man, I'm glad you're here," Skylar said when Tyler entered the house. "I think something's wrong with Dallas."

"What?" He dropped his things near the door and took off his suit jacket, tossing it over one of the kitchen chairs. "Where is she?"

"In her room."

"Why didn't you call me?" he asked over his shoulder and moved toward the stairs.

"I tried, but wait. Before you go up there I need to show you something." She led him into the living room.

"Sky, if Dallas is sick I…" he started, but stopped when she handed him the vase with the dozen blue roses. He turned the vase several times as he inspected the flowers in awe. The dark blue petals with their exotic look were like no other flower he'd ever seen. "Wow, these are amazing, but I didn't order them. Hell, I didn't even know blue roses existed. But now that I know I mig—"

"Well, if you plan to buy any in the future, don't buy any for Dallas," Skylar said dryly. "She almost fainted when she saw them."

His eyes narrowed and he sat the flowers down. "What?"

"She hyperventilated when I walked in with those flowers. She looked spooked. You should've seen her. I promise you her face turned two shades lighter. It was the weirdest thing I'd ever seen. Mind you, she was perfectly fine before I brought those flowers in here."

Tyler ran a hand over his mouth and down his goatee. "Did they come with a card?"

"Yep." Skylar searched the space. "I placed it here on the table before I left the room, but I don't see it. Maybe Dallas took it upstairs with her."

"You should've called me."

With her hands on her hips, Skylar glared at him. "I told you I tried. Your phone kept going to voice mail."

He pulled his cell from his belt, glanced at it, and then looked at his sister sheepishly. "Sorry. Dead."

She rolled her eyes. "Anyway, I called the florist who delivered *your* flowers and the owner said they don't carry blue roses. What's interesting, though, is that she said most places don't sell them because of the work involved to get them blue. Can you believe those are white roses dyed blue?"

Tyler touched one of the petals expecting some of the color to come off on his finger tips, but nothing. So if his florist didn't deliver them by accident, then who else sent Dallas flowers?

*****

He paced at the foot of her bed like a caged animal. She knew he'd be upset, but she had no idea he'd carry on like this. She didn't know which was worse, his marching back and forth in front of her with his fists balled at his sides or listening to him rant and rave about how much she'd disappointed him. As if he were the only one hurting.

"I can't stand to look at you right now. You've ruined everything," he growled through gritted teeth as he approached the left side of the bed. "I have worked my butt off trying to set up a good life for us, but that has never been good enough for you has it? With your one track mind to make partner, you probably let this happen on purpose!"

Dallas reared back as if she'd been struck. His caustic words were like a scalpel scraping against her bones. How could someone who claimed to love her treat her like this? She'd already lost so much, yet all he could think about was himself. "You know that's not true. How can you blame me for this?" she cried. "I wanted this more than you'll ever know."

"No, you didn't!" He grabbed and shook her. "Stop lying. You tried to do this. It was your way of defying me wasn't it? Answer me, dammit! Wasn't it?" He shook her harder but she fought back.

"Stop! You're hurting me!" she screamed. "Stop! Let me go!"

"Dallas. Dallas, wake up. You're having a bad dream. Baby, wake up."

Dallas continued to fight until she recognized Tyler's voice calling out to her. "Dallas, wake up," she heard him say again, and her eyes flew open. She lunged into his arms as deep sobs racked her insides like never before.

The dream seemed so real. The memories. The fear. The anger. Everything came flooding back. Over the years, working long hours had helped to suppress the hole in her heart. But seeing those blue roses brought all the pain and heartache back.

Hearing Tyler call her name, she finally looked at him. Despite the tears clouding her view, she could see the concern on his face.

She eventually pulled herself together, but it felt like she'd been run over by a semi-truck. Her eyes burned, her head throbbed and her body ached. If only she could've met this kind, gentle man who was now cradling her in his strong arms, first.

****

Tyler didn't know what to think when he found Dallas thrashing against her pillows. He reached out to wake her only to have her fighting him with balled fists. And damn if she didn't hit hard. He still could feel a twinge in his right shoulder blade.

He wiped the last of her tears and noticed some of the tension had left her body. "Are you okay?"

She blew out a weary breath. "Yeah. I'm sorry about all of this."

"Hey, don't apologize. I'm glad I was here. That must've been some dream. Do you want to talk about it?"

She shook her head. "No."

"Do you remember any of it?"

"No."

Tyler stared at her. "You don't remember *anything* about it?"

"No. I don't," she said, her attention locked on the crumpled tissue in her hand.

He could tell by the lack of eye contact that she was lying, but why? "Dallas, did the dream have anything to do with the blue roses that came today?" He felt her stiffen in his arms. "Well, tell me this. Who else besides me is sending you flowers, because I sure as hell didn't send any blue roses?"

She glared at him and shook out of his grasp. "I don't know who sent them, and I don't appreciate you talking to me like that."

He moved closer to her and turned her to face him. "I'm not sure what's going on with you right now, but let me tell you something. I don't like to share! And I don't plan to share you. Honey, I love you.

You might not be ready to hear me say it, but I do. If you have someone in the wings, you need to tell me now. So, who sent the flowers?"

"Tyler." She glided her soft hand down his cheek until he stopped her, covering her hand with his. "I don't know who sent them ... and it doesn't matter because there is no one else."

Without breaking eye contact, he lifted her small hand, turned it and kissed the inside of her wrist. "I hope you know you can trust me. Whatever's going on, I'm here for you." He kissed her lips and pulled back to see eyelashes laced with tears.

He leaned in closer and allowed his hand to travel down the back of her head to the curve of her neck. He'd told himself to follow her lead and not rush her into anything, but God if he didn't want to kiss her. Their eyes held for a second before he moved his mouth over hers and eased her back against the pillows. What started as a gentle kiss, turned into passion filled tongue aerobics. He couldn't get enough of her. Even with her trembling in his arms, she pulled him closer, deepening their connection. The caress of her lips on his mouth sent the rest of his body into a tailspin, and he held on for the ride.

"No wonder Mom wanted you to have a babysitter while Dallas was staying here," Skylar said from the doorway.

Dallas pulled away and Tyler dropped his head on the pillow and growled. "God! You've got to be kiddin' me! Don't you have someone else you can harass?"

She laughed like she'd just learned the secrets of the universe. "Whatever. I guess you didn't hear the doorbell. Quinn's downstairs," she said and turned to leave.

Tyler rose up on his elbow and returned his attention to Dallas. "Are you feeling any better?" The back of his hand glided down her cheek in a gentle caress. He hadn't forgotten the fact that she'd lied about not remembering her dream, or at least he was pretty sure she'd lied. What was it going to take for her to trust him?

Her lids lowered as if enjoying his touch. "Yes. Thank you," she said, and looked at him. "About that declaration you made earlier...I..."

"Shh." He put a finger to her lips. "You don't have to say anything right now. I just wanted you to know how I feel." He couldn't believe he'd said those three words to her again. He kissed her lips and climbed off the bed. "We'll finish this up tonight, but in the meantime, let me go change my shirt and see what's up with Quinn. While I'm gone, why don't you get dressed? We have some serious celebrating to do. It's not every day a woman turns 34. How about some dinner and then we'll check out a new spot I heard about that plays live jazz?"

"I'd like that," she said and smiled for the first time since he'd entered her room.

He walked to the door and turned back to looked at her. "Remember, you know you can talk to me about anything. I meant what I said earlier. I'm here for you."

****

Twenty minutes later Tyler walked down the stairs making a mental note to have his assistant find out who, in the area, sold blue roses.

"What's up, man? Why haven't you been answering your phone?" Quinn asked when Tyler walked into the office.

Tyler finished buttoning his fresh shirt and tightened his tie as he made his way to his desk. "Thanks for reminding me. My battery died. I didn't realize it until I got home." He unclipped his cell phone from his belt and hooked the phone up to the charger. "What's going on with you?"

"I have some information." He pushed his long dread locks back over his shoulders and closed the office door. "It's about Dallas's firm."

Tyler lifted his head and raised an eyebrow. "What about it?"

"Rumor has it that the Weisman and Cohen Group are being investigated by the Security and Exchange Commission."

Tyler studied his friend. "The SEC doesn't get involved unless there's some mess going down."

Quinn nodded. "It's in the beginning stages, and I'm sure the firm doesn't know yet."

"Really? How's that?"

"My sources say the SEC has been watching them from a distance for the past couple of months. They haven't requested any detailed information from the firm yet, but it's coming."

Tyler sat on the corner of his desk, his arms folded. "This isn't good. Dallas is busting her butt, trying to make partner while they're doing who knows what."

"You can't say anything, Ty."

"Man, I can't keep this from her."

"You can, and you will. The SEC hasn't said what's behind the initial probing. We have no idea what … or who they're looking at."

Tyler pushed away from the desk. "I know you don't think they're investigating Dallas, do you?"

Quinn leaned on the back of the sofa. "Man, chill. We both know Dallas takes her job very seriously, and I doubt she'd do anything to jeopardize it. So don't—"

They both turned to the door when they heard a knock. "Come in," Tyler said.

Dallas stuck her head in before walking further into the room. "Hey, you almost ready?" she asked Tyler. "Hey, Quinn."

"How you doin' Ms. Dallas? You're looking mighty fine tonight." She smiled. "Thank you."

Tyler admired her from across the room. He didn't think she could get any more beautiful, but each time they went out she surprised him. Her hair was all done up with curls on top of her head with curly wisps of hair framing her face, which was perfectly made up. And the fact she didn't take forever to dress, always impressed him. Tonight she had on a strapless black fitted dress that reminded him of the one she had worn the first time they met. He remembered following her around that evening like a puppy dog, and tonight probably wouldn't be any different.

"Uh, give me a second, baby. I'll meet you in the kitchen."

"Okay. Good seeing you, Quinn."

"You too. And happy birthday."

"Thanks." She closed the door behind her.

Tyler grabbed his back-up cell phone and patted his pocket for his wallet. "Quinn, I don't feel good about keeping this from her. She already has trust issues, and I'm doing everything I can to change that."

"Yeah, I know. Give me a little more time and then you can tell her."

"So what you got goin' on tonight?"

"Not too much." He leaned on the desk. "Ty, I'm serious, you can't tell Dallas about what we just talked about."

"Q, man…" The look his friend shot him stopped Tyler from protesting. "All right, I won't say a word, but did you find out anything else?" Tyler searched the top of the desk for his keys and didn't look up until he realized Quinn hadn't answered. "Well?"

Quinn hesitated. "Nah, that's pretty much it for right now. I gotta get going. Have a good time tonight," he said on his way out the door.

Tyler watched him leave. He knew Quinn held something back.

****

"Bianca, I'm glad I caught you." David rushed to Dallas's assistant's desk. He ignored the fact that her computer was black, and she was standing with her purse over her shoulder and her briefcase in her hand. "Before you leave, can you give me Dallas's client files again? I didn't realize I needed some additional information from them."

"I'm sorry, Mr. Weisman, but Dallas has those files. If you'd like, I can contact her in the morning and let her know you need them again."

David swore under his breath and gripped the edge of the desk to ride the wave of nausea. He was screwed. If he left his makeshift ledger in Dallas's files like he thought he had, it would be impossible to get them back without raising suspicion.

"Mr. Weisman?" Bianca tilted her head. "Are you okay?"

David blinked to clear his mind. "Uh, what were you saying?" He wiped his sweaty palms down the side of his pants.

"I said I can call Dallas in the morning regarding the files."

"No, no, that won't be necessary. Do you know when she's expected back?" He rubbed the back of his neck and rolled his shoulders.

"I think in a couple of weeks, but I'm not sure."

"Okay, I'll wait until then and talk with her. Thanks." He rushed out the door and back to his office in time to see a person in the hallway, who wasn't supposed to be in the building during business hours.

"What are you doing here?" David growled and looked around to see if anyone saw him. He hurried his visitor into his office and closed the door. "I told you never to show your face around here. We can't risk anyone seeing you."

His visitor took a seat in one of the chairs positioned in front of David's desk. "Nobody saw me."

"Well, why are you here?" David rounded his desk and sat down.

"Are you ready for me to finish the job?"

"Not yet. I'm not convinced she knows anything."

"I think you're wrong. She's probably known for a couple of months, which is why I suggested we put a little fear into her."

David stood and leaned across the desk. "Listen to me, you two bit piece of trash. I don't pay you to think. When I'm ready for you to make another move, *I'll* let *you* know."

****

"This was a great choice, Tyler." Dallas smiled as they walked into one of her favorite restaurants. With the lobby's impressive décor of expensive artwork and dark wood paneling, each time she stepped through the door, she couldn't help but think of old money.

"I thought you'd be pleased. It's been awhile since we've been here."

They moved up to the hostess. "Hi. We have a reservation for two – Hollister." Tyler wrapped his arm around Dallas's waist, pulling her closer. "Are you sure you're okay using only one crutch this evening?" he asked for her ears only.

"I'm fine," she whispered back, feeling much better than she had earlier. Thoughts of the roses that totally freaked her out and the dream were tucked away in the back of her mind. She planned to enjoy her evening with this wonderful man who had professed his love for her again. No more pushing him away and insisting on them just being friends. *It's time to give love another try.* The last couple of weeks reminded her of how much she'd missed him and what they once shared.

"I'm glad you two could join us this evening," the hostess said. "Mr. Hollister, Mr. B. is here tonight and asked me to let him know once you and your companion arrived. He'll be stopping by your table shortly. Please follow me."

The hostess led them through a dimly lit dining room and over to a secluded circular booth in the corner. "Is this okay?"

"This is perfect." Tyler helped Dallas get adjusted in her seat, and leaned her crutch against the wall next to her.

Moments after the hostess walked away, Dallas recognized the owner walking toward them with a bottle of wine and a large grin. Apparently, Tyler spotted him at the same time.

"So what, you're slumming now, Joe? You couldn't get anyone else to wait on our table?" Tyler's voice was filled with the love and respect he had for his long time friend.

Joe placed the bottle of wine on the table and greeted Tyler with a one arm hug. "Man, where the hell have you been? I haven't seen you around here in over a year." Then he turned to Dallas and lifted her hand to his lips. "Ms. Dallas, you're even more stunning than I remember. I'm glad you decided to celebrate your birthday with us." He kissed the back of her hand.

Dallas blushed. "Thank you, Joe. It's good seeing you again. I can't think of any other restaurant I'd rather dine in on my birthday."

His hand covered his heart. "If I didn't think this big guy over here would come after me with a gun, I'd whisk you away from here."

"You're damn right. So don't go getting any ideas." Tyler said, and they all laughed. "But seriously, it's good seeing you again, man. You're looking good."

"I'm feeling good." Joe lifted the wine bottle and poured them each a glass. "Out of 230 wines, this is one of my favorites, so I figured I'd share it with my two special guests. Oh, and dinner is on me tonight." He lifted his glass. Dallas and Tyler lifted theirs as well. "To old friends."

****

Once the waiter cleared away the empty dessert plates, Tyler propped his elbow on the table and with his chin resting on his hand, his eyes scanned boldly over Dallas. Every day, his feelings for her intensified, making him want to make their reunion permanent. She looked healthy and the spunky attitude she wore like a badge of honor had returned. It was only a matter of time before she started talking about going home.

"And here I thought you were taking me to some boring hole in the wall. I still love this place, and I got to have dinner with the most handsome man in Milwaukee, making it even more special. Thank you for celebrating my birthday with me. I'm thinking maybe you can give me my other gift when we get home." She lifted her eyebrows up and down suggestively.

Tyler's face spread into a devilish smile. "Girl, I love it when you talk dirty. As a matter of fact, I do have a little *sumthin' sumthin'* planned for you tonight." He eased closer to her in the circular booth. They'd been exchanging flirtatious comments since they left the house. He looked forward to acting on them, especially now that it seems he'd been given an open invitation. Whatever was bothering her earlier in the day had been pushed aside.

"Did I tell you how good you look tonight?" He placed an arm around her shoulders and a kiss near her temple.

"I think you might have mentioned it once or twice, but I don't mind hearing it again," she said, her voice smooth and confident.

Tyler felt the heat of the sensuous flame in her eyes. Tonight would be the night he laid his cards on the table, and prayed she'd give their love another chance. He wanted her back in his life, permanently. She had yet to voice her love for him, but her actions spoke volumes. Could they possibly pick up where they had left off months ago, when she ran from their growing passion?

"I had planned to take you to this cool jazz spot I ran across recently, but now I'm thinking I'd rather take you home."

"And gyp me of an evening out on the town? I don't think so … unless you're planning to dust off your baby grand and play something for me tonight."

He laughed. "I haven't played in months. I'm not sure I want to embarrass myself like that."

"I remember the first time you played for me," she said, laying her head on his shoulder. "We were in Chicago, and after leaving the theater we stopped by that lounge around the corner from the state building. Do you remember?"

"I think I might remember a little something about that evening."

She punched him in the arm. "Quit playin'. I know you remember. They had that shiny black piano in the corner and you asked the manager if you could play a little something. After a couple of songs, you had me sit next to you. Then you played one of my favorite songs, *Don't Go*, by Alex Bugnon."

Tyler chuckled. "Yeah, and then the manager asked me if I'd be interested in a permanent gig there."

"If only he knew he was offering a job to a self-made millionaire." Dallas laughed. "You have a gift, Tyler. Remind me, do any of your other siblings play?"

He shook his head. "My mother wanted at least one of her children to play an instrument. Guess who drew the short straw. Not many people know I had to suffer through ten years of lessons."

"I'm glad you drew the short straw. Now you can take me home and play something for me … before you give me my other birthday gift."

****

The thought of her and Tyler coming together again in the most intimate way made Dallas giddy. She would no longer have to fantasize about how it would be to make love to him again.

Tyler slid his arm around her as he guided her out to the lobby. "It has to be hard walking around with one crutch. Are you sure you don't want me to get the other one out of the car?"

"I'm positive. Besides, without the other crutch in the way, this gives me a chance to be a little closer to you." She smiled up at him.

"I like it when you're close to me. If I had my way, I'd have you by my side like this all the time."

"I'd like that. These crutches are cramping my style. We can't even walk hand in hand like we used to."

He kissed the top of her head. "You won't be on crutches forever, and then we can go back to doing a lot of other things we used to do." He grinned mischievously.

Dallas couldn't help but remember why she fell in love with Tyler the first time. The attention he showered on her went deep and being with him felt right. Making partner at the firm should be her main focus right now, but the more time she spent with Tyler the more time she wanted to spend with him. *Don't think, Dallas. Just enjoy the moment.*

"Before we leave, let me stop by the ladies room."

"Sure. It's this way."

"Hello, Dallas," someone said from behind them. They both stopped and turned to see who the voice belonged to. "How's it going Hollister?"

Anxiety gushed through Dallas's veins when she stared at the man of her nightmares. Unable to speak, she grabbed hold of the front of Tyler's shirt. Chilling images of her past flashed before her eyes.

The small shimmer of security that settled on her when Tyler's protective grip tightened around her waist only lasted a minute before anger pierced her heart. The hell Mark had put her through years earlier came flooding back. It had been ten years since she'd last seen him, and if she had her way, it would've been longer.

"I don't even get a hello? No hug, no kiss, nothing?" He stepped closer to her, but Tyler stiff armed in the chest, causing Mark to stop.

Tyler turned to Dallas. "How do you know Mark?"

Her mouth dropped open. "How do you know him?"

"It's good seeing you, Dallas," Mark interrupted and glanced at Tyler, and then back at her. "I guess congratulations are in order. I heard you two are married." He gave them a tight-lipped smile that didn't reach his eyes.

Dallas, still in shock, cast sad eyes up to Tyler. His anger-filled eyes were intense and bore into her as if searching her soul.

"What's going on here?" He tightened his hold on her waist.

Her eyes filled with tears, but she refused to let them fall. Instead she swallowed and said, "Tyler, this is…."

"Her other husband," Mark volunteered.

Chapter Twelve

Tyler's hands felt raw from the grip he'd had on the steering wheel on the drive home. He still couldn't wrap his brain around the fact that Dallas had an ex-husband. Mark Darley no less. He hadn't like the guy the first time he met him, and he liked him even less now.

For the past half-hour Tyler's mood went from angry to shock, back to angry. Why would Dallas keep this from him? When were her and Mark married and for how long? And why did this guy assume he and Dallas were married? He had more questions than answers and based on her silence in the car, it wasn't going to be easy getting the answers.

The panic in her eyes when Mark showed up at the restaurant bothered Tyler most. He'd never known her to be afraid of anything, but tonight he saw fear. What had this guy done to her?

He walked upstairs with a glass of water for Dallas. When they arrived home, she had asked him to help her to her room and requested some water, but said nothing else. He couldn't stand to see her distressed and withdrawn, and he knew it would take more than a glass of water to get her to talk. Maybe he should've opted for the glass of wine, like he'd originally thought.

"How do you feel?" He set the water on the side table. She had curled up in the center of the bed, still in her clothes. Weary eyes followed him around the room, but she said nothing.

He sat on the side of the bed and moved loose strands of hair away from her eyes. "Dallas, baby, I need you to tell me what happened tonight. Why haven't you mentioned you've been married before?"

The look of uncertainty covered her features, and her lids slid closed shielding her eyes as tears streamed down her face. Sadness tugged on Tyler's heart, and he climbed further onto the bed. He rested his back against the headboard and pulled her into his arms.

His intent wasn't to cause her more pain, but he needed to know about her and Mark. "When was the last time you saw him?"

"Over ten years ago," she mumbled and then glanced at him. "How do you know, Mark?"

"He's the architectural engineer who's working on our condo project in Chicago."

When Dallas didn't comment, he continued. "I met him a few weeks ago in Chicago. Another architect from his firm was overseeing our project, but he got ill and Mark took over. Based on Quinn's gut feelings and your reaction toward Mark, we're going to have someone else finish up the project." Tyler thought back on the day they'd met Mark and now understood why he kept making reference to Tyler having a wife. For whatever reason he thought they were married.

"Was he the guy you told me about from grad school?"

She nodded against his chest.

"Dallas, I don't get it. Why didn't you mention you were once married?"

"Didn't want to think about him, let alone talk about him."

Tyler sighed, frustrated by the short responses. "I can understand that, but you and I were once very close, and I thought we were heading in that direction again. Don't you think I had a right to know?"

"You never asked."

Stunned by her scathing retort, he took several deep breaths to steady his pulse and to get his anger under control.

"Why did he think we were married?"

Dallas lifted her head to face him. The dejected look he saw in her dismal eyes was that of a person in a great deal of pain. "I don't know. I haven't seen, nor have I talked with him since he.... As far as I'm concerned, Mark could fall off the face of the earth."

He placed a kiss on her temple and rested his chin on the top of her head. "Talk to me, baby. I can tell whatever transpired between you two was traumatic." He rubbed her arms hoping to bring some comfort. "What happened?"

She sniffled a few times. "Mark and I were a long time ago. There's nothing to tell."

Tyler stilled his hand and lifted his head. The edge in her voice let him know the stubborn, closed-lipped Dallas had shown up to replace the distraught one. After the good time they'd had earlier, he thought they were finally getting back to where they once were.

"What do you mean there's nothing to tell? You guys were married. I would say there's a lot to tell."

Dallas wiped her face with her hands and scooted to the opposite side of the bed. "What part of nothing to tell don't you understand? I really don't want to talk about this right now."

With her chin held high and her now passionless eyes trained on him, Tyler knew he'd have to dig deep down into his soul to find patience. "I bet he has something to do with you holding back when it comes to us. If we're ever going to make it you have to talk to me … and trust me."

"Just because I don't want to talk about this doesn't mean I don't trust you. It means I don't want to talk about it! Besides, I don't owe you an explanation for something that doesn't concern you."

"This sure as hell does concern me. I care about you and I know you feel the same way about me." He swung his long legs to the floor and walked to the other side of the room, never taking his eyes off of her. He ran a hand over his head, frustration covering him like a thick wool coat. What did he have to do to get her to open up? "With this jacked-up attitude of yours, you're acting like I asked for a kidney or something. All I want to know is what happened and why you never mentioned him."

Dallas huffed and folded her arms across her chest. The tears were now replaced with anger. "What happens in my life is my business. I'm trying to forget my past, not relive it. So let it go!"

"What's wrong with you? Don't you understand you have to make peace with your past, so it doesn't ruin your present? Baby, we're never going to be able to have a future together if something in your past is holding you back."

Dallas lowered her eyes and fiddled with the rumpled comforter. After a few moments of silence, she scooted back on the bed until her back touched the headboard and shook her head. "I can't do this anymore," she mumbled. "I care about you, but ... I'm not ready. You've been wonderful these past few weeks, and I appreciate everything you've done for me. I'm sorry if I led you to believe there could be more between us. Right now, the only thing I can offer you is a friendship. Nothing else."

Ahh, here we go again. Her mixed signals would be the death of him. But he wasn't letting her off that easy. "Is that why you didn't tell me your little secret? You had plenty of opportunity. What other secrets are you hiding besides being married?"

"Past tense. I was married. Let's get something straight, Tyler. There is nothing but a friendship between you and me. And since we're just friends, I don't have to tell you everything."

His eyes bore into her, not believing what he was hearing. A few hours ago she was all lovey dovey and ready to take their relationship to the next level. Now she sounded like she did when he'd asked her to marry him, as if it would take nothing for her to toss him away without looking back.

In a low threatening voice he said, "Do you even know what it means to be a friend? Friends talk to each other, trust each other. What you and I have ... aw hell I don't know what the heck we have. For some reason, I thought we'd be able to pick up where we left off and eventually build a life together. Guess I was wrong." He turned to walk away, but stopped and looked back at her. "I'm done."

****

Dallas jumped from the thunderous boom that shook the room when Tyler slammed the door. She collapsed onto her stomach and screamed into the pillow, pounding the bed with her fists. *What is wrong with me? Why do I keep doing this to him?* If she hadn't agreed to stay with Tyler, none of this would be an issue. She knew she couldn't be around him and not fall for him again. "Ugh," she screamed, her voice muffled by the pillow.

Her thoughts quickly went to Mark. The nerve of him introducing himself as her husband. He hadn't been her husband in years and even then it was in name only as far as she was concerned. She turned over on her back and hurled a pillow across the room. Irritation coursed through her veins at how vulnerable she still felt around him. *I hate you Mark Darley?*

Dallas heard a door downstairs slam shortly before hearing Tyler's motorcycle come to life and peel out of the garage. "Darn it," she screamed. She knew a simple apology wouldn't be enough this time. He'd given her every opportunity to tell him everything, and she didn't. *He probably thinks I'm crazy. Heck, I'm starting to think it too.*

Two hours later Tyler hadn't returned to the house. Dallas debated on calling him on his cell, but what could she say? "Sorry I keep pushing you away, but I'm never telling you my horrible, pathetic story." Why bother calling him if she couldn't share everything with him? He deserved so much better. She sighed in frustration. There was only one thing left to do. She grabbed her crutches and went to the closet for her travel bag.

****

Skylar walked into the house, just as Dallas reached the front door. "What's with the car outside?" She looked down and noticed the bag sitting in the hallway. "And where are you going?"

"Home. I've overstayed my welcome. It's time for me to get back to my life." Dallas leaned heavily on her crutches. It took her forever to get down the stairs and the little energy she had left she didn't want to use explaining her decision to Tyler's sister.

Skylar walked further into the house and glanced in the kitchen before running to Tyler's office. "Tyler," she screamed out several times.

"He's not here. He left hours ago."

She walked back over to Dallas. "Does he know you're leaving?"

"It's better if I go before he comes back."

Skylar pulled her cell phone out of her purse and dialed. "Dallas, it's eleven o'clock at night. Why not wait until the morning?"

Dallas had thought the same thing, but why put it off. She had to get back to Chicago and as far away from Tyler as possible. Better to leave now before things got even more complicated.

"Shoot. Where is he?" Skylar said out loud after getting Tyler's voicemail. "Ty, come home...now. Dallas is leaving," she said, urgency in her voice. She put her cell back into her purse and blocked the door, preventing Dallas from passing. "At least wait until he gets here."

Dallas sighed. "You know Tyler and I are like oil and water. We don't mix. Aren't you sick of us arguing all the time? I know I am. I can't do this anymore and besides, he deserves better than what I'm able to give."

"I can tell this isn't what you want. Look at you. You're a wreck. Based on your red, puffy eyes, I'd say you've done your share of crying. And you look like you're on the verge of tears now. Besides, they still haven't found the person responsible for your car accident and the threats. It might not be safe for you to be alone right now."

Dallas had thought about that, but she couldn't live her life in fear.

"Why don't you stay and talk to Tyler. I know, whatever the problem is, you guys can work it out together."

Dallas looked away from Skylar. That *was* the problem. They couldn't work it out because Dallas didn't know how to tell Tyler or anyone else about her life with Mark. She'd done everything she could to block it out of her memory and talking about it brought it all back.

"I'm sorry, Skylar. I have to go. Thanks for everything, and please tell Tyler … I'm sorry."

****

Tyler threw back his forth shot of whiskey and chased it down with a swig of beer. He hadn't drunk like this since college, but tonight he was celebrating. *No more Dallas.* That meant no more arguments; no more stress; no ex-husband; and no more chasing after her like a puppy dog. He was done.

Fifty million women out in the world and he had to be in love with the *one* who didn't want the 'happily-ever-after.' What was it about her that made him give up his bachelor's life? He had dated beautiful women who had catered to his every need. Why'd he ever give up that freedom? *Stupidity.*

"Hey what's up Q?" the bartender greeted as Quinn took the bar stool next to Tyler. "I was wondering when you were going to show up. Your boy here is at his limit. What are you havin'?"

"How about a cup of coffee? Looks like I'm the designated driver tonight."

"You got it."

Tyler could feel Quinn's eyes on him. "Go ahead and say it."

"Say what?"

"I told you so."

Quinn shook his head. "That's not what I was going to say. I was going to ask if you were all right, but I can see you're not."

"Actually, I'm great." Tyler slurred his words and lifted his half empty beer bottle. "I'm celebrating. No more Dallas. I'm done with her."

Quinn took a sip of his coffee before saying, "You don't mean that."

"Oh, but I do." Tyler spun around on the bar stool and would've fallen had Quinn not caught him.

"Lenny, how about a couple of aspirin and a gallon of water. He's worse off than I thought."

The bartender chuckled. "You got it, man."

Quinn stood and helped Tyler over to a booth. "Ty, how many drinks have you had?" he asked once he'd gotten Tyler settled in.

"Did you know Dallas is married?"

"*Was* married."

"She's married to that...." Tyler stopped and stared at his friend, even though things were blurry. "You knew?"

Quinn didn't speak until the bartender left the aspirin and water on the table. "I wasn't positive but I checked some things out. And, it was confirmed."

"So I guess it's true." Tyler took the aspirin and let his head fall back on the back of the booth's seat and closed his eyes. No doubt he was going to have a helluva headache in the morning. "Did you know you almost had to bail me out of jail tonight? When I saw how Dallas reacted to seeing Mark, I wanted to kill him. And I might've if she hadn't insisted on getting away from him."

"I figured as much. So instead of bailing you out of jail, I'm here watching you drink yourself into oblivion."

Tyler opened one eye and looked at his friend. "When'd you start using big words? And how'd you know I was here?"

"Lenny called, and Skylar's been looking for you … Dallas left."

"Good riddance. She's good at running, and I'm done chasing her."

"I'm sure you'll feel different in the morning. Besides, she might be in danger and I know you don't want anything to happen to her."

"Dallas can take care of herself. Or at least that's what she always says. So let her." Several moments of silence passed before Tyler opened his eyes and looked at Quinn. "So what, no comment?"

"Why bother. You probably won't remember this conversation in the morning anyway."

Tyler let his head drop back down. "Yeah, you're probably right. But I am starting to remember why I cut out the hard liquor after college."

Quinn laughed. "I bet. Just wait until in the morning. You're probably going to want to cut off your head. Come on, let's get you home."

****

Curled up in the corner of her sofa, Dallas fiddled with the tassels on her brown throw blanket. Scanning her large living room she was still trying to get used to being back in Chicago and at home. She glanced at her wilted plants too lazy to toss them, and grunted in disgust at the dust that had accumulated on the glass cocktail table. She laid her head on the arm of the sofa and her eyes automatically went to the picture above the fireplace. Tyler had purchased the Yeb, Ghana silk painting on their first vacation together.

Dallas turned on her side and dabbed at the tears in the corner of her eyes. Despite her best efforts to forget Tyler, her mind continued to take her there. She wondered how he was, if he were still mad at her, and whether or not Desiree had moved in to play house. That last thought alone sent her back into a frustrated fit. As time went on, there would be many more Desiree's and there was nothing Dallas could do about it. She only had herself to blame.

Why couldn't she just answer his questions? She'd been asking herself that for the past two days. The look on his face when she refused to tell him about Mark will forever be ingrained in her brain. He was nothing like Mark, but yet, she made him suffer because of her history with her ex-husband. Now it was too late. She'd walked away from the only man she'd ever truly loved - again. And for what? To protect her precious past?

When she left this time it was even harder than the last time. Before, she could at least function without having him in her life, but now, she couldn't even stop crying. And it didn't help matters that she was inundated with work, which was the last thing she felt like doing.

She glanced at her laptop and groaned. The extra responsibilities and clients were proving to be too much, and right now she wanted to forget she had a job. But people were depending on her.

Eager for peace of mind, she grabbed her painkillers and bottled water. For the past couple of days, the pills had been the only way to dull the ache in her heart and the pounding in her head. Minutes after taking them, numbness traveled through her veins, stilling her mind and relaxing her body. Before she knew it, she had succumbed to a deep sleep.

The shrill of her cell phone woke her early the next morning.

"Hello," she answered groggily.

"Dallas?"

"Yeah."

"Are you awake?"

"No," she answered, and tried to force herself to wake up, but sleep kept pulling her back.

"Dallas, wake up," Simone said. "I've been trying to reach you for days. Are you okay?"

"I'm exhausted. Can we talk later?"

"No. We need to talk now. I've been worried sick about you. Why haven't you been answering your phone?"

Dallas had wondered when Simone would call again. She had intentionally not called her and didn't return any of her calls. Simone was good at chewing people out and Dallas didn't want to hear her rant and rave about leaving Tyler the way she had. How could she tell her best friend, who happens to be Tyler's sister-in-law, she had screwed up … again?

"So, are you okay?"

Dallas, surprised by the concern she heard in Simone's voice, almost cried. But she didn't. She couldn't. She was all cried out.

"No. Actually I'm not. I really blew it this time."

"I heard. Tyler told Tim about how you guys ran into Mark after dinner. Honey, I can only imagine how that was for you, especially considering what happened the last time you saw him."

"I couldn't believe it was him. And he had the nerve to act like nothing happened; like he hadn't abandoned me during the worse time in my life; like I was supposed to greet him with open arms or something."

"I'm glad I never met that jerk. He sounds like a real piece of work."

"And poor Tyler," Dallas groaned. "I was awful to him. He wanted to know everything about my relationship with Mark and I wasn't ready to talk about it. I said some things that I will forever regret."

"Do you love him?"

"Who? Tyler?"

"Of course, Tyler! Do you love him?"

Dallas released a frustrated breath. "Yeah, more than he'll ever know."

"Then why haven't you talked to him? If you truly love him, tell him everything about your past. Tell him about your dysfunctional family growing up, your marriage to Mark, everything Dallas. Are you trying to lose him?"

"I've already lost him." She sat up and ran her hands through her untamed hair. "He'll never forgive me for the things I said to him the other night. Heck, I don't even know if I can forgive myself."

"You have to talk to him Dallas. We all have things in our past that we're not proud of, but we deal with it. You remember everything Tim and I went through before we got it together. My delusional mother, Tim's baby momma drama, and don't even get me started on his and Tyler's lunatic brother, Kenny."

Dallas remembered all too well. If they could survive all the challenges they endured, she wanted to believe she and Tyler could to.

"I know the memories are painful," Simone continued, "but you need to face them. Once you talk about them out loud, they won't have the same control over you as they do now."

Dallas listened to her friend, who was closer than a sister, and knew she was right. Besides talking to a therapist years ago, as well as Simone, she'd never shared what had happened between her and Mark with anyone. "He probably won't take my call."

"He might, but you'll never know if you don't call him. Now how are you doing physically? Are you sure you should be at home by yourself?"

"I'm okay. I've been over compensating for my broken leg and now my hip has been killing me, but I'm sure it'll be better in a few days."

"Well, try not to overdo it. I'd come and hang out with you if I could, but my doctor said no more traveling until the baby is born."

"Stay put, I'll be fine. The cast comes off in a couple of weeks, and then I'll be back to normal."

"Oh, God, I hope not." Simone chuckled. "Normal for you would mean working 60 hours a week and living only on bread and water. That's one of the reasons why I wanted you to stay with Tyler. I knew he'd take care of you."

Dallas reached for a tissue to catch the tears streaming down her face, surprised that there were any tears left. She thought back on the first couple of weeks at Tyler's house and how they bumped heads at every turn. Her desire to get back to work right away and her lack of food intake practically drove him crazy. God she missed him.

****

It had been months since he'd played the piano, but for the past few days since Dallas's departure, Tyler had done little else. He had people in place to run his businesses and decided it was finally time to use them.

His fingers traveled effortlessly over the ivory keys as he closed his eyes and played the old classic, *Stardust,* by Hoagy Carmichael. He let the melody seep into his tattered soul. Between sleepless nights and trying to keep his mind off of Dallas, some days he didn't know if he was coming or going.

"When are you going to stop sulking and go after her?" Skylar sat on the bench next to him, interrupting the piece he'd been playing when she pecked on a few keys. "It's been three days. Have you called to make sure she's okay?"

Tyler stopped and stared into eyes identical to his. "Why would I do that? She's the one who left."

"If it'll make you feel any better, it didn't look like it was easy for her to leave. She loves you Tyler. Why she's fighting it, I'm not sure. But I can tell she cares."

He went back to playing, but talked over the music. "Maybe, but I can't do this anymore. Whenever we start to get close, she clams up or bolts. Then I'm the one looking stupid with my heart in my hands. And don't even get me started about the fact she has an ex-husband who she never mentioned."

Moments passed before Skylar spoke. She put her hands over his to stop him from playing. "I remember when Hadrian tried courting me," she said of her military husband. "I wouldn't give him the time of day, because I knew his plans of going into the Marines. I didn't want to be a part of a military family where he's home one week and shipped out the next."

"So what made you give in?"

Skylar chuckled. "He wouldn't give up. He was there at every turn. Not like a stalker, but he integrated himself into my life like a bee to honey. He was adamant about us getting together, telling me how much he loved me and how he needed me in his life. I eventually fell in love with him, partly because of his determination to make me his."

"Well, my hat goes off to Hadrian, but I'm not going after Dallas again."

"For weeks you said the two of you belong together, and you couldn't imagine your life without her. Why are you giving up?"

"Because she doesn't want me. I feel like I'm swimming upstream in shark infested water. The harder I try to reach my goal, the more it feels like sharp teeth taking out chunks of my ass. I'm fighting against something that's stronger than me. Dallas will have to come to grips with her past before she can let me in."

"Do you still love her?"

"Of course I do."

"Then don't give up. Give her time to get herself together, but not too much time. Dallas is a beautiful woman. If you don't pursue her, someone else will."

Tyler grimaced at the thought. Even though he couldn't have her, he didn't want her with anyone else. Still, he listened to his sister, but he wasn't ready to talk to Dallas. If she didn't know how much he loved her by now, she never would.

Chapter Thirteen

Mark looked intently at the picture in his hand. During his internship, he and Dallas had posed for it at his company's holiday party. Everyone thought they were the perfect couple, destined for great things. The partners at his company made it no secret that family was very important, which made it important to him.

He and Dallas were going to have it all: the big house, fancy cars and three kids, two boys and a girl. But Dallas didn't stick to the plan. Mark had it mapped out. He'd get his career started with one of the top engineering firms, and she'd stay home and raise their children. If only she'd kept her end of the deal.

He stared at the picture. Her kissable lips smiling back at him. After seeing her in Milwaukee, he realized the old photo didn't do her justice. The years had been good to her. She was more stunning than he'd remembered. Seeing her also reminded him of one of the biggest mistakes he'd ever made - letting her go. He knew she wouldn't be happy to see him, but he had no idea she'd react the way she had. *I'm not the monster you think I am.*

Upon arriving in Chicago, he'd read an article featuring the *Weisman and Cohen Group*. Dallas was one of their top investment managers. Mark remembered she'd always been good at investing, probably because she lived and breathed her work.

"We could've had it all, Dallas," he said to the photo.

He jumped at the sudden knock at the door, and shoved the picture into his desk drawer. "Come in."

"Hey, Mark, sorry to disturb you, but this just came." His secretary handed him a large white envelope.

"Thanks. I've been waiting for this information. Oh, and can you cancel my ten o'clock appointment with David Weisman, for tomorrow? I'll need to reschedule it for sometime early next week."

"Sure, no problem. Anything else?"

"No, that's it, thanks." Mark waited until she closed the door and pulled papers from the envelope. His lips curled into a wide smile. *Just what I needed.*

****

Dallas felt like a stranger in her office. She ran her hand slowly across the mahogany desk and let her fingers stop at the hideous paperweight that Tyler had given her as a gag gift over a year ago. Toying with the ceramic one-eyed frog, a slight smile graced her lips. She remembered the gorgeous box it had arrived in, a true contrast to the actual gift.

Shutting out the memory, she glanced around the rest of the office. Surprisingly, she hadn't missed being there. During the four weeks she'd been away, Tyler had served as more than her protector. He was also a wonderful distraction, and being with him reminded her of the importance of creating a balance between work and play.

"Boy I'm glad you're back." Bianca said, and walked into Dallas's office, closing the door behind her. "How do you feel?" she asked and moved around the desk to give Dallas a hug.

"I feel okay. I'm looking forward to getting this stupid cast off though."

"I bet." Bianca sat in one of the chairs in front of the desk. "This place wasn't the same without you. Everyone has been on edge, and David has been on a warpath."

Dallas frowned. "Why?"

"I'm not sure, but about a week ago, I was leaving for the day, and he stopped to ask me about your client files. I thought it was strange because he asked for them after you were already back to work on those files."

"Did he say why he wanted them?"

Bianca shook her head. "When he found out you had them, Dallas, I thought he was having a heart attack. His face turned beet red. He was perspiring real bad and you know the one vein in his forehead that usually pops out when he's angry?"

Dallas nodded.

"It showed up. I wasn't sure whether to call 911 or just get the heck out of here. He eventually calmed down, and said he'd talk to you when you returned. And then he left."

"Did you tell him I was coming back this week?"

"I gave the message to his secretary. I know she gave it to him, but the other day she told me he called and said he'd be out of the office this week. Call me crazy, but I think he's hiding something. He's been acting weirder than usual."

Dallas rocked back in her office chair, twirling a pencil between her fingers. "Well, you're not crazy, 'cause I think something strange is going on, too. I even thought you had sent me the papers that had the handwritten notes on them intentionally." Dallas leaned forward and studied her assistant's reaction. When Bianca's gaze dropped to the floor, Dallas had her answer. "Bianca, I'm going to need your help in digging into this a little deeper, but promise me you won't say anything to anyone."

Several hours later, Dallas glanced at the clock and realized she had missed lunch. She'd been there since six in the morning and it was now after two and she couldn't believe how fast the time had gone.

She propped her elbows on her desk and rubbed her tired eyes. She'd read the same material over and over for the past thirty minutes and didn't have a clue about what she'd read. She needed to talk to Tyler. Apparently that was the only way for her to get any real work done. If he'd forgive her, she'd tell him everything.

With her hand on the telephone, she recalled how he'd catered to her every need, wiped away many tears, and changed his schedule to accommodate her. And how did she repay him? She declared them *just* friends and stomped out of his life. When she knew good and well they were much more than that.

Dallas groaned and removed her hand from the receiver. *I can't call him. I'm the last person he'd want to talk to.* She folded her arms on top of her desk and dropped her head. *What am I going to do? I need him. I want him back.*

"Dallas?"

Dallas's head flew up. "Yes?"

"Are you okay?" her assistant asked.

Dallas straightened in her chair. "Oh, yeah, I'm fine, just resting my brain. What can I do for you?"

I need to make a run, but should be back in about thirty minutes. Do you need anything while I'm out? Maybe lunch, since you skipped it?"

"Nope, I'm good. I'm not really hungry, so take your time."

Five minutes after Bianca left, someone knocked on Dallas's door. "Come in." She stood and began to hobble around her desk when David flew in.

"Hey, Dallas. Welcome back. You look good." He rounded the desk and captured her in an awkward hug. "We've missed you around here."

Dallas backed away and reclaimed her seat. "Uh, thanks, Dave. It's good to be back."

He plastered a fake smile on his chubby face. She couldn't believe how different he was from William, the other partner. Throughout her time away, William often called to check on her, encouraged her to take as much time as she needed, and had offered to lighten her work load. David, on the other hand, had done none of those things. Outside of the flowers he'd sent on her first day telecommuting, she hadn't heard from him.

He took a seat in one of the chairs facing her desk and crossed his right ankle over his left knee. "I know you're probably busy, so I'll make this quick."

It was no secret she and David only tolerated one another because they had to work together. Dallas found him to be shallow, selfish, and extremely arrogant. All the qualities she hated in a man. Her face burned as her thoughts went to Mark, who possessed similar qualities.

"Looks like William will be out of the country for another two to three weeks."

"Yes, I talked with him today. He told me his brother's surgery went well, but that he'd planned to stay a little longer."

"Yeah, I told him to take as long as he needed. Also, I'm not sure if Bianca mentioned to you, but I misplaced some papers that I might've left in one of your client's files. I was so busy working on several things at once I think I might have misfiled them."

I just bet you did. "Yes, she did mention it to me. I looked through the files the other day, and I didn't notice anything out of place. But you're welcome to go through them yourself. They're on the table over there." She pointed to the round meeting table in the corner of the spacious office. When Dallas looked back at David, she noticed him fidgeting in his seat and beads of sweat laced his eyebrows. He pulled on the collar of his shirt and loosened his tie. "Dave, are you okay? You don't look so good."

He placed his feet on the floor and stood. "I'm fine." He snapped. "I'll take the files and go through them. I should have them back to you in a couple of hours."

"No problem. I won't need them for the rest of the day." Dallas watched him gather the files and make a hasty exit.

David, I know you're up to something, and I'm going to find out what.

****

Fourplay, one of Tyler's favorite jazz groups played through the speakers of his favorite barbershop. The ten-chair establishment held a professional vibe that appealed to a vast clientele, including players from the *Milwaukee Bucks*. Unlike some shops, offensive rap music would never be heard in this place. The owner, one of his best friends, favored jazz and at times, some old school R & B, which often had the barbers and customers singing along to familiar favorites. Though Tyler kept busy with all aspects of real estate, as well as other ventures, he often made time to stop by and hang out with the fellas at the shop.

"You want a shave today?" Craig asked.

"Nah, I'm good. I need to head out after you finish my cut."

"Okay, but do you have time for us to talk? Remember I told you about a business idea I wanted to run by you?"

"Oh yeah, I do."

"Well I was hoping we could do it today. It'll only take about fifteen or twenty minutes, tops."

"No problem. Sorry it's taken me so long to get back with you on that. I'm curious to hear your idea."

Even with the music bumping, Tyler heard the door chime, announcing that someone had just entered the shop. He glanced at the door as the barber finished lining him up, and his surprised expression quickly surrendered to rage. The last person he wanted to see walked over to the chair like he owned the place.

"What do you want?" Tyler barked.

Mark seemed unfazed by Tyler's rude greeting. "What's up Hollister?" he asked before giving his attention to the person cutting

113

Tyler's hair. "I was told this is the best place to come for a haircut. Can you squeeze me in?"

Tyler turned in his seat and made eye contact with the barber.

"Sorry, man. I'm booked for the rest of the day," Craig said.

Mark shrugged and directed his attention back to Tyler. "Hollister, can I talk to you when you're done?"

"We don't have anything to talk about."

With the cockiness Tyler had grown to hate, Mark said, "Actually we do. It'll probably be better if we talk outside."

Tyler wondered what they could possibly have to talk about, but noticed the attention they were getting from the barbers and some of the patrons. His coldness towards Mark hadn't gone unnoticed. The fellas and their customers who knew him were probably shocked at the way he had spoken to Mark, but Tyler didn't like the guy and had no intention of pretending he did.

He waited until Craig removed the cape from around his neck and brushed him off.

"You a'right Ty?" Craig asked.

"I'm cool. Be right back." His long strides carried him outside and away from the shop windows. In case he decided to punch Mark, he didn't want any witnesses. "Okay, what do you want?"

"Dallas," Mark said without hesitation.

Tyler stared the man down. He had Mark by at least four inches and easily thirty pounds, but apparently Mark wasn't intimidated by that fact. Maybe he was just arrogant, no, stupid would be more like it. What else could he call a man, bold enough to step to another man, and tell him he wanted the woman he loved more than life?

Tyler closed in on him and in a hard, ruthless voice asked, "What makes you think you can have her?" It took everything he had not to wipe the smug, condescending look off Mark's face.

Mark put some distance between them and for the first time since arriving looked uncomfortable, but not defeated.

"Hey, I'm gonna be straight with you. Since I found out you and Dallas aren't married, I figured; why not go after what I want? We were once very good together and I'm sure it wouldn't be hard to pick up where we left—"

Tyler grabbed him by the collar and threw him against the brick building. "Man, I don't know where you get your information, but I'm about to beat your ruthless a—"

"Ty," Craig yelled from behind him. "You got a call."

"Take a message." Tyler glared at Mark, knowing that Craig was just trying to get him away from Mark.

The barber walked to Tyler's side and put a hand on his shoulder. "Ty, whatever he's done, it's not worth it. Let him go and come on back inside."

Tyler jerked Mark's shoulder and released him. "If I catch you anywhere near her, there won't be anyone who'll be able to pull me off of you."

Mark stumbled back. "I thought if I came to you like a man, we could talk about this, but apparently I was wrong. I'll leave it up to Dallas to decide who she wants."

Tyler lunged at him, but Craig grabbed him by the arm, and they watched Mark walk quickly to his car.

"Man, we've been friends for a long time, and I've never seen you like this. What's goin' on?"

Tyler jerked out of Craig's grasp. "Give me a minute." He trudged to the back of the building, feeling like a volcano on the brink of eruption. He had never fought over a woman before, but for Dallas he'd consider it.

The knot in his throat demanded release, but cleansing breaths didn't dissolve it. He stomped back and forth between the buildings until he could get his breathing and temper under control. Somehow he knew he hadn't heard the last of Mark Darley.

****

Chicago, Illinois

"It's nice to finally meet you," Dave Weisman said and shook Mark's hand.

"Same here. Sorry I had to postpone our meeting. I had to leave town for a few days."

"No problem."

"I'm curious to hear more about this irresistible opportunity Ray told me very little about. I also understand you and I know someone in common."

"Oh, yeah, who?" David motioned for Mark to have a seat in the small conference section of his office.

"My wife, Dallas. Well, my ex-wife, but I'm sure that's going to change soon."

Of all the people Ray could have sent David, he sent Dallas's ex-husband? All these years and he had no idea she'd ever been married. Even if Mark did have money, there was no way in hell he could do business with him. David wasn't sure how much, if anything, Dallas knew about his dealings. And until he did, it was important he tread lightly.

As casually as he could, he asked, "What do you mean by *that's going to change soon?*' Are you guys planning to reunite?"

"It means I messed up, but I plan to get her back. That's why Ray Gardner thought it important we meet. If I invest with your firm, it'll make me look good in her eyes."

"I see." *Ray has some serious explaining to do,* David thought of his silent partner. "Can I get you some coffee or maybe something stronger?" David stood and walked to the bar. Whether Mark wanted a drink or not, David needed a stiff drink to calm his nerves. He needed this money, and Ray assured him Mark could deliver, but at what cost?

****

Dallas hobbled around her kitchen preparing dinner, thinking about work. She hadn't seen David since the other day in her office, and her research into his documents kept coming up empty. At first she'd thought it was a list of potential stocks or businesses he'd planned to invest in. But with further checking, she realized they didn't exist. Tomorrow she'd call Paige, her friend from grad school who now lived in Chicago. Paige was a corporate lawyer, but minored in finance, and loved to uncover mysteries.

Dallas moved the brown rice to the back burner and seasoned the grilled vegetables. She glanced at the oven timer. The salmon would be ready in five minutes. The only thing missing from this perfect meal was a glass of wine...and Tyler.

Just call him. The thought had played in her head for the past few days. It was time to surrender to her feelings for him and make things right. If nothing else, he deserved an apology. What would she do if she told him everything, and he couldn't handle it? She'd have to take that risk. She wanted another chance with Tyler, and this time she wasn't going to blow it.

She turned off the burners on the stove and grabbed her cell phone. While she waited for him to pick up, she wiped her palms on her apron and turned off the oven timer. Hearing his voicemail, she tapped her fingers on the counter and wondered again if calling him was a good idea.

"Tyler." She pinned the telephone between her neck and shoulder as she opened the oven. This is Dall...ouch!" Her arm brushed the hot pan and her cell phone tumbled to the floor. "Ugh." She practically threw the baking pan at the cooling rack on the counter, as she scurried for her phone. She swore under her breath, seeing it on the floor in pieces.

"Well so much for that idea." She picked up what was left of the telephone and laid the parts on the table.

Her arm hurt, but the door bell rang before she could grab some ice. Removing her apron, she tossed it on the counter and shuffled out of the kitchen. The person on the other side of the door started banging on it before she could get to it.

"I'm coming." Seconds later she peeped through the peephole and swung the door open.

"Harmony! Oh my God." She grabbed her sister's hand, and pulled her inside, and then looked out to see if anyone was with her. When she was sure Harmony was alone, she closed and locked the door. "Come in here. What happened?"

Her sister's face was swollen. Her eyes were red and mascara streaked her honey brown cheeks. Dallas grabbed her arm to escort her further into the house, but released it when Harmony winced. She waved a hand at the sofa for Harmony to sit down and then hobbled into the half-bath, off of the kitchen, for a hand towel.

When she walked back into the room she asked, "What happened? Who did this to you?"

"It doesn't matter."

"It does matter. Maybe I should call the police or get you to emergency," Dallas said as she dabbed at the mascara stains on Harmony's face.

"No. Don't."

"Then tell me who did this."

"Jerome," she whispered.

"Jerome? The guy you brought over to Tyler's house?"

Her sister nodded, and fresh tears flowed down her cheeks. "I'm so stupid."

"Oh, sweetheart, no matter what you did or said no one deserves to be beaten." Her sister's anguish brought back Dallas's humiliation from when Mark treated her like crap. Maybe the therapist Dallas had seen after grad school was right. Maybe their poor judgment in men had something to do with the fact they didn't grow up with a positive male role model in their lives.

Harmony sat further back on the sofa. She looked as if she was going to say something, but her withdrawn eyes were soon covered when she pressed her hands over her face and wept. Deep sobs flowed from her sister as Dallas gathered her into her arms, and allowed her own tears to fall freely.

Chapter Fourteen

Morning sunlight through the window played with the shadows on the tray ceiling over Tyler's bed. He wanted to bang his head against a wall for letting Quinn talk him into double dating last night, a blind date at that. At least Michelle, Tyler's date, hadn't taken his funky attitude personally. He hadn't said a word about Dallas, but when he walked Michelle to her car, she had kissed him on the cheek and surprised him when she said, "You must love her very much. I hope she knows how lucky she is."

Tyler sat up and dragged his legs over the side of the bed. He had enough work and other commitments to keep him busy for a lifetime, yet, it wasn't enough to keep him from thinking about Dallas. The woman had a hold on him and no matter what he tried he couldn't seem to shake it. Quinn's words from the night before came back to him. *You either do something about Dallas or get over her. This is crazy. You're a brotha' who has it going on, but for the past couple of weeks you've been acting like a punk. If Dallas means that much to you, go get her!*

Tyler ran a hand down his face and then looked over at the night stand. Seeing his cell phone reminded him that he hadn't checked his voice messages the night before. He grabbed the phone and punched in his access code.

The first message was from Desiree, apologizing again for her behavior weeks ago and asking if she could make it up to him. "Yeah, like that's going to happen," he said and deleted the message. But his heart leaped in his chest at the next message.

"Tyler, it's Dall...ouch." He heard a lot of racket, and then the call went dead. *What the heck?* He glanced at the clock. *Seven forty-five, maybe she hasn't left for work.* Before he could call Dallas, his phone rang.

"Hello," he answered on the first ring. He heard a person breathing on the other end. "Hello?" Again there was no response, and the hairs stood on the back of his neck. "Who is this?"

"Someone who is looking forward to getting to know your woman."

Tyler rose slowly from the bed. Mark entered his mind first, but the guttural tone didn't match Mark's tenor. Besides, he was too cocky to stoop to this level. He was more of the type to handle things face to face.

Weeks had gone by with no threatening calls. Why now? If only he could wrap his hands around the person's neck and shake information out of them.

"Oh, so what, you don't have anything to say?" The caller taunted.

"Who is this?"

"Like I'm going to tell you. All you need to know is that your woman has been warned."

Tyler cursed under his breath. "Warned about what? What do you want from her?"

"I have a feeling I'll be getting what I want very soon."

Tyler gripped the phone as if it were a lifeline. "If you do anything to hurt her, I will hunt you down like the worthless piece of shit you are!"

A ruthless laugh boomed through the phone line before the caller disconnected.

Damn. Tyler hung up the phone and used speed dial on his cell to call Dallas's home number. *The number you have dialed is being checked for trouble. Please try your call again later.* He disconnected and tried her cell only to have the call go directly to voicemail.

"Dallas, what the hell is going on?" he said to the empty room.

He searched through his telephone contacts for her work number. Again he got her voicemail. This time he left a message for her to call him the moment she got into the office.

He grabbed his travel bag from his closet while he dialed Quinn's number. He pulled his pre-packed toiletry carrier from the top shelf and shoved it into the bag while Quinn's phone rung several times.

"Yeah," Quinn finally answered.

"Q, I'm heading to Chicago."

"Well it's about time. I guess my little talk last night helped."

Tyler tossed a few more items into his bag and zipped it. "Your talk helped, but that's not why I'm going. I think Dallas is in trouble."

"What do you mean?"

"I just received another threatening call."

"Shit. I thought that was over. What did they say?" Tyler filled him in on the call and they both agreed that it would be good to let Detective Davenport know.

"Well, this is probably as good a time as any to tell you I have someone watching Dallas," Quinn said.

"What?"

"Yeah. I put Hank on her the day after she left. I thought you would've hooked back up with her by now, but since you haven't, I figured I'd give it a month before I pulled my guy off her."

For the first time since hearing Dallas's message, Tyler felt like he could breathe.

"Man, you claim you're done with her, but I know you're crazy about that woman. If something happened to her you'd never forgive yourself."

Tyler shook his head. Whether he and Dallas were together or not, he wanted her safe. "Yeah, you're right. So what's going on?"

"Not too much. From what I understand, she puts in crazy long hours at work, and then goes home. There's been no sign of the ex-husband. Everything seems normal, although, last night she did get a visitor – some woman. Hank hasn't checked in this morning yet. So that's all I have right now."

"Okay," Tyler said pacing the length of his bedroom. Since Dallas didn't know that Hank was watching her, he wasn't sure he wanted her to know at this point. "Tell you what. Keep Hank on her until I get to town. Once I arrive at her office, I'll relieve him of his duties and take over from there. But have him to call me if he notices anything suspicious."

****

121

Dallas leaned against the doorjamb of the guest bedroom where Harmony was staying. She had no doubt that her sister knew she was standing there, but Harmony ignored her by sifting through a fashion magazine.

"Don't you have to go to work or something?" Harmony asked, still not looking at her.

"Nope. Not until later." Dallas walked in and sat at the foot of the bed. "Oh, and before I forget, the phone still isn't working, so hopefully you don't have to call anyone."

"Who am I going to call?"

Dallas wasn't sure how to reach out to her sister. They'd been close growing up, but they'd drifted apart as adults. Lately, their conversations had evolved into Dallas berating her for her poor choices. Now Harmony needed compassion - not one of Dallas's strengths.

"If you don't want to talk, we don't have to," Dallas said. "But you might feel better if you tell me about last night."

"It's hard admitting you're stupid."

Dallas's brows knitted. "You're being a little hard on yourself, don't you think?"

"No, not really. You've been right all these years. I attract scum, like flies attract shi—"

"Hey! Stop that. We all make bad choices. God knows I've made my share. But it doesn't help to beat yourself up."

Looking at Harmony's bruised face was like looking into a mirror for Dallas. Her life with Mark flashed before her eyes. She couldn't relate to the swollen face and busted lip, because Mark never hit her. A wife with bruises on her face would have messed up his "family first" image. Yet, that didn't stop him from yanking on her arms or pushing her into things. Like Harmony, her spirit had been crushed, which hurt more than the physical pain.

"Oh, don't tell me Little Miss Perfect has made bad choices. Say it isn't so!" Harmony mocked her. "What do you know about making mistakes when your life is perfect? You have a gorgeous house, the perfect job, more money than you probably know what to do with, and a fine boyfriend who worships the ground you walk on. So don't try to play like you know how I feel!" She screamed and threw the magazine across the room.

Dallas' brows drew together and her lips parted in surprise. "Is that what you think? That I have this perfect life with no problems?"

Harmony didn't say anything. Instead she sat on the bed, with her back against the headboard, arms folded, and her eyes closed. Her hair was swept up in a ponytail on top of her head, giving Dallas a better view of the side of her face that didn't seem as swollen as it had the night before.

For the first time, Dallas saw how fragile her sister looked. She was way too thin and appeared older than her twenty-five years. Dallas thought about herself at that age. She'd already been married and divorced and had experienced more grief than a person should be allowed to endure. She studied her sister. Even with a nine-year difference between them, they looked so much alike.

"All right, Harmony. Let me enlighten you on a few things."

Dallas started with stories about their love starved mother, things Harmony never knew. And then Dallas went on to share things about her own life - details about her years in Louisiana, away from family, and how she struggled to work two jobs to put herself through college. When Dallas mentioned her ex-husband, Harmony's eyes grew to the size of saucers.

"You were married?" Harmony moved closer, folding her legs Indian style. "When? Don't tell me it was to Daddy Warbucks."

For the first time Dallas noticed Harmony seemed more interested in what she had to say. A smile tipped the corners of Dallas' mouth. She couldn't help but chuckle at Harmony's reaction to her news as well as the nickname she'd given Tyler.

"Yes, I was married, and no, it wasn't to *Tyler*. I didn't know him back then."

Harmony's brows furrowed, and she moved to sit back against the headboard, her arms refolded across her chest. "Am I the only one in the family who didn't know?"

Dallas shook her head. "Simone found out years later, but I never told anyone else. We were married shortly after I finished graduate school. It didn't last a year. It was the worse year of my life." Dallas told her about the marriage and the abuse, intentionally leaving some things out. No one would hear her complete story until she could share it with Tyler; that is, if he'd listen.

Moments passed before Harmony spoke. With eyes laced with tears, she finally said, "All this time I thought you were hard on me because you thought you were better than me."

Dallas reached for her sister's hand. "I never meant for my words to hurt you. You're such a beautiful woman with so much potential. I didn't want to see you go through the stuff I'd gone through." Dallas hugged her, and they stayed that way until Harmony pulled away.

"So where does Daddy Warbucks come in at?"

Dallas shook her head and laughed. "Girl, his name is Tyler."

"Okay, where does Tyler come in at?"

On a sigh, Dallas said, "He's a whole different story."

"I got nothin' but time right now."

"Fine. I'll give you the short version." Dallas ran her fingers through her hair. "We met about a year-and-a-half ago and dated for a while. When he started talking marriage, I wasn't ready, so we broke up. After my car accident, he was the first person I saw in the hospital." She paused, smiling at the thought. "When it was time for me to be released, he insisted I stay with him until I got better."

"I should be that lucky. That was some house," Harmony mumbled.

"Yes it is. A few weeks ago Tyler and I had a fight and I left. I haven't heard from him since." Dallas stood and stretched. "That's about it."

They talked a few minutes longer before Dallas left the room and went to get ready for work. She wanted Harmony to go to work with her, but her sister didn't want to be seen in public with her bruises. Harmony assured her she'd be fine at the house.

Dallas wondered if her sister would ever tell her what happened with Jerome. The only thing she said was that she had left his apartment in a taxi. Dallas was surprised he lived in Chicago. Harmony resided in Milwaukee and she assumed Jerome did too.

She turned at the sound of a knock at the bedroom door. "Come in."

Harmony stuck her head in. "The telephone people are outside."

"Thanks. Hopefully they have some good news." She shuffled down the hall and to the front door.

"How you doing? Sorry to bother you." The young man's gaze traveled approvingly over the length of her body before his eyes made it back up to her face.

Dallas rolled her eyes. *Men.* "I hope you were able to fix my house phone."

"No. I'm … I'm sorry. I wasn't." The young man stuttered. He rocked from one foot to the other. "It's going to take a little more than expected to fix it. Your phone line was cut."

"What do you mean it was cut? How'd you do that?"

He shook his head. "Wasn't me. Whoever did it, though, knew what they were doing. It's a clean cut. I checked with a few of your neighbors, and it looks like your line is the only one that's been tampered with."

****

Hours later Dallas moved carefully toward her office building as the wind practically carried her to the entrance. Today Chicago was living up to its *Windy City* nickname.

She had gone to her doctor's appointment before going into work. And despite the fact that it had lasted longer than expected, she had no complaints. She was ecstatic to be rid of the heavy cast, even though it had been exchanged with a hideous air cast. Still needing at least one of the crutches, her walk felt lighter than it had in weeks as she strolled to the bank of elevators.

"Hold the elevator," she yelled. Once over the threshold the steel doors closed behind her and she thanked the older gentleman.

"What floor?" he asked.

"Thirty-eighth, thanks." Dallas moved toward the back of the semi-empty elevator and leaned against the wall to catch her breath. She did a mental inventory of the rest of her afternoon. Things had been so busy, that in order to keep up with her new workload, she had to put in as many as twelve to fifteen hours a day. But once she made partner, it would all be worth it.

She checked her watch, one fifteen. She had to prepare for a two o'clock meeting. The morning had been crazy after finding out her house telephone line had been cut. No way did she want to leave Harmony alone. And after much discussion, Harmony agreed to hang out at a friend's house. Dallas could only hope the friend in question wasn't Jerome.

The metal doors glided open and she stepped out onto the plush beige carpet and walked to her office.

"Hey Bianca."

"Hey there. I was just changing your calendar. Your two o'clock meeting has been cancelled," she said following Dallas into her office.

"Wonderful. Now I can stop rushing."

"I see you got your cast off. I guess that means you're almost back to normal."

"Almost. I still have to wear this one." She pointed at the walking cast. It's much lighter than what I had though." Dallas put her briefcase near her desk. "Well, since the meeting's cancelled, I'll go grab some lunch."

"Do you want me to run and get you something?"

"No, that's okay. I'll go downstairs to the café. Do you want anything?"

Bianca shook her head. "No thanks. Their prices are getting ridiculous. I'm protesting by not eating there anymore."

Dallas chuckled. "What, another protest? You keep this up and you'll only be able to eat at home."

Once downstairs, Dallas realized she needed cash, so she stopped by the ATM and stepped into line. A nostalgic moment washed over her as she stared down at the baby girl in the stroller. There was a time in her life that she thought she'd have a couple of kids by now. She moved her purse strap to her other shoulder and tried to redirect her thoughts.

"Brings back memories doesn't it?"

Fear and anger knotted inside her at the sound of the voice that irritated her more than someone scratching their nails across a chalkboard. She turned slowly and came face to face with the man she hated more than anything in the world. Mark.

"What are you doing here?"

"I have a client in this building. Funny running into you."

Dallas didn't see anything funny about it. Was it a coincidence he had a client in the same building, or was he following her? Not interested in a conversation, she tried to step around him, but he blocked her path.

"Do you mind?" She hoped her voice sounded steadier than her erratic heartbeat. *Okay, Dallas, just calm down. He can't hurt you anymore.* She limped around him and walked a few feet before he grabbed her arm. Despite the lightweight cast on her leg, she turned ready to do battle.

Mark threw his hands up and took a few steps back. "Come on, Dallas. At least give me a chance to apologize. Maybe I can buy you lunch or something."

Dallas stood before him and studied his features. The irrefutable strength in his face hadn't changed. He still exuded an air of command. Though she had seen him a few weeks ago, today she really looked at him. His ruggedly handsome face, the color of walnut, now sported a thin mustache and a perfectly trimmed beard, whereas back in grad school he was bare faced. His tailored suit hung perfectly on his trim, but fit body, and his shoes were top notch and shiny as usual. No one could ever accuse him of being a slacker when it came to dressing. It wasn't until her gaze traveled back up to his dark, emotionless eyes that she saw him for who he really was. A coward.

****

Tyler took the elevator to the thirty-eighth floor. On one hand, he was anxious to see Dallas. On the other, he still harbored unresolved feelings about the way she left.

He glanced at his watch. One forty-five. He should've arrived at her office hours ago, but between traffic and the power outage in five of his Chicago condo units, he was way behind schedule. It worked out having Quinn's guy, Hank, trailing Dallas. He kept Tyler abreast of her whereabouts throughout the morning. Once she arrived at her office Hank called him and Tyler relieved him of his duties since he knew he was only minutes from her.

It had been months since he'd been in her office building, but nothing had changed. He turned the last corner leading to her office and walked up to her assistant's desk.

"Hey, Bianca," he said and the secretary looked up from her computer screen.

"Oh my goodness, Tyler! It's so good to see you." She rounded the desk to give him a hug.

He'd once been a regular visitor and had befriended the young assistant. She'd allowed him to surprise Dallas with visits or presents. Bianca would do whatever she could to help him please her supervisor. "Is the boss in?"

"She's here, but she went down to the café." Bianca glanced at the time on her computer screen. "Actually she's been gone a while. She should be back any minute. Do you want to wait in her office?"

He hesitated, unsure that he'd even be welcomed there. He also didn't know how much Bianca knew about their situation.

Apparently noticing his delay, Bianca said, "I heard what happened. And between you and me, she's been miserable since she's been back." She stood and walked toward the door. "Come on in. I know she'll be glad to see you."

Tyler smiled. "Thanks."

"No problem."

He walked in and glanced around the spacious office that looked so much like Dallas: browns and beige in the sitting area, rich

127

mahogany bookshelves, and a smooth mahogany desk near the center of the room. Everything seemed to have a place in her tidy workspace.

"Can I get you some coffee?"

"Uh, no, I'm good. I'll just wait for Dallas. I left her a message this morning. Do you know if she received it?"

"Probably not. She's been out all morning and arrived in the office maybe twenty, twenty-five minutes ago."

He ran a hand down his face, glad that Dallas was okay, but anxious to see her again. "She isn't expecting me, so I'm not sure how it's going to go," he said with a weak smile.

Bianca walked to the door, but turned back. "She's going to be very happy to see you. Funny, you're her second surprise visitor today. An old friend of hers stopped by less than five minutes ago looking for her. He said they attended grad school together."

Tyler's pulse quickened and he moved closer to Bianca. Anger singed the corners of his control, but as calmly as he could manage, he asked, "Did he give his name?"

"Yeah. He said his name was Mark."

Tyler's thoughts raced dangerously. Could Mark actually be behind the phone calls? When they had their encounter a couple of weeks ago, Tyler didn't take him as the type that would stoop to that level. "Where'd you say Dallas went?"

"Downstairs to the café."

"I'll go down there. If she comes back up before I get here, let her know I'm here and have her call me on my cell."

"Is anything wrong?" Bianca asked.

"I hope not," Tyler said over his shoulder.

Chapter Fifteen

For too long Dallas had allowed Mark to manipulate her and treat her like crap. She had run from her past, never allowed herself to enjoy her present, and a happy and successful future was questionable – all because of him. And he had the nerve to only offer lunch?

"So what do you say?" He stood before her, his hands in his pants pockets. "Can I buy you lunch?"

"No thanks. I'm suddenly not very hungry." Tempted to say something scathing to hurt him the way he had hurt her, she turned and limped toward the main doors. Anything she said could set him off, and she knew the consequences.

"Face it, Dallas. You can run, but you can't hide," he said and followed her. "Sooner or later we're going to talk. I want you back in my life."

"Well, we don't always get what we want."

A few yards from the front entrance, he grabbed her arm and pulled her into the nearest corner.

"Get your hands off of me." The venom in her voice matched the wild, crazed look he surely saw in her eyes.

"You've gotten tough over the years. I like that."

"I said get your hands off of me." The Mark she hated was showing his true colors, thinking he could bully her into submission. No longer the scared little girl he once controlled, she stood her ground. Though he held her arm, she maintained a death grip on her purse strap. Her free hand clenched and unclenched as if pulsing with mounting fury.

"Or what?"

"Or this." She brought back her hand and let it rip across his cheek, forcing him to grab the left side of his face. The gratification of knowing she caused him pain pulsed through her veins.

"Why you little…."

"Little what? Oh, yeah, this is when you start calling me names and yank me around right? Well, Mark, things have changed." Her breathing ragged, her heart pounded, but no way would she back down. He wanted a fight, she'd give him one. "If you ever and I mean ever, put your hands on me again I'm going to make two phone calls: One to the police, and the second to a reporter with the Chicago Tribune." Mark's reputation meant everything to him. The confident look she'd grown to hate no longer covered his face.

"So now you're throwing out useless threats?" His scornful laugh unnerved her, but she stood her ground. "Dallas, baby, I'm not afraid of you."

"You should be. I wonder what your boss would think if he knew his top engineer used to abuse his wife. Or what his reaction would be if he knew you had left her alone, in a hospital, after she miscarried *your* child." Dallas chest heaved and tears rolled down her cheeks. It was awful enough losing her baby, but the way he'd tossed her to the curb hurt just as much. "Oh, and that's only a little of what I would share. Who knows, I might also add the part about how you disappeared by the time the hospital released me."

Marked grabbed her forearms. "If you ever threaten me again, I'll—"

"And I told you what I'd do if you ever came near her again." Tyler grabbed Mark by the shirt collar, jerked him away from Dallas, and smashed a right hook into his left jaw. Before Mark could react, Tyler lifted him off the ground and slammed him against a wall and punched him in the gut.

Dallas's jaw dropped. Where had he come from? It wasn't until security charged through the small crowd gathered around them that she responded.

"Tom!" She screamed at the security guard who pulled Tyler off of Mark. "This is just a misunderstanding, please let him go," she said of Tyler.

"Are you sure, Ms. Dallas? All I need to do is make a phone call and they'll both be hauled out of here."

"Get your hands off of me." Mark yelled at the other security guard. "He's the one you should be roughing up. I ought to call the cops myself. Assault is a felony and he just assaulted me."

"Please let him go." Dallas pointed to Tyler. "As for you..." She walked to Mark, still restrained by the guard. "Go ahead. Call the cops. Then I can show them your handprint on my forearm."

When the guard released Mark, he glared at Dallas. "This ain't over." He huffed away.

When Mark left, Dallas turned to Tyler. Bent over, his hands on his knees, he struggled to catch his breath. She took two tentative steps toward him, but then he looked up and their eyes met. *Those beautiful eyes.* For Tyler to show up in Chicago, meant more to her than she'd ever be able to express.

He stood to his full height. "Are you okay?" She nodded, walked into his arms, and held on tightly around his waist.

Moments later Dallas leaned back, without letting go, and looked at him. Tears of joy traveled down her face until Tyler wiped them away. What did she ever do to deserve this wonderful man who continued to come to her rescue? She placed her hand against his cheek.

"I'm so sorry for the way I left and the horrible things I said to you," Dallas said. "I love you. I love you so much. I just want—." Her words were halted in her throat when his mouth came down hungrily over hers. Anything she'd planned to say was lost somewhere in the back of her mind as she enjoyed the tantalizing kiss that was like the soldering heat that binds metals. With one hand on the back of her head, and one at the small of her back, he pulled her closer, deepening their connection. For weeks she had longed to be in his arms and feel his mouth against hers and he didn't disappoint.

When he eventually pulled away, she couldn't bring herself to open her eyes, still reveling in the feel of his lips against hers.

"Now what were you saying?" He stroked her hair, trailed gentle fingers down the side of her face, and lifted her chin. His gaze stayed on her lips, as if he'd plan to kiss her again.

"I was saying, uh...please give me another chance to tell you everything."

He stared into her upturned face, and kissed her again. "Has it only been three weeks since I've seen you? It seems like forever. You look amazing. And I guess you were right. You can take care of yourself."

Dallas shook her head. "No, Tyler, I wasn't right. I do need you. Baby, I need you more than you know. Give me another chance to tell you everything. Please."

He placed a light kiss across her lips. "Okay, okay. Calm down. What time do you get off?"

****

An hour later, Dallas and Tyler sat on a park bench overlooking Lake Michigan. The wind had died down and they took advantage of what was probably one of the last few warm days of summer.

Dallas intertwined her fingers with his and rested her head on his shoulder. A loud sigh slipped through her lips. So far her day had been like something out of a thriller movie. Running into Mark and finally standing up to him was scary and invigorating all in one.

Having Tyler come to her rescue yet again, confirmed within her how much she needed and wanted him in her life. Despite the fact she'd treated him like crap, he was still right there. How would she ever be able to make it up to him and convince him to give her another chance?

"I'm not sure where to begin," she said staring at the sun's rippling reflection on the lake.

"Why don't you tell me what happened between you and Mark to make you so uncomfortable around him?" He squeezed her hand.

Dallas took in a cleansing breath and let it out slowly. "From day one, I wasn't myself with Mark. I can't explain the power he had over me and how I used to deteriorate whenever I was in his presence. When we parted ways, I went through a year of therapy, but I didn't walk away with answers."

"What do you mean?"

"My therapist began to drop hints that my behavior with Mark had something to do with growing up without a father, and my mother's ridiculous devotion to every loser who came into her life. I didn't give the therapist a chance to develop any of those theories. I needed a change in my environment and when the opportunity to work for Weisman and Cohen became available, I left Louisiana. I moved here, vowing to heal myself."

She told him about her internship and how she'd met Mark. They had only dated for a short period of time, yet she thought she loved him. So when she ended up pregnant and he asked her to marry him, she didn't think twice. Then he'd asked her to quit her job and let him support them, and their problems started.

"What happened to the baby?" Tyler asked.

Dallas lifted her head from his shoulder, released his hand, and angled her body to face him. "When I was five months pregnant I had a miscarriage."

"Aw, baby, I'm sorry."

"I almost died. They saved me, but not my baby. And of course I blamed myself. My doctor had warned me about working too much and that I needed to take better care of myself. I cut my work hours and made sure to eat right, but it wasn't enough. I begged God to save my baby."

Tyler wrapped his arms around her. "That had to be devastating."

Not wanting to lose her nerve to tell him everything, she pushed away from him. "It was. I hated myself for putting my career before my child. But I don't know what was worse, losing the baby or having to endure Mark's wrath when he found out. He arrived back into town, and instead of coming to the hospital to comfort me, he came blaming me. Oh my God, he was like a mad man. His company was really big on family, so Mark's main focus was on having a family."

"You're telling me he was more concerned about what they'd say at his job, than losing his child and almost losing his wife?"

She nodded. Of course it would sound unbelievable to Tyler. He had been raised to care about people, not to view them as assets or the means to an end. "He told me I had ruined everything. He ranted and raved about how much he hated me and how I was good for nothing. Then he left. And that was the last time I saw him. I'm not positive, but looking back, I think he was seeing someone on the side."

Tyler swore under his breath, got up from the bench, and walked closer to the water. "There's more," she said to his back. He stopped and turned, his face clouded with fury. Silently he reclaimed his seat and took her hand.

"When Mark walked out of the hospital room, a part of me left with him. I had lost my baby and my husband all in the same day. And though he was a lousy husband," she shrugged, "at that moment I felt like he was all I had."

Tyler kneaded her shoulder and neck with his free hand. "Dallas," his voice choked, "I can't believe how he left. I ... damn, I can't imagine anyone treating you like that. No wonder you left me when I had asked you to marry me last year. So many things make sense now."

"When Mark showed up at the restaurant, everything came back as if ten years ago happened yesterday. He left me like it was the easiest thing in the world to do. I had nothing, Tyler. I was on track to making partner back then, and he told them I wouldn't be returning to the firm because I was too distraught from the loss of our child. That's what my supervisor told me when I returned to work." Dallas shook her head. "I freaked out, started yelling and pounding on desks. Needless to say, she told me I needed more time to heal."

Tyler released her hand and leaned forward, his elbows resting on his thighs. He sighed loudly, but said nothing.

"He left me with a boatload of bills," Dallas continued. "And he cleared out our joint bank account. If that wasn't enough, within two weeks of my release from the hospital, he served me with divorce papers."

Tyler glanced at her. Dallas didn't miss the flare of anger that crossed his handsome face. She hated reliving her pain and loss, but it felt good to share it with the man she loved.

"Did he ever try calling you?"

"No. The night of my birthday, was the first time I'd seen or heard from him. "Wait." She shook her head. "That's not totally true. When I saw the blue roses, I feared they were from him. Actually, I knew they were from him. He used to send them to me regularly when we were together."

Tyler moved from the bench. "He is so lucky I didn't know all of this sooner, especially before I ran into him this afternoon."

Dallas stood next to Tyler and wrapped her arms around his waist. They stood that way for the longest time until she felt some tension leave his body. "I've been meaning to ask you," she said. "Why did you come to see me at my job?"

Tyler turned in her arms to face her. He ran his hand through her hair, and let the long strands sift through his fingers. "Part of me wanted to move on and forget we'd ever met, but my heart wouldn't let me. I needed to see you. Baby, not a day has gone by that I haven't thought about you."

Dallas rested her head against his chest and held him tighter. She didn't know what to say. If he had moved on, it would've been her fault. This was the second time she'd walked away from him.

"The other reason I'm here is because you received another threatening call."

She lifted her head and stepped back? "When?"

"This morning, right after I listened to your voice message."

"What did they say?" she asked, but after seeing his expression, she said, "Or do I even want to know?"

Tyler shrugged half-heartedly. "Something about getting to know you, and that you've been warned. Then they said that they will be getting what they want from you soon."

"This is crazy!" She rubbed her temples, and reclaimed her seat on the bench. "What is this about?"

Tyler sat next to her. He had his cell phone in his hand. "I called the detective and told him I'd have you get in contact with him as soon as I saw you. By the way, what's going on with your telephones?" He searched for the detective's number.

"I dropped my cell phone while I was leaving you a mess—."

"Here, it's ringing," Tyler said handing her his cell.

She put the phone to her ear. "So what did the detective have to say about the call?"

"At the time, not much. They still don't have any leads."

She lifted a finger for Tyler to give her a minute. "Hi, Detective Davenport, this is Dallas Marcel."

"Hi, Ms. Marcel. I'm glad you called," Davenport said.

"Wait. Hold on sec, I'm going to put you on speaker phone. Tyler is here with me." She handed the cell back to Tyler and he switched it to speaker.

"Okay, Detective, go ahead."

"We traced the call to a phone booth on the south side of Chicago. We're waiting for word as to whether the police could lift prints from it."

How could this be happening? For the past few weeks there had been no incidents, no calls, nothing. Why all of a sudden are the calls starting again? Dallas wondered.

Tyler put his arms around her and pulled her close. "Detective, did you guys get any fingerprints from the car?"

"No, none that we could use, but we're doing everything we can to put the pieces together. Ms. Marcel, have you thought of anyone who would want to harm you?"

She looked up at Tyler. "The only person I can think of is Mark Darley, my ex-husband." She told the Detective about the flowers and their run-in with Mark. Since Tyler had used Mark's company for his condo project, he gave the detective all of Mark's information.

"I'll follow up on this and let you know the moment I have additional information. In the meantime, Ms. Marcel, please be careful."

****

Tyler drove through the busy streets of Chicago marinating on all that Dallas had shared. He looked over at her as she stared out the passenger side window. What an afternoon. First fighting with Mark, and then taking in Dallas's history. After hearing her story, he loved her even more, if that were possible.

"Are you okay?" he asked pulling up to a stop light. She turned to look at him, and his heart slammed in his chest. There were no tears, but she looked to be on the verge of crying. Misery glittered in her tired brown eyes. He hadn't seen her like this since the night they'd run into her ex-husband. He reached for her hand and squeezed it.

"Do you think Mark had something to do with the car accident and the calls?" she asked.

The light turned green and Tyler pulled off. "No, I don't."

"You don't?"

"No. I think Mark is too cocky to hide behind a telephone and threaten you. And he still cares about you in his twisted way. I can't see him having anything to do with slamming a car into you."

Dallas stared straight ahead. "I don't think he's behind it either, but I'm not sure. I haven't seen him in a long time and I don't know what he's capable of."

"Mark came to see me a couple of weeks ago."

Dallas turned to look at him. "He did? Why?"

"When Craig finished cutting my hair, Mark walked into the barbershop. Needless to say I was shocked to see him." Tyler stole a glance at her then returned his attention to the road. "Anyway, he asked if we could go outside and talk. So I went. I asked him what he wanted, and he wasted no time in telling me he wanted - you."

Tyler released her hand and rubbed his forehead. He felt trapped by the memory of his own emotions that afternoon. "Dallas, if Craig hadn't intervened, I'd probably be in big trouble with the law right now. When Mark said he wanted you and that you two were once very good together, I snapped. It wasn't only because of what he said; it was the way he said it. He was arrogant and … well, anyway I remembered what you told me about him. Before I'd realized it, I had grabbed him and thrown his sorry butt against the wall."

Dallas touched Tyler's arm. "I am so sorry. I've brought you so much grief these past couple of months."

"Baby, you've brought me way more than grief." He smiled. "If Simone hadn't of introduced us when she did, I'd still be lovin'em and leavin'em. Quinn and I used to joke that no woman alive could capture our hearts. Then you came along and everything changed.

"I don't know what I've done to deserve you. But thank you for coming today."

"You're welcome." He brought her hand to his lips and kissed it. "I honestly don't think Mark had anything to do with all of this, but I plan to find out."

"How?"

"I had Mark investigated." Tyler hopped on the expressway in route to Dallas's house.

"Really?"

"Yeah. He knew too much about you and about us. Since he was bold enough to step to me, at the barbershop, I knew I had to see what I was up against."

"Sooooo."

"So what?"

Dallas punched him in his arm. "So what did you find out?"

"OW."

"Tyler, quit playing."

"Okay, seriously though, he's clean. He's been in Louisiana since grad school and in Chicago for a few months. You already know where he works. There's not much more to tell. He knew so much about you because he hired someone to check up on you."

"So why didn't you say anything to the detective."

"I figured I'd let them do their own investigation. As far as I'm concerned, they took too long to find the car. Who knows how long it'll take for them to find the person responsible. Quinn and I have already started turning the soil on this thing."

"But it wouldn't be a bad idea to stay away from Mark. We don't know what he's capable of."

"I'll stay away from him, as long as he stays away from you."

****

Tyler pulled onto Dallas's street. The small hairs on the back of her neck rose when she saw two police cars parked in front of the house, and her front door standing open.

"What the heck is going on?" She asked when they pulled into her driveway.

"Only one way to find out." Tyler cut the engine and hurried around to help her out of the truck.

Dallas stepped across the threshold of her home and gasped. "Oh, my God, what happened in here?"

Someone had broken the lock on the door, shattered the bay window, and toppled over the book shelves and furniture.

"It wasn't me." Harmony leaned against a wall in the hallway with a police officer who looked up from his note pad. "Are you her sister?" the officer asked. Another officer entered the hall from the kitchen

"Yes and the owner. I'm Dallas Marcel. What happened?" Dallas's eyes scanned her living room and dining room. Anger swept through her at the thought that someone had invaded her home and destroyed her personal items.

"It was like this when I got here," Harmony said. "I used your neighbor's phone and called the police. They just got here."

Tyler introduced himself and walked through the house, leaving Dallas to answer the second officer's questions. She told him about the car accident, the calls, and the new information detective Davenport had given her. She also mentioned the cut telephone line and that the alarm system didn't work without it. Tyler chose that moment to return to the room. Dallas didn't miss the tightening of his jaw and the way his dark piercing eyes bore into her. She knew he'd broach the subject later, especially since she hadn't taken time to call the police.

"Ms. Marcel, in light of the information you've given us, we're going to have someone come dust for fingerprints. In the meantime, don't touch anything. I'll check in with Davenport."

"Are you okay?" Tyler asked when the officer walked away.

Dallas swallowed the sob rising in her throat and nodded as she surveyed the wreckage. A chill ran down her spine. Someone definitely wanted her attention.

Standing in the middle of her bedroom, she wrapped her arms around herself and her tears flowed freely. Her beautiful home destroyed. Her favorite vase and Tiffany lamp scattered in pieces around the carpet. It would take forever to pull her home back together.

She felt Tyler's presence the moment he walked into the room. He wrapped his arms around her, pulled her close to his body, and the weight of all that had transpired over the last few weeks finally took its toll. Dallas broke down in his arms and cried; accepting the fact that her life was in serious danger. She didn't know who was out to get her, but she knew she'd had enough.

A couple of hours later, she laid stretched out on the sofa still reeling from her horrendous day. After the living room had been dusted for prints, a flurry of activity surrounded them. Tyler hired his contractors to replace the windows and the door. The crew righted the furniture, made the space somewhat presentable, and assured Tyler they'd take care of the rest in the morning.

Once everyone was gone, Tyler joined them in the living room. "You know, Harmony." He stood over her, his arms crossed. "I'm a little surprised the officers didn't ask about the bruises on your face. How'd you get them?"

Harmony shot him a "none of your business" look. "It's nothing, just a minor disagreement." She turned her gaze back to the television and continued her mission of channel surfing.

"If your black eye and swollen cheek don't make big deal status, then what does?" Tyler walked over and turned the T.V. off.

"She and Jerome had a fight," Dallas offered. She sat up and planted her feet on the floor.

Tyler's eyes narrowed. "The guy she came to the house with?"

"Yep. Since she won't give me details about why her boyfriend got mad enough to hit her, maybe she'll tell you."

Harmony glared at Dallas. "Why you puttin' all my business out there?"

"Harmony, did Jerome know where Dallas lived?" Tyler asked.

Dallas hadn't thought about that and eyed her sister, waiting for an answer.

"I don't know. I sure didn't tell him. That was one of the reasons why we had a fight the other night. He wanted to know how to get in contact with Dallas here in Chicago."

Dallas leaned forward. "Why? I don't know him."

Harmony shrugged. "I didn't think you did. He's not a guy you'd hang out with." She paused and tilted her head. "Now that I think about it, that wasn't the only time he'd mentioned you."

"It wasn't?"

"No. When I heard about your car accident and found out you were in Milwaukee, he's the one who convinced me to call you. I needed a few dollars to pay for the room I rented and he said, 'call your sister.' I don't ever remember mentioning you."

With his hands locked behind his back, Tyler paced the length of the room. "What's Jerome's last name?" He stopped and pulled out his cell phone. When Harmony didn't respond, he looked up at her. "Harmony?"

She shook her head. "I don't know."

"You're dating a guy, and you don't know his last name?" Tyler said in a raised voice.

"Tyler," Dallas warned.

He looked from her to Harmony and shrugged in confusion. "What? Forgive me if I don't understand this. How can you date someone and not know his last name?"

Harmony stood with her hands on her hips. "Well, it's not like we went out a long time. We only kicked it for a few months. I don't know everything about him."

"Okay, how about this? How did you and Jerome meet?"

"I met him a few months ago here in Chicago. Actually, at Dallas's job."

Dallas's eyebrows shot up. "When was this?"

"Remember when I showed up at your office a few months ago? I had stopped by to have lunch with you. While I waited for you to come downstairs, he came up to me and started talking. I gave him my number, and we've been kickin' it ever since."

Tyler shook his head. "I don't know about this, Dallas. For all we know, this guy might be behind this mess. Or worse, responsible for your accident."

"What do you mean responsible for the accident?" Harmony moved closer to Dallas.

"It turns out someone intentionally slammed that car into me."

"And you think it was Jerome?" She looked from Dallas to Tyler.

"Based on the little you've said, I'm not ruling him out. When you and Jerome had your fight, did he say why he wanted to get in contact with Dallas?"

Harmony shrugged. "Something about her having something of his or something he needed. I don't know. I can't remember exactly. By that time, I was so mad at him I was half listening."

"Ah, hell." He turned to Dallas. "Get your things. You're not staying here."

Chapter Sixteen

"I don't care what you have to do. Get those papers!" David yelled into the telephone. Anger raced through his veins as he thought about the incompetent people he had working for him. "I've paid you a great deal of money and saved you from a life in prison, Jerome. So I expect you to take care of this. Sooner than later."

"Man, I tore her place apart and came up empty handed. We should've made a move when I suggested it before. Now her boyfriend is in the picture and it's going to be hard to get to her."

"I don't care how hard it is, get it done."

"I know you think she's on to you, but do you actually know if she has the information?" Jerome asked.

"Would I have you going after something if I weren't sure?" David paced behind his desk. There was no doubt in his mind Dallas had those documents. And since she didn't give them to him willingly, he would have to take them at any cost. "Do whatever it takes, or else." He slammed down the telephone not giving Jerome a chance to respond.

David walked over to the small bar in the corner of his office and poured himself a drink. A few years ago this had all started as a side hustle. His plan was to make a quick million and stop, but he didn't. He found more investors and he couldn't help himself. Now things could blow up in his face.

He should've destroyed those notes when he had the chance. There was no way he was going to let some over ambitious girl like Dallas ruin what he'd built. Sure she brought in a lot of accounts to the firm, and her financial savvy could rival any investment manager, but he didn't like her. There hadn't been an office meeting or situation where she didn't challenge him on at least one subject. Had it not been for William, he would've gotten rid of her years ago.

His telephone rang as his glass touched his lips. He gulped his drink and poured himself another one, taking his time getting to the telephone. "Weisman, here."

"I think we need to close up shop and cut our losses. The SEC is sniffing around."

"Ray, I'm the one who calls the shots here," David yelled at his silent partner and tossed back his whiskey. He shook his head wildly as the liquid burned the back of his throat. "Quit worrying, everything is fine. As for the Securities and Exchange Commission, they're not the smartest guys in the world. There's no way they know what we're doing."

"My gut tells me they're smarter than you think. We started off careful, Dave, but you've gotten careless lately. Maybe you should tell me how you've been handling these investments, just in case."

David dropped into his office chair and grabbed his head. The two quick drinks made him lightheaded. "Nah, you don't need to know. You're a silent partner in this project, remember? If the commission starts asking you questions, they might trip you up to draw out information. The less you know, the better you are," he said, his words slurred. "If they contact you, tell them what I told you to say. You'll be all right."

"I don't know," Ray said, doubt in his tone. "I have a bad feeling about this, and I have too much to lose."

"Aw, quit your worrying and don't call me again unless you have another investor." David disconnected and rested his head against the back of his chair. There was no way the SEC was on to them. He'd been too careful.

****

Dallas paced the floor in Tyler's bedroom like a caged animal. Yes, he was right about her and Harmony not staying at her house, but how dare he man-handle her into staying at his penthouse.

"Dallas?"

"Not now, Tyler."

143

"Then when?" He walked into the huge bedroom and closed the door behind him.

She stopped in front of the floor-to-ceiling windows and stared out into the night. She could see Tyler's reflection where he stood in front of the door, his hands stuffed in his front pockets. It was hard to stay mad at him when she knew his main concern was her safety, but that didn't negate the fact that he'd behaved like his usual domineering, possessive self when he demanded they leave the house.

"I get that you're angry. But what did you expect me to do? Someone runs you down, leaving you for dead. There have been threatening calls, a mysterious note, and an idiot ex-husband to show up. Who I *just* found out about and who is brave, *or stupid*, enough to attack you in a public place, and if that isn't enough, a break-in at your house. What did you expect me to do?"

Dallas sighed audibly but didn't move from her position, her back still to Tyler. She continued to stare out into the night, and couldn't ask for a better view. The bright lights from nearby buildings bounced off the darkness creating a spectacular sight. Tyler had told her about his Chicago project, but she didn't expect all of this. Though dusk had settled over the city, she could easily see Lake Michigan lit up by the lights from Navy Pier. She couldn't wait to see the view in the daytime.

She turned away from the window and roamed around the room, aware of Tyler's eyes on her, but making sure not to make eye contact. It felt good to move around without the bulky cast and pain-in-the-butt crutches. Although the crutches were nearby, she didn't need them at every turn.

A heavy sigh slipped through her lips. She needed to figure out what was going on, who had broken into her home, and what they were after. Her life was turning into something out of a James Patterson novel. Okay, well maybe it wasn't that bad, but geesh.

"I'm so tired," she mumbled. She plopped down on Tyler's huge bed, laid back, and placed her arm across her eyes. Moments later, he sat next to her.

"You can continue to ignore me, but I'm not going away."

With her eyes still covered, a small smile touched her lips. "I'm counting on that."

The mattress shifted under her, signaling that he stretched out next to her. He brushed a few strands of hair away from her forehead with his hand, and placed a kiss near her temple. "While I was hanging out in the living room with Ms. Harmony, I noticed some similarities between you two."

"Oh yeah? What?"

"You're both very beautiful and equally stubborn."

Dallas laughed. She could imagine the conversation between him and Harmony. He probably told her she couldn't leave the apartment, and most likely her sister responded with a few choice words punctuated by a neck roll. Dallas removed her arm from over her eyes, and looked at Tyler.

"Thanks for everything, especially for putting up with me and Harmony. She's still young, but I was hoping to be rid of my stubbornness by now."

He awarded her with a smile, and a kiss that ended way too soon.

"Well, your stubbornness is starting to grow on me, which is something I've wanted to discuss with you. I came to Chicago to check on you, but I also came to talk … about us. Unfortunately, the day hasn't gone quite like I thought it would."

"You can say that again."

"The day hasn't gone—."

Dallas elbowed him.

"OW. What? You said I could say it again."

"Yeah, but I didn't think you'd actually say it."

Tyler chuckled and then turned serious. Dallas's eyes drifted shut when the back of his fingers stroked her cheek ever so gently. The mere touch sent a tantalizing surge from the top of her head to the tip of her toes.

"I've missed you," he said. "Before I heard your voice message this morning, I did everything to get you out of my mind." He drew in a deep breath, released it, and stilled his hand.

Dallas turned her head slightly to look at him. He turned on his back and stared up at the ceiling. "But I couldn't. I couldn't stop thinking about you."

"Tyler, why me?" It was an unusual question, but she needed to know. Needed to find out what it was about her that kept him coming back. "Why haven't you given up on me? On us?"

"Good question. And one I've asked myself many of times. I know this is going to sound cliché, but you complete me."

"Will you be serious?"

145

"I am." He said without laughing. "When we're together, I feel complete, whole. I love the way you make me feel. Haven't you noticed how my chest sticks out more when I'm with you? I love the way you listen to what I have to say. And I enjoy our deep, intellectual conversations. You're brilliant, gorgeous, and when you're not giving me a hard time, you make me feel alive and powerful. I can't explain it any better than that. It's like what Tim told me when he fell for Simone. When love hits - you know. And Dallas ... baby, I love you. I've never stopped loving you."

A lump formed in her throat and Dallas fought back tears. No one, not even her mother, had ever made her feel so loved. And with Tyler, it wasn't just lip service.

"I don't deserve you."

He lifted up on one elbow, looked at her and frowned. "Why would you say that?"

"Because I don't. I've given you hell since day one. Not because I don't find you excruciatingly attractive, inside and out, but because I'm afraid. I've been fearful of letting my guard down around any guy who has been interested in more than a friendship with me. You know how I use to be. It was about having a good time with a guy, and then I'd move on."

"Yeah, I remember. When we met, I knew I'd met my match. Trying to get you to agree to an exclusive relationship with me was like trying to take your wallet. Now I know how some of those other guys you shot down felt."

"What other guys?" "Oh, don't try to play innocent with me. I heard about how you used to love'em and leave'em, breaking hearts all over the place."

Dallas smiled. "Simone talks too much. And you should talk! Your brother warned me about you Mr. men-weren't-meant-to-have-just-one-woman. I know you're an amazing man and there are plenty of women who would kill to be with you."

"I don't want any other woman. You are the only woman for me, and I will fight 'til the end to have you. Dallas, you're my other half. We're supposed to be together."

"Tyler, I—"

"Please ... let me finish. I already know how important your career is to you. I know how determined you are to make partner."

"Ty—"

"Dallas." He exhaled in frustration. "I want you to have everything you want, your career and a family. With me, you don't have to choose one or the other. I'm not Mark. And I'm tired of you treating me like I am. I don't expect you to stay at home and raise kids. I know you want more, and I want you to have it all. But I need for you to give me a chance. Give us a chance."

"And that's what I've been trying to tell you. I love you, *dammit*! I have been a total jerk. I'm so sorry it has taken me this long to get my act together. But months ago, when you asked me to marry you, it scared me. Despite how wonderful you are, I was afraid I'd end up the way I was with Mark. And for the record, I know you're not him. I feel things for you that I've never felt with another man."

He wiped her tears and pulled her into his arms. "I hope you know I'm looking for more than just a girlfriend. I want forever. This is not a proposal, 'cause I know we still have some things to work out, but I want you to be clear about my intentions. I'm in this for the long haul and I need to know if you feel the same way, otherwise, this is not going to work."

Dallas gazed into his eyes and cupped his face with her hands. "I want forever, too."

He stared at her with dark penetrating eyes and flashed his beautiful smile and twin dimples that still made her weak in the knees. "That's all I needed to hear."

In one smooth motion Tyler rolled her onto her back and covered her body with his. He lowered his head and kissed her so tenderly that all the stress from the day melted away and a raging fire rippled through her body. For the first time in a long time, she was ready, ready to give all of herself to a man, this man.

"Just so you know, if your sister knocks on that door, or barges in here, I'm not stopping. I'll be damn if I let another interruption stop me from getting reacquainted with your luscious body," he said against her mouth, his hands making quick work of unbuttoning her blouse.

"You'll get no arguments from me," she said breathlessly, feeling the hardness of his erection against her inner thigh as she clawed at his shirt. She groaned when his greedy lips replaced his hands and seared a path from the lobe of her ear, down her neck, and over the swell of her breast where he lingered.

"We have on too many clothes for what I have in mind," he said and pulled his lips away as if it were the hardest thing to do. He stood. Breathing hard and not taking his eyes off of her, he ripped off his shirt, not caring that buttons went flying. He tossed the garment aside, toed off his shoes and started undoing his belt.

"Mmm, let me," she said scooting to the edge of the bed and pulling him closer by the waistband of his pants. She took her time sliding down the zipper and smiled as his eyes fluttered closed and a throaty groan erupted from within him when she wrapped her hand around his throbbing manhood. "You like that, baby?" she crooned loving the effect her touch was having on him.

"Oh, yeah, but if you keep that up, this will be over before we even get started," he said, and gently eased away from her before she could really make him cry out. He took a breath and wasted no time in sliding his pants and briefs down his long muscular legs.

Turned on by the mere sight of him, Dallas scampered back, raised her hips and shimmied out of her skirt, tossing it to where Tyler's shirt and her blouse had landed. She looked up to find him staring, and enjoyed the way his sexy eyes made love to her semi-naked body.

"Damn, girl, I think red is my new favorite color," he said of her lace bra and barely-there panties. "You're even more beautiful than I remember."

"I guess I could say the same about you." She stared up at the tall, amazingly built man, whose smooth toffee skin, broad shoulders, and long, thick shaft could make the strongest woman drop her panties without being asked. Zoning in on her favorite part of his anatomy, she couldn't help but think of how generous God had been when handing out the part of Tyler's body that made him all man.

She shuddered in anticipation and inched back against the mound of pillows and opened for him, inviting him to have his way with her.

A devilish smile graced his lips as he ripped open the condom package and quickly covered himself. He did a slow crawl onto the bed until he was directly over her. "I wanted to take this slow, but the way you're looking—"

"We'll go slow next time 'cause right now, all I want is for you to be inside me."

"Anything you want, baby," he said, quickly discarding her skimpy undies, and before she could take her next breath he had slipped inside her, filling every crevice of her interior walls.

She cried out with pleasure as her body adjusted to him, savoring every tantalizing inch of his thickness. Still wanting more, her bold hands grabbed his ass, pulling him even deeper. She'd gone months without the feel of him inside her and she wanted all of him.

Their hips rocked to a familiar beat and everything within her pulsated when he grabbed her butt and with each thrust he dove deeper, and deeper sending her to the edge of her control. All too quickly, she bucked uncontrollably against him unable to hold back, her head thrashing from side to side against the pillows. Waves of ecstasy throbbed through her and she screamed out surrendering to the whirl of sensation that took her over the edge.

Tyler was right behind her, growling out her name as his release came with such force Dallas felt the turbulence of his passion swirl around her before he collapsed on top of her.

After a second round, she placed a lingering kiss along his jaw and curled up to him. His strong arms securely wrapped around her, was more than perfect. This is where she belonged and where she planned to stay.

****

Cradling her in the crook of his arm, Tyler outlined the roundness of her breast with the tip of his finger.

"Mmm, that feels good, but you're going to have to feed me before we do a round three."

"I have no problem with that," he said, knowing she'd be asleep before he could ease off the bed. Seconds later he chuckled when he heard her soft snores. *Talk about role reversal.* He covered her naked body with the sheet and got up to take a quick shower. At the moment, he was more hungry than tired.

A little while later, Tyler exited the bedroom and walked into the living room surprised to see Harmony and Quinn tidying the kitchen.

"Hey, you just caught me. I was getting ready to head out," Quinn said.

"Well, I'm glad you're here. I wanted to talk to you about a few things."

"I guess that's my cue," Harmony said and placed the last dish in the dishwasher. "Thanks for keeping me company, Quinn. I hope I see you around."

"You will," he said grabbing her around the waist when she attempted to step past him. He pulled her close and placed a friendly kiss on her cheek before releasing her. "Take care and have a good night."

"You too," she smiled at him and headed down the hall humming.

Tyler shook his head at his friend. *Unbelievable.* "So, what did I miss?" he asked looking through the large stainless steel refrigerator for something to eat. Dallas was still a firecracker in bed, draining him of all of his energy, yet he couldn't get enough of her. But right now, he needed food.

"Why didn't you tell me Dallas had a gorgeous sister?" Quinn asked. He took the bottle of beer Tyler offered and moved into the living room, making himself comfortable in one of the upholstered chairs.

Tyler chuckled, and took a seat on the sofa, a beer in one hand and two slices of cold pizza in the other. "Didn't think about it. Besides, she's too young for you."

"As long as she's legal, she's old enough for me. She's cute, but having a boyfriend who knocks her around sounds like bad news."

"Yeah, I know. I've seen him, and he is bad news. I'm just glad she got away from him."

Quinn rubbed his chin. "Me too. It'll be easier getting to know her if there's nobody else in the picture."

Tyler shook his head and laughed. "Q, don't start nothin'. She seems like a nice young lady. She doesn't need you to come along and corrupt her." He joked.

"Ha, ha, very funny. For all you know, she might be the one."

Tyler's eyebrows knitted together. "Yeah right. Like you'll ever settle down." Quinn had been in love once, but when the love of his life was killed, he never let another woman get close again.

"Hey, it can happen. Look at you."

Tyler nodded. "True."

"So I take it all is well with you and Dallas. I can't help but notice you seem more...ah, what's the word I'm looking for," he snapped his fingers a few times. "Oh, I know, satiated, or maybe it's happy."

Tyler laughed. "You're right about that. My girl definitely knows how to bring a smile to my face, but we still have some things to work out."

Quinn nodded. "Well, while you're working things out, you might want to sound proof your bedroom. You too were making enough noise to make me blush, and you know I don't blush easy."

Tyler choked on his beer and fell into a coughing fit, pounding his chest.

"Hey, I'm just sayin'"

"Uh, thanks. I'll take that under advisement," Tyler hurried to change the subject. He filled Quinn in on the day's events, including his concern about Jerome's possible involvement.

"So back up a minute. Let's talk about you knocking Mark around? I can't believe you, a grown man, fighting over a woman."

"I wasn't fighting over Dallas. I was getting dude off of her. The way he grabbed her, he's lucky security stopped me when they did."

"You think he has anything to do with this nonsense that's been going on with her?"

"Dallas asked me the same thing, and my gut tells me he's not out to physically hurt her. But I want us to dig a little deeper on him. I also want to see what we can find out about this Jerome dude."

Quinn slouched down in his chair and rubbed his goatee. "Maybe Harmony and I can go for a little ride in the morning and pay her boyfriend a visit. It'll also give me an opportunity to see how he likes being knocked around."

Tyler shook his head. "I don't know Q. Maybe we should let the cops handle the face to face stuff. I want you to find out about Jerome's background, where he works, and any other information that might be helpful. Besides, I've seen the way you knock people around and I'm sure you wouldn't want to scare Harmony with your dark side."

He remembered a bar fight Quinn was involved in years ago. They'd always had each other's back, but when Quinn returned from active duty, he was like a one man wrecking machine. He not only tore the place apart, but broke a man's nose and his arm, as well as the knee cap of another man, putting them both in the hospital. His behavior that night got him a night's stay in the county jail. It probably would've been longer, but Quinn knew people. He was out the next morning, with all charges dropped. Since then, he usually kept a low profile.

Quinn stood holding his beer, walked to the patio door and looked out. Several minutes passed and he said, "Yeah, you're probably right."

****

Sitting at her desk, Dallas released a wistful sigh when touched one of the delicate petals of the gorgeous floral arrangement she'd received from Tyler earlier in the day. Last night had been amazing. She and Tyler never had a problem in the bedroom, and last night proved they still were in sync. The thought of them being a couple again made her warm inside. Maybe this time she'd get it right.

"Dallas," Bianca said over the intercom.

"Yes."

"Paige Logan is on line one for you."

"Okay thanks."

"Hey Paige, thanks for getting back to me so quickly."

"All right, so let's talk about these mysterious documents."

Dallas recapped what she'd told Paige over the telephone the day before and her concerns about the things going on at the firm.

"I've been thinking about everything you've told me: the firm's cutbacks, David's strange behavior, your conversation with the client in Milwaukee, and now these notes. What if David is involved in something illegal - like a Ponzi scheme?"

"I don't know Paige that seems a little out there."

"I know it sounds far-fetched, but hear me out. Look at that guy in New York, Bernard Madoff. He turned his wealth management business into one of the largest Ponzi schemes in history. Defrauding thousands of clients of their money, fabricating gains, and even today, federal investigators don't know if his business was even legit."

Dallas sat speechless. She remembered when the story broke because many of their clients were concerned about their investments. Would David put the firm in jeopardy, and even worse, take money from innocent people? The thought made her skin crawl.

She shook her head. "I can't see him doing something like that. He'd have too much to lose. Yes, I think he's like the lowest form of human life, but this? I don't think so."

"I don't think you should rule it out, but I hope you're right. Maybe you can ask him a few questions and see if he gives any clues to it. I'm not sure if you're privy to this type of information, but has there been any money missing from any client accounts? How much do you know about the firm? Is there another branch or arm of the company that he might be using to run money through?"

Dallas let her head fall back against her chair and closed her eyes. She hoped Paige was wrong, but the more she thought about it, the more things were becoming clearer.

A few months ago she'd returned to the office around ten o'clock in the evening for a file and was surprised to find David meeting with several men in his office. Whatever they were discussing was heated.

The raised voices traveled down the hall to her office and she remembered hearing David talking about needing more investors. She had stuck around a little longer to check her voice messages and recalled how surprised he'd been to find her in the building when he was leaving. Since then he'd been acting stranger than usual toward her.

Dallas raised her head. "Oh my God, Paige, you might be on to something. I have to find out what he's up to."

"Uhh, I don't know Dallas. If he is involved in some nonsense like a Ponzi scheme, he's probably not someone you want to tangle with."

****

From the patio of one of the condos in his building, Tyler looked down at the busy street below. He'd been lucky to get the building in such a prime location, right near the Magnificent Mile. Some days he couldn't believe how their company had grown. He and Quinn had made some good investment decisions and were now reaping the rewards.

Upon hearing a door slam, he turned to see Quinn walking into the empty unit.

"Hey man, how long you been here?" Quinn asked and placed the large box that he was carrying on the kitchen counter.

Tyler stepped back into the apartment and closed the patio door behind him. "Not too long."

"What do you think of the place so far?"

"It's coming along, although I expected the last three units to be done this week."

"Yeah, about that, looks like it'll be another two weeks. But don't worry we're still coming in under budget."

"Good. Best news I've heard all day."

Quinn leaned against the counter. "Well, now for the not so good news. I got some information on Jerome. The guy is bad news. He's been in and out of trouble since he was fifteen, even spent a bout in jail last year after beating a guy so bad, the man ended up in the hospital for weeks."

"So why isn't he behind bars?"

"He was. Dude did a few months until his hearing, and should've done more time due to some other accusations and warrants, but somehow the case was dropped and all of his fines paid."

Tyler swore under his breath. He knew Jerome was trouble the day he came by the house with Harmony. He had walked in as if he was casing the joint.

"I know you said not to, but Harmony and I did go by his apartment this morning."

"Q…"

"Don't worry, nothing happened. He wasn't there. I talked to a couple of his neighbors and no one has seen him in the last few days. The cops have been there, but no Jerome. I have someone watching the place, but, Ty, there's something else."

"What?"

"The Securities and Exchange Commission is definitely investigating Dallas's firm. The shit is about to hit the fan. Rumor has it they suspect one of the partners is involved in securities fraud."

"You gotta be kiddin' me." Tyler stood in front of him with his arms crossed. "Are you sure?"

"Positive. And if Dallas were my woman, I'd want her to know what's going on. I'll let you decide if you want to tell her, but if ever it gets back that I told you anything, I'll deny it."

He knew his friend was serious. Being ex-special ops for the government, Quinn had a way of finding out things, but he'd never betray a source – not even for him.

Tyler had a bigger problem. How was he going to tell Dallas that all of her hard work to make partner may be in vain? Once the SEC was done with them, the firm may no longer exist. "Are we talking a Ponzi scheme?"

"Most likely."

"If that's really what's going on, that low life David Weisman is probably the mastermind behind it."

"I don't know, but if you tell Dallas any of this, make sure she keeps her mouth shut. If it's a Ponzi scheme, someone's going to jail. And since they don't know who all the players are you definitely don't want her sharing information with the wrong person."

Chapter Seventeen

Dallas covered her face with her hands and groaned. If she had to be a part of one more meeting today she would scream. The day had been crazy from the moment she'd stepped into the office. Her only excitement had been when she signed a millionaire client, who requested her personally.

"Hey there."

Dallas dropped her hands when Bianca knocked and walked in. "I'm heading out, but just so you know, David just called to see if you were still here. He says he wants to talk to you before you leave for the day."

"Did he say what it was about?" She opened her desk drawer and put away some personal stuff she'd been working on.

"Nope. Do you want me to stick around?"

"Oh, no. Go on home. I appreciate you staying this late."

"Are you sure? I can stay a little longer."

"I'm positive." She glanced at her watch. "Besides, Tyler should be here any minute. So go on, leave." She waved her hand in a brushing motion. "Have a good night, and I'll see you in the morning."

"All right, if you insist. But remember, security is a phone call away if David gets out of hand."

Dallas smirked. "I'll keep that in mind, though I'm sure he has more sense than to get crazy with me." Or at least she hoped he did.

Last night when she told Tyler about Paige's theory and showed him the documents she thought were linked to it, he told her he had recently found out the SEC was investigating her firm.

"I'm glad I caught you before you left."

Startled, Dallas looked up to find David walking toward her. She scanned his appearance. His hair looked as if he'd run his fingers through it one too many times, causing several unruly strands to stick straight out. His brown and tan striped tie hung loose around his neck with the top button of his wrinkled white shirt unbuttoned and the tail of it sneaking out of his pants. He looked as ragged as she felt.

"What's up, David?" She stood and walked around him to get to her file cabinet. By the looks of his disheveled appearance, she wondered if the SEC had made contact. Tyler told her she couldn't say anything about the investigation to anyone, not even William.

"Not much. I'm trying to finish up a few things before heading out," he said. He first stood with his hands in his pocket, but when she looked back, he had taken a seat in one of the chairs in front of her desk. "I wanted to congratulate you on the Miller account. That's some portfolio you'll be managing. We were all surprised when Mrs. Miller requested you by name."

"I wasn't surprised. I've been in contact with her for months."

David glanced over his shoulder and shot her a "whatever look" but said, "At this rate, you'll make partner in no time."

Dallas leaned against the file cabinet. Making partner had been her number one goal for the past few years, and it suddenly wasn't important anymore. Building a relationship with Tyler took precedence now. "Thanks, David," was all she said.

"Uh, Dallas, seeing you do some of your filing just reminded me. I was wondering if you've run across those documents I've been looking for. I was hoping maybe they had turned up in some of your other files by now, since they weren't in the files I looked through."

Dallas slammed the file drawer closed and walked back to her seat. With her elbows resting on the desk and her fingers interlocked under her chin, she looked at him. "No, sorry I haven't seen them. Maybe if you tell me what they pertained to, I'll know them if I see them."

David pounded his fist on her desk and leaped from his chair. "Don't screw with me little girl. You know damn well what I'm talking about!"

Dallas pushed back from her desk, her heart thumping erratically against her chest. She knew David didn't like her, but he had never disrespected or verbally attacked her before.

"I…I don't have your papers," she managed to get out. "Let's calm down and maybe we can figure out where—"

With one clean swipe of his hand across her desk, everything went flying across the room. A high pitched scream that sounded like she was blowing her lungs out flew through her lips, when David lunged at her.

"I'm not sure what type of game you're playing." He growled, grabbed hold of the arms of her chair, and pulled her and the chair toward him. His face inches from hers. "But those papers are very important, and I plan to get them back. Either you can hand them over, or find out the hard way how I handle people who cross me." Without another word he released the arms of her chair, turned and walked out of the office.

The breath she didn't realize she was holding escaped her in a burst moments after David left the room. Her body was shaking so badly she could barely push herself up to her desk. *What have I done? I should've just given him the papers.* She had already handed over a copy of the documents to Tyler, to give to his SEC contact. What harm would it do to give David back his originals?

With her hands covering her face, she took several cleansing breaths. She'd hand over David's papers, but not before he confessed to what he was doing. Fear knotted inside her. If David was bold enough to come after her in the office, she knew he was serious about getting his information back.

On shaky legs, she moved from her desk and began picking up the items David had thrown on the floor. The glass pencil holder was in tiny pieces and papers were strewn everywhere. As for the broken glass, she picked up the big pieces, but would leave a note for the cleaning service to pay extra attention to the area.

David had knocked things off the desk with such force, that there was now a small dent in the wall from where the paper weight made contact. Thankfully it wasn't broken.

It was only a matter of time before he got what was coming to him. When the SEC made a move, she'd be ready to help them in any way she could.

"Hey, baby, you…."

Dallas jumped and dropped the paperweight she held in her hands. When she looked up and saw Tyler, tears welled up in her eyes. She had never been so happy to see anyone in her life. And had it not been for her awkward position on the floor, she would've run into his arms.

"What happened in here?" He reached out his hand to help her off the floor.

"David." His name hitched in her throat.

"David what?" He held her at arm's length and she felt his body tense, and watched his eyes turned flat and hard.

"He ... Tyler it doesn't matter. It's over and—"

"What happened, Dallas?" His voice was low and demanding as he looked her over. "Are you hurt?"

"He wants his papers back. I said I didn't have them, and he told me not to play with him." She wiped at her tears. "Then he got angry, shoved everything off of my desk and came at me."

"What?" he yelled. "Did he touch you?"

Dallas rested her hands on his chest. "Tyler, nothing happened. See. I'm fine." She wrapped her arms around his waist. "Everything's fine."

He grabbed her shoulders and held her back, forcing her to look at him. "Dammit, Dallas, everything is not fine! When your boss comes at you over some stupid papers, there's something very wrong." He dropped his arms and turned to leave.

"Please. Don't leave me," she cried. It was the only thing she could say to keep him from charging out of the office, in search of David. The last thing she wanted was for him to take matters into his own hands. Yes, she wanted David to pay, but if he was doing something illegal she wanted him caught and put behind bars.

Tyler walked back and pulled her into his arms. "Then I'm calling the police."

"No, don't. Technically he hasn't done anything. Maybe scared me a little, but that's it. I believe David is the one the SEC is after and when they finish their investigation they'll put him away for life."

Still holding her, he rested his chin on top of her head. Dallas could feel the rapid beat of his heart when his arms tightened around her.

"Come on let's get this stuff cleaned up and get out of here," he said.

He picked up the items on the floor while she straightened her desk and locked her file drawers. After one last look around, Dallas walked over to Tyler. She could feel his anger when he put his arm around her waist and led her to the door.

"I'm okay. He didn't hurt me," she said.

"Maybe not this time, but what about next time?"

"There won't be a next time."

He kissed her lips. "Damn right there won't be."

****

Mark walked into his favorite downtown bar, a place that was quickly becoming his second home. Since he worked and lived in downtown Chicago he had his choice of great restaurants, but this place offered it all. Good food, sports, and a comfortable atmosphere. It was the perfect spot to unwind after a busy day. He took a seat at the bar and looked around the quaint space.

"Hey, handsome. Second time in four days, must be a heck of a week for you," one of the bartenders said, bringing him his usual.

"Yeah, something like that," Mark said. He wrapped his hands around the bottle she placed in front of him. "I could say the same for you. Do you ever get a day off?"

She cast a toothy smile at him and leaned over, giving him a good view of the assets hiding behind her low cut shirt. "I only take off when necessary. Besides, if I don't show up I might miss seeing your good-looking face."

Mark grinned but didn't comment. He didn't want to encourage her to keep flirting, which she did every time he came in. He took a swig of his beer, placed the bottle down, and glanced around the bar. Besides a few of the regulars, there weren't many people there tonight. When he turned to his left, his gaze landed on a woman who reminded him of Dallas.

He rubbed his tired eyes as frustration mounted at the thought of how he'd botched his encounter with her. He definitely hadn't set out to scare her, but when she threatened to call him out on things from his past, he lost it.

What made him think he could walk back into her life and pick up where they'd left off? He wanted to make amends for how he had abandoned her, but not even the fact that she was rich, thanks to him, could fix what he'd done. He never had the chance to tell her about the investments he'd made with the money he had taken from their joint account years ago. Now he might never get a chance to make things right with her.

Yesterday he had received a visit from the cops, asking him questions regarding his whereabouts months ago. They wanted to know about his face to face contact with Dallas, and whether or not he'd been making threatening calls. Somehow they'd found out that he had her investigated and wanted to know if he knew anything about a break-in at her house. He had no idea she'd been going through so much craziness, otherwise he would've found a different way to approach her once he arrived in town.

"I'll have what he's having," the familiar voice said to his right.

Mark looked over only to find David Weisman taking the seat next to him. "David," Mark said simply. Seeing him reminded Mark that he hadn't gotten back in touch with David after their meeting. Originally when Ray, his old college friend, had told him about an unbeatable investment opportunity, his interest was sparked. Especially since he found out it was with Dallas's company. But after his run-in with Dallas and Tyler, he knew there was no chance for reconciliation, and he was no longer interested in anything David had to offer.

"So this is where the rich and powerful hang out." David slurred, taking a swig of the drink that sat in front of him.

Mark shook his head. He hated being around people who couldn't hold their liquor, and it looked as if David had already had a few. "I wouldn't know." He wasn't in the mood for David, or anyone else for that matter. The whole point of being there was to unwind, watch a baseball game, and not think.

"Haven't heard back from you since we talked. You still interested in investing in my project?"

"Nah, I think I'll pass."

David leaned toward him and Mark could smell the liquor on his breath. "Too bad. You gon' miss out."

Tuning his unwanted guest out, Mark faced forward looking at the mirror behind the bar, surprised at how quickly the bar and grill had filled up. He enjoyed the exhilaration that always surrounded him whenever he was there. Several TVs showed different games, while guys cheered for their favorite teams. He couldn't think of a better place to forget about his problems.

"I see you ain't got much to say. I wish your wife was more like that, but no, she always got something to say."

Mark heard the bitterness in his tone when he mentioned Dallas. If David was like most drunks, he'd keep talking without prompting, and Mark waited for him to step out of line.

"I see why you kicked her to the curb. She's a pain. Been a thorn in my side since the day William hired her. But that's going to change soon."

Mark put his drink down. "What's that supposed to mean?" He and Dallas might not be on good terms, but he didn't want anything bad to happen to her.

"I can't stand that bi—"

"Hey, watch yourself. Drunk or not, I won't have you disrespecting her. If she's anything like she used to be, I'm sure she's brought more money into your firm than your sorry butt deserves."

David stumbled to stand up. "Oh, so you're defending that tramp? Well, go ahead, 'cause when I get done with her, she's going to need—"

Before he realized what he was doing, Mark sent a left hook to David's jaw. "Say somethin' else."

The manager walked over holding a baseball bat. "All right you two. If you're going to fight, take it outside."

Mark emptied his drink, grabbed his jacket and left David standing there holding his face.

****

"What do you think about us finding a nice cozy restaurant to eat at before going home?" Dallas asked. Tyler hadn't said much since they left her office and she couldn't stand the tension between them.

"Where'd you have in mind?"

"How about Liza's? It's been a long time since we've been there."

"Sounds good."

After their meal, they talked over coffee. Tyler told her about an opportunity he and Quinn had to purchase some land near Schaumburg, Illinois that would be perfect for a strip mall. She was glad he was loosening up. She wanted to keep him talking, but his cell phone vibrated for the second time in ten minutes.

"Are you going to answer that?"

"No."

When it vibrated again five minutes later, he said, "I'm sorry, baby. I'm not sure who this is, but let me take it real quick. Tyler Hollister."

Several minutes into the telephone conversation, Tyler grew quiet. Dallas wasn't sure who he was talking to, but it must've been someone he didn't like, or they were telling him something he didn't want to hear. His eyes narrowed, his lips thinned, and his words were few. He didn't look happy.

When he finally ended the call, Dallas couldn't help but ask, "What was that all about?"

Without looking at her, he said, "Nothing much. Just something I need to take care of tomorrow." He moved his empty plate off to the side and reached for her hand. "Thanks for suggesting we stop for dinner. I've been so caught up in getting these condos done and—"

"Looking after me," Dallas said. "I'm sorry we haven't had a chance to spend much quality time together since you've been in town."

Tyler shrugged. "It's okay, I'm sure we'll make up for it. My main concern now is figuring out what's going on at your firm and keeping you safe in the process."

"I appreciate that. I'm going to make it easier for you."

"How so?"

"For starters, I'm working from the penthouse for the next couple of days. My encounter with David this evening kinda shook me up." The moment David's name came out of her mouth, she regretted it. Tyler immediately tensed and a swift shadow of anger swept across his face. She squeezed his hand. "I'm sorry I brought that up, but I want you to know I'm cutting back my work hours."

His eyebrows arched. "Now that's something I thought I'd never live to hear you say."

She smiled. "My priorities have changed."

"Oh, really?" He leaned forward in his seat and smiled for the first time that evening. "Tell me about this change of priorities."

"Well, you might find this hard to believe, but my quest to make partner is no longer my main concern. Thanks to you, I finally realize there is so much more to life than making partner."

"Like what?"

"Like you. Like us. Like spending more time with you and less time at work." Dallas stopped talking when the waitress approached their table with their bill.

"I'm glad you're willing to invest in us," he said after the waitress walked away. "I promise - you won't regret it." He pulled her hand to his mouth and kissed the back of it.

The touch of his warm lips against her skin sent a smoldering sensation through her, and it was going to take a miracle for her to restrain herself from ripping off his clothes before they arrived home.

"You ready?" he asked.

You have no idea.

****

Mark drummed his fingers against the tabletop. He glanced at his watch for what seemed like the hundredth time, only to find that it was a mere ten minutes since the last time he had checked. He'd give Tyler another five minutes, and then he was leaving. Mark was beginning to think that calling him yesterday evening might not have been such a good idea. Of course Tyler wasn't happy to hear from him, but reluctantly agreed to meet after the mention of David's name.

Mark released a frustrated sigh and then spotted Tyler making his way through the small cafe. He put his coffee cup down, wiped his mouth, and stood to greet him.

"Hey, how you doin'? Thanks for meeting me," he said stretching out his hand.

"This ain't a social visit, Darley. Just tell me why it was so important that we meet." Tyler took the seat across from him.

"I think Dallas might be in danger."

****

Dallas grabbed a bag of chips, went into the living room, and sat on the sofa next to Tyler. He had come in shortly after lunch, but hadn't said much. "Want some?" She offered.

"No thanks," he said without taking his eyes off the TV.

"So are you home for the rest of the day, or do you have to go back out?"

"I'll be here for awhile, but Quinn and I have a meeting in about an hour. Why? Do you need something?" He glanced at her, but quickly returned his attention to the television.

"I was just wondering how long I'll have you all to myself." She leaned against him and played with the buttons on his shirt. When she undid the top few buttons, and he didn't respond, she snatched the remote and turned the TV off. "What's wrong with you? You haven't said much of anything since you got here. What's going on?"

He leaned back against the sofa. "I have a lot on my mind."

"Like what?"

After a long pause he said, "You. I'm worried about you."

She moved her hands up and down his thigh and felt his muscles tighten under her touch. "Tyler, I'm fine. The cops are on the case, and you, Quinn and Hank have been watching me like a hawk. Why are you worried?"

He sat up and turned to look at her, his eyebrows knitted together. "Because of all of this mess that's been going on! How can you even ask me that, especially after your run-in with David last night? He better hope the SEC get to him before I do because … damn, Dallas. I don't know what I'd do if anything happened to you."

Dallas wrapped her arms around his neck and climbed onto his lap. "You fellas have been taking good care of me. I'm not worried because I'm not going to put myself in any unnecessary danger, and I'm definitely staying clear of David."

He caressed her cheek with the back of his hand. She couldn't read his expression, but his brilliant dark eyes studied her. "I met with Mark today."

Her body stiffened and she leaned back. "Mark who? 'Cause I know we're not talking about Mark Darley, my ex."

"Actually, we are. He was the call I received when we were at dinner last night. He wanted to meet."

Dallas pushed away from Tyler and stood. It didn't make sense for her boyfriend to meet with her ex-husband. "What could you two possibly have to talk about? There is nothing between he and I, and I already know you can't stand him. So what was there to talk about?"

She grabbed the bag of chips and stormed into the kitchen. "What were you doing, comparing notes or something?" Angry, but still hungry, she grabbed an apple from the refrigerator and a knife from the drawer to slice it.

Tyler walked up behind her and put his arms around her waist and nuzzled her ear. He placed a kiss on her temple and slowly removed the knife from her hand.

"Hear me out before you start jumping to conclusions. Mark called because the other night he ran into David Weisman."

Dallas turned in his arms to face him, and he held her tighter.

"Seems your boss made some not so nice comments about you and Mark popped him. That's probably the only thing I like about your ex-husband."

She pulled back to look at him. "How does he even know David?"

"A few weeks ago David contacted him about investing in a *special* project. Unfortunately, Mark doesn't know any details about it because once he realized you didn't want anything to do with him, he was no longer interested in investing with David."

"So what did David say to Mark to make him want to call you?"

"David told him you were a thorn in his side, but that was going to end soon. At any rate, Mark said it sounded like a threat. He wanted to call you directly, but didn't think you would give him the time of day."

"And he thought you would?"

Tyler shrugged. "I don't know, but I'm glad he called. I'm not sure what David's plan is, but at least we know to be careful, especially where he's concerned."

Dallas rested her forehead against Tyler's chest. *Maybe I can come up with a plan to get David to confess what he's doing.* She quickly shot the idea down since she'd told Tyler she wouldn't put herself in harm's way.

"I'll go ahead and contact the police about this latest incident with David. I guess I was holding off because I want the SEC to find out what he's doing and put a stop to it. If the police start sniffing around, they might screw it all up."

Tyler kissed her cheek. "I get what you were trying to do, baby, but this is too dangerous. I'm already not comfortable with you being at the office with David. At least if the cops know what's going on, if something should happen, you're covered as far as not withholding any information. Oh, and one more thing," he said pulling a white envelope out of his pocket and handing it to her.

"What's this?"

"The money Mark used from your joint account was invested. That's your half of the proceeds. He assured me that though he'd hope to rekindle some type of relationship with you, he understands that's impossible."

****

"Where you going?" Harmony asked when Dallas walked past her in the living room.

Dallas grabbed her jacket from the coat rack near the door. "Hank is taking me by my house to pick up some more of my things. It shouldn't take too long."

"Are you sure that's a good idea? Quinn said Tyler didn't want you going out without one of them."

"Hank will be with me. Besides, it's only going to take a few minutes. I'll be back before you know it. Do you need anything while we're out?"

"Nope. I'm cool," she said, but then stood up. "On second thought, maybe I'll go with you. At least I'll get out the house. Who knows, maybe I'll even be able to talk Hank into taking us to *Garrett's*. I can go for some of their world famous popcorn right about now."

"Mmm...that does sound good. We can stop there first. Grab your coat, I told Hank I'll meet him downstairs."

Chapter Eighteen

As big and tall as Quinn, Hank had a gentleness about him that made Dallas think that he grew up with some younger sisters. His ruggedly handsome face was bronzed as if he'd spent a lot of time in the sun and his toned body, from his thick neck to his tree trunk thighs made the average man look like a chump. But despite his intimidating presence, he had the patience of a saint and Harmony had tested it for the past hour having him to make several additional stops before they finally arrived at Dallas's place.

After he checked the house and put his gun away, Hank gave Dallas and Harmony the okay to go in. Dallas walked through the front door of her home with trepidation. She stopped in the hallway, and glanced into the living room. True to his word, Tyler had the space looking like new. Same with the dining room, everything was back in its place and the items that had been broken were replaced. But it didn't feel like home.

When Dallas left the house days ago she hadn't thought about what it would be like returning, and now she wasn't sure she'd ever be able to stay there again. Someone had invaded her privacy, gone through her things and destroyed the comfort that she'd created.

"I'll stay here in the living room while you do your thing," Harmony said grabbing the remote from one of the end tables and turning on the television.

Hank double checked the front door to make sure it was locked, and then he shadowed Dallas as she moved from room to room. Hank didn't say anything, as if he understood her need to take it all in and deal with the empty feeling lying dormant in her gut. Her peace of mind had been stripped and she would never be able to regain the serenity she always felt when arriving home after a long day of work.

Apprehension raced through her veins when she stopped in front of her semi-opened bedroom door, keeping her from walking across the threshold.

"It's okay," Hank said from beside her, and pushed the door open.

"Do you need some privacy?" he asked from the doorway.

"No, it'll only take me a minute to grab a few things."

She went about pulling dress pants, blouses, and business suits from the closet and filled a few pieces of luggage. It was at that moment she decided she wouldn't return. She couldn't sleep in her bed, or use her shower without wondering if someone had planted a video recorder, or worse, returned to the scene of the crime.

Besides Jerome being a person of interest, the police still didn't have any major leads. The question she had though, was why? If Jerome was behind the break-in, what was he looking for? Tyler started his own investigation citing that the cops were taking too long. She agreed.

Hank grabbed her bags, and she took one last look around her bedroom. There had been some wonderful years in her house, and though she'd miss it, she was looking forward to the next chapter in her life.

****

"You said that you're sure she has those documents, but we've looked up and down this office," Jerome said. "They're not here." He lounged in Dallas's office chair, stretched out his legs, and put his size 12 up on her desk.

"Get your feet down. We can't leave any sign that we've been in here snooping around. I don't understand why we haven't found that information. The papers have to be here somewhere."

Jerome put his feet on the floor and shook his head. "Dave, man, I'm telling you, they aren't here. And before you ask me again, they're not at her house either."

"Then you'd better step up your game and find them. Your life depends on it," David threatened.

Jerome stood to his lean six-foot height and walked around the desk. The lethal look in his dark, intimidating eyes sent David a few steps back. "Oh, so now you're threatening me?" he growled.

David raised his hands to stop Jerome's approach. "Wait. Months ago, I hired you to do a job. Not only did you botch it up, but you made things much worse by almost killing her with that stupid car accident. You were supposed to find out if she was on to what I've been doing, not put her in the hospital.

Jerome shrugged. "Yeah, I kinda messed that up."

"*Then*, after realizing my notes were missing and that I was pretty sure Dallas had them, you were supposed to help me get them back."

"And I've tried. I hooked up with her sister thinking I could get close to Dallas, but that didn't work out. Not only is the woman you have working for you beautiful, she's no dummy. If she has those papers, then she has them very well hidden."

"Or she's given them to someone," David mumbled, running his hand through his hair. The SEC had contacted the firm, requesting a meeting with the partners in two days. Granted, they might not be on to him, but just in case, he didn't want any loose ends. Besides that, the cops had showed up today asking questions. Good thing he could talk his way out of anything. By the time they left, he had them thinking that Dallas was the one not wrapped too tight.

He turned and walked toward the door. With his hand on the doorknob, he glanced back and scanned the room before letting his gaze fall on Jerome. "Come on, let's go. One way or another, she'll hand the information over."

****

Dallas sat in the back seat of the luxury vehicle, staring out the side window. Her world had changed so much in the past couple of months. Despite the car accident and the threats against her life, something good had come out of it. Tyler. She couldn't have planned a more timely reunion even if she'd tried. If anyone had told her that she and Tyler would be back together; that she'd be considering leaving her firm; or that she would ever contemplate marriage again, she would've told them they were crazy. Yet, all of those things were rattling around in her mind.

The thought of having a life with Tyler almost brought her to tears. It was a miracle that he was willing to give them another chance. She ran a hand through her hair thinking about how she had ruined things between them more than once. No way would she mess it up again.

Things were still a little tense between them thanks to the turmoil in her life. She had a feeling that when they put a stop to David's plans, things would miraculously go back to normal. If Tyler and Quinn's theory was right, David was the mastermind behind all her misery. All she needed was proof. It was still hard for her to believe that he had anything to do with the car accident and the threats. And what role did Jerome play in it all, assuming he was involved? Surely they weren't trying to harm her because of the documents. Dallas shuddered at the thought.

She dug through her purse for her new cell phone. A quick glance at her Blackberry revealed she had a text from Tyler. His meeting was taking longer than expected. She also had several emails, two from new clients who had signed on a couple of days ago. Neither she nor Bianca had time to put their information into the database yesterday, which meant she needed to stop by the firm to pick up their files.

"Hank, do you mind swinging by my office before taking us back to the penthouse?" Dallas asked.

"Aw, come on, Dallas. Don't you ever get sick of working? This was supposed to be a quick trip," Harmony said from the front seat.

"Hey, nobody told you to come along. So wherever we go, you go. But don't worry I'm only going to run in and run out."

"Yeah, right."

"Do you mind, Hank?" Dallas ignored whatever else Harmony mumbled under her breath.

"No problem." He made a u-turn and headed in the opposite direction.

****

I need a vacation, Tyler thought as he sat at the table with Quinn and three other men discussing a possible joint venture. Quinn had already told him he wasn't interested in joining forces with another group unless they were forced too, and right now their company was solid. But Tyler wanted to at least hear them out. Unfortunately, he hadn't heard much since his mind kept straying to Dallas.

She'd sent a text message saying Hank was taking her by the house to pick up some things. Tyler was glad she hadn't insisted on going back to the house to stay, otherwise, he'd have to move in too. No way would he let her stay there alone, at least not until they caught whoever was behind the threats and the break-in. And as far as he was concerned, her house was too small for them to live in for any long period of time, comfortably.

Tonight it took everything he had to leave her at the penthouse. Though he had complete confidence in Hank's skills as a bodyguard, Tyler had been on edge ever since David confronted her. And the meeting he'd had with Mark hadn't helped. The cops said they'd check into it, but Tyler knew how that was going to go. They'd ask David the right questions, he'd give the right answers, they'd leave, and then David would turn up the heat on Dallas.

Maybe I can get Dallas to go away with me for a few days. They could use a few days of R & R, but knowing her, she'd probably look at the idea as running or hiding from her problems. No, they needed to find whoever was behind all of this and end it.

"So what do you think, Tyler?" the guy in the pinstripe suit sitting across from him asked.

Totally caught off guard, Tyler said the first thing that came to mind. "Hollister and Associates prides itself on developing premier communities and your ideas sound like they would fit our mission. Unfortunately, we're not looking to move in the direction you're proposing at this time. I think Quinn would agree with me that we appreciate you giving us the opportunity to join forces, but right now, we'll have to pass."

A quick glance at Quinn confirmed that he had answered appropriately. For the rest of the dinner meeting, Tyler made sure he stayed focus on what was being said. He didn't want to be caught off guard again.

****

David paced the length of his office. He needed to come up with a plan to get Dallas alone. Lately, she'd been seen with that boyfriend of hers and it was hard to get to her. He thought the scare he'd given her the other day would do the trick, but it didn't work. She still hadn't handed over the information. Instead, she'd been working from home. He'd give her one more chance to come clean, after that he'd have to show her how serious he really was.

Tapping his pen against the desk he racked his brain trying to come up with a way to force her hand. One thing he knew about Dallas was that she was a sucker for new clients. He could always tell her that there was a potential client who he wanted her to meet.

A sly smile crept across his face. He'd set up a meeting, and once she arrived in the office, he would tell her they cancelled. *On second thought, maybe the meeting should be someplace else.* That way he could take her somewhere and make her talk. Then once she spilt her guts, he'd make her disappear. He laughed out loud and rubbed his hands together triumphantly.

"I take it you have a plan," Jerome said from across the room. He placed the newspaper he'd been reading on the table and stood.

David looked at Jerome. He had forgotten he was still there. Now, what should he do with him? So far Jerome had been more of a hindrance than an asset. He had botched every job that he'd given him and now that the SEC was on the scene, David stood the chance of losing everything. He couldn't afford for Jerome to be the cause of his downfall, although, he might come in handy when it came to getting rid of Dallas's body.

"Actually, I do. Right now I need to work out the details, but I do have a plan. Once I put a few things in place, I'll call you. Until then, I need you to lie low."

Jerome nodded. "Alright. Call me when you're ready for my talents." He turned to leave, but snapped his finger and stopped. He glanced around the office as if looking for something.

"What?"

"I thought I brought my gloves in here." After back tracking to the sofa and moving the newspaper that rested on the table around, he shrugged. "Well, maybe I didn't."

David felt his temperature rise. Hiring Jerome was turning out to be his biggest mistake. "Did you leave them in Dallas's office?"

"That's possible. I'll check on my way out. But first I gotta take a whiz."

David stood. "Better yet, I'll check her office and you go and … handle your business. I'll meet you by the elevators."

****

"I promise it'll only take me a couple of minutes to grab a few files, especially since Harmony decided to stay in the car. I definitely don't want to hear her mouth," Dallas said to Hank when they exited the elevator on the floor that housed her firm's offices.

"No problem. Take your time. While you're doing that, I'll run to the men's room."

"Okay. It's that way." She moved to the right of the elevators and stopped at the end of the short hallway. "Go to the end of this hall and turn left. Once you make that left, it'll be the third door on the right."

172

"Got it, but let's go check out your office before I leave." They went to her office and Dallas unlocked the door. Hank walked in first and looked around before ushering her in. "Make sure you lock the door when I leave."

"Okay." With all that had been going on, he didn't have to tell her twice. She did as instructed, no longer taking any unnecessary risks.

She shuffled to her desk and grabbed the mail out of the inbox before sitting down. "Junk, junk, and more junk." She tossed most of it in the trash. The rest she'd take with her. *Shoot, I should've brought my handbag upstairs so I could put everything in it.*

She grabbed her keys from the top of the desk to unlock her file drawer. "Now, that's strange?" Rarely did she leave the office without locking her desk drawers, but then she remembered. She'd been in such a hurry to leave the day David showed up that it was possible she had forgotten.

She pulled out the files she needed, locked the cabinet and sat back in her chair. The last time she was there, David had come in demanding his papers. *I'll never let him intimidate me like that again.*

She planned to help the SEC anyway she could. Tyler had already given copies of the documents to his contact person. Hopefully it wouldn't take them long to catch David. She wasn't working herself to death so that he could do whatever the hell he wanted with their client's money. There was too much to lose if the firm collapsed.

Where is Hank? She peeked at her watch. *And they say women take forever in the bathroom.* She'd give him a couple of more minutes before she went in search of him.

Glancing around her office for the first time since arriving, she noticed some things out of place. An empty water bottle lay on the floor near a conference table chair that was pushed up to the file cabinet. Maybe Bianca had been working in here today. Dallas quickly shot down that idea. The nightly cleaning service was excellent. And they should've made their rounds by now. No way would Sally, the one who usually cleaned her office, leave an empty bottle on the floor and a chair out of place.

Dallas's gaze moved to the sitting area. She saw leather driving gloves resting on the coffee table. *Someone's been in here.* She pushed back from the desk prepared to stand when she heard someone at the door. *Finally.*

Glad that Hank had returned, Dallas quickly grabbed her mail, files and walked around the desk, but stopped when the door flew open.

Her eyes grew large when David walked in. She wasn't sure who was more surprised, him or her. But he recovered first.

"Well, well, well." He walked farther into her office, with a smug grin on his face. "So, what brings you here this time of night?"

Initially taking a few steps back, Dallas stopped herself. The last thing she wanted to do was get trapped behind her desk again. With her knees shaking so bad, she didn't know if she'd be able to get to the door without collapsing. *Okay, be cool, keep it light.*

"Hey David, I just stopped by to pick up a few things. What are you doing here?"

He put his keys in his pocket and moved toward her. "You and I have some unfinished business to take care of."

Chapter Nineteen

Dark clouds had settled over the city, releasing a light drizzling rain when Tyler and Quinn stepped outside the restaurant. Dinner had been good, their host kind, yet, Tyler was ready to go home. Funny how his penthouse felt more like home now that Dallas was there.

"That was a nice save during dinner," Quinn said after they'd climbed into Tyler's truck and pointed the vehicle in the direction of the highway. "I wondered if I was the only one who had noticed you daydreaming most of the evening, but when Mr. Pinstripe Suit asked you what you thought about their plans, I almost burst out laughing."

Tyler smiled, shaking his head. "If I hadn't sat in on so many meetings like that one, I definitely wouldn't have been prepared. I knew I had to come correct so that I could wipe that smug look off his face. He acted like he'd caught me doing something inappropriately."

"Man, I'd say ignoring them during their presentation was inappropriate. They invite us to a five-star restaurant, pour their hearts out about their project, and you totally disregard everything they shared."

"It wasn't that bad." Tyler signaled as he merged onto the expressway. "I heard most of what they said, and I thought they had some good ideas. But you were right. With all that we have on our plate, we don't need to collaborate with another group right now. It's been bad enough trying to work with On Point Development Company in North Carolina. It'll be awhile before we join forces with another company."

"I agree. See, if you would've listened to me in the first place, we could've saved ourselves a forty-five minute drive to Schaumburg and two hours of semi-boring conversation."

Tyler agreed. He would've definitely preferred hanging out with Dallas tonight. He was ready for them to get on with their lives and put the past couple of months behind them.

He pulled out his cell phone and speed dialed her. He and Quinn were about thirty minutes from Chicago, but he couldn't wait to hear her voice. Her phone rang three times before it was picked up.

"Hello."

Tyler frowned. "Harmony?"

"Hey, Tyler."

"Why are you answering Dallas's phone? Where is she?"

"Oh, don't get me started about that girlfriend of yours. She's had me sitting in this car for at least fifteen minutes."

"Why? Where are you? I thought you guys would've been back at the penthouse by now."

"We would've if she didn't have to stop at her stupid job. I'm telling you, Tyler, I think she's possessed. I bet she puts in more hours…"

Unease crept through Tyler's body as Harmony rattled on. "Harmony," he said, but she kept talking. "Harmony!"

"What?"

"Please tell me she didn't go upstairs by herself."

"No. Hank's with her."

Well, at least she's not alone. Hank served in the military with Quinn, and now did personal security detail on occasion. That made Tyler feel a little better, but he still didn't like that she was at her office. He glanced at the clock. Eight-ten. Way too late for anyone to be there, and hopefully that included David. But there was always a chance.

"Did she say why she needed to stop there?"

"Something about a file for a new client."

"How long has she been gone?"

"Almost twenty minutes now and I'm starting to get pissed. I'm giving her a little more time, and then I'm going to hotwire this car and leave her tail here."

Tyler wasn't sure what Harmony's carjacking skills were, but he wasn't going to assume she wouldn't follow through on the threat.

"Okay, before you do that, give it five more minutes. If she's not back by then, call me." He disconnected and immediately dialed Dallas's office number. It rang four times before the voicemail picked up. He didn't bother to leave a message.

"So what's going on?" Quinn asked.

"I'm not totally sure, but Dallas is at her office. Harmony stayed in the car, but says Hank and Dallas left about twenty minutes ago."

"Well, you know Dallas. She probably started doing some work and lost track of time."

"Then she should've answered her office phone. They have caller ID and she would've saw that it was me calling. Nah, I think something's wrong."

"I'll call and see if I can catch up with Hank."

When Quinn didn't get a hold of Hank, Tyler said, "Reach under your seat for me."

Quinn bent down and pulled out a small case. "What do you plan to do with this?" He lifted the handgun out of the case, checking it for bullets.

Tyler took his eyes off the road briefly and glanced at his friend. "Hopefully nothing, but I've been carrying it around for the past few weeks, just in case."

"At least you knew enough to keep it in the case unloaded."

"Well, if I don't hear from Dallas in the next couple of minutes, I'm going to need you to load it for me. What about you, are you packing?"

"Yeah," he said drawing out the word. "But if I'm caught with a gun, I can get around a - carrying a concealed weapon charge. But you on the other hand, can't."

"I'll take my chances." He glanced at the clock and stepped on the gas. Harmony still hadn't call, so he called her again.

"Hey." She answered on the first ring.

"I take it she hasn't returned."

"Nope, and I'm about ready to cut out."

"Okay, but I need you to do something first. Go to her office."

"Tyler." She grumbled.

"Harmony, Quinn and I are on our way there, but it'll probably be another twenty or twenty-five minutes before we arrive."

"Why are you coming here?"

"Because I want to make sure everything is okay. Dallas is not answering her office phone and Quinn can't reach Hank. It might be nothing, but we need you to go up there and check on things. Oh, and when you leave the car, take Dallas's cell phone with you."

"Let me talk to her," Quinn said reaching for the telephone.

Tyler handed it to him and Quinn gave Harmony further instructions. He told her to put the phone on vibrate and to listen for anything unusual before going into Dallas's office. "If anything is out of the norm, or if something doesn't seem quite right, get the hell out of there and call the police. Then call us," Quinn told her.

Tyler had a death grip on the steering wheel as he plowed down I-94 toward Chicago. He had a bad feeling - something was definitely wrong.

****

The telephone rang several times, but Dallas didn't dare make a move toward it. She hadn't had a chance to gauge David's temperament this evening, and didn't want to do anything to set him off. As long as she didn't let him see how nervous she was, maybe she could get some answers out of him.

"So what unfinished business do we have to discuss?" she asked. She sat the files and the pieces of mail that were in her hand down, and leaned heavily against the desk. Suddenly her idea to leave her crutch in the car didn't seem like such a good idea. So much for running in and out. The thought made her think of Harmony. That was probably her calling.

"This is your last chance to hand over those papers, Dallas. I've been very patient with you." He paced the length of the office, his head down and arms linked behind his back as if he were deep in thought.

She only had one shot at getting him to fess up about what he was involved in, but didn't quite know how to broach the subject. All she knew was that she was so sick of hearing about those papers and was ready to put an end to whatever he was involved in.

"So where are they? I'm not asking you again."

His tone was no nonsense, and she had no doubt he was serious. But she had to know whether or not he was really behind a Ponzi scheme, and why. "David, I—"

"Cut the crap, Dallas. Hand them over."

"*Fine.* I've had enough. You can have your damn papers," she said with more bravado than she felt. She moved behind her desk and opened her middle draw. After a few minutes of searching, she yanked out the folder and pulled out the stack of papers. She stood and shuffled back around to the front of the desk, her leg throbbing with every move.

I hope I'm doing the right thing. Since the SEC had copies, what harm would it do to give David his originals back? "Before I give you these, I want to know why they're so important to you."

A wicked snarl covered his chubby face. He crossed his arms. "I have reason to believe you've already figured that out. But since you want to play dumb, I'll tell you what they are. They are a list of investments made for my own special project."

Ugh, I can't stand his pompous ass. "Oh, so is that what they call it now? A special project? And all this time I thought they referred to it as securities fraud or better yet, a Ponzi scheme." She slammed the papers down on the desk in frustration, but kept a firm grip on them.

When the smirk on his face quickly turned to anger, Dallas braced herself as he moved closer. Stopping inches from her, he said, "You're too damn smart for your own good, which is probably why I never liked you."

"Why, David? Why would you risk everything like this? Why take people's hard earned money to use for your own gain when you probably have more money than you know what to do with?"

His eyes narrowed. "What are you doing, recording this conversation or something? Why all the questions?"

"Because I want to know how can someone, who is financially secure, steal from people? You probably have plenty of money. Why do this?"

"Dallas, Dallas, Dallas. Don't you know you can never have too much money?" He leaned against the back of a chair. "If people are stupid enough to give me money for my special project, then they deserve to lose it. Besides, some of them made a nice little chunk of change, and the others … well, they'll soon find out that the investments just didn't work out."

"Is William involved in this nonsense?" She hoped not. William was like a father to her, and she couldn't imagine him stealing money from people. And no way would he know about this and not do anything.

"Of course not. His holier than though attitude would never allow him to take any risks like this and live on the wild side."

"So where do I come in at? Why did you run me down with a car? And what was the point of the telephone threats and ransacking my home?" She wasn't sure if he was behind those things, but she decided to test Tyler's theory.

He laughed and shook his head, moving away from her to stand near the bank of windows. "For awhile I didn't know what you knew or if you were going to cause trouble for me. But when my notes turned up missing, I knew that if you didn't know anything before, you'd probably figure it out. And just for the record, I didn't do those things you're accusing me of. I might have an idea of who did, but it wasn't me."

Dallas leaned against the edge of the desk for support. "You know, David. I'm a little surprised you're admitting to any of this. What gives?"

He turned toward her and chuckled. "I can say whatever the hell I want to now. I told you that this would be your last chance to come clean. I just have to decide how I want to handle things from here on out."

He walked up to her and snatched the papers from her hand before she could react, but at this point she didn't care. As he examined them, she glanced at the door wondering what was taking Hank so long to return.

"We got a problem." Jerome stormed in, but froze upon seeing Dallas standing near David.

Jerome? What's he doing here? Fear gripped her as realization dawned on her. *He and David must be working together.*

She hadn't seen Jerome since the time he and Harmony stopped by Tyler's house. She hated the way he had looked at her back then, and she definitely didn't like the way his dark, lethal eyes bore into her now. Her stomach clenched and panic gnawed away at her confidence at the thought of being in the office with the two of them.

"Now, what's the problem?" David turned impatiently.

Without taking his eyes off of Dallas Jerome said, "I had to take care of a little situation in the men's room. But it looks like you're having more fun in here."

"What situation?"

"The bodyguard."

"What in the hell are you talking about?"

He finally looked at David. "Didn't I tell you? She has a bodyguard. I guess my threats freaked her and the boyfriend out so much that they had to get her some protection."

"What did you do to him?" Her voice quivered despite her efforts to put on a brave front. Jerome crept closer to her, and she inched her way back until the back of her thighs bumped into the arm of the sofa.

"Ah, he'll be alright in a couple of hours," he said touching her cheek. She flinched and knocked his hand away, but he grabbed her. His hand was like a vice-grip around her wrist as she struggled to pull away. "You're even more beautiful up close." He held both her arms and pulled her toward him, slamming her body against his rock hard chest. When he lowered his revolting mouth to hers she scratched his face.

"Why you little bi—"

"Knock it off and tell me what you've done. Where is this bodyguard now?" David yelled.

Jerome increased his hold on her and Dallas didn't know what he'd do next. Instead of retaliating, he released her and caused her to stumble back.

He turned to David. "I left him in the bathroom with a nice gash on the back of his head. Where do you want him?"

David looked down at the papers in his hand and then back at Jerome. "Since I have what I want. You can do whatever the hell you want with him as long as you get them both out of here … now."

Dallas was going to be sick. It was all starting to come together. Jerome's role in all of this was to do David's dirty work.

"What are you saying?" She croaked and watched David exit the office without responding, leaving her with Jerome.

"That means I can finally have my way with you. I've wanted to tap that ass since the moment I laid eyes on you in Milwaukee." His hands snaked around her waist and pulled her close to him.

"Get your hands off of me!" she seethed. Her arms thrashed against him, pounding his chest, his shoulders, and she even managed to whack him one good time across the face. With that, he backed up, but not before she saw the raw fury in his eyes. "Please … just let me go. I promise I won't say anything."

With the speed of lightning, the back of his hand came up and across her face with such force she fell back onto the sofa. He pounced on her, temporarily knocking the wind out of her, but she kept fighting. She cried out when he ripped her shirt open and kept swinging at him in an effort to get away, but he was too strong.

"Get off of me!" They fell to the floor with him on top of her, a searing pain charged up her back. Yet, she continued to kick and scream to no avail. She couldn't move him.

"So you want to play rough huh? Baby, I like it rough," he said and brought his mouth down over hers.

She sputtered and spat, moving her head side to side to keep his lips from hers, as his large, callused hands explored under her shirt. Suddenly, through her tears, she saw Harmony ease up behind him with a lamp held over her head. Jerome must have seen something in Dallas's eyes because he turned at the moment the lamp came down. He blocked the blow and pushed Harmony into a wall, knocking her out cold.

"Harmony!" Dallas kicked him in the groin and tried to crawl away, but all it did was make him angrier. She cried out when he grabbed her bad leg and pulled her back, ripping her skirt in the process.

"Help me!" she screamed. "Please, somebody help me!"

"Shut up! Or so help me, I'll give you something to really scream about," Jerome said and slapped her.

In the next second he was jerked off of her. Dizzy, Dallas attempted to scramble away, but stopped when she heard Tyler's voice.

"I am going to kill you!" he said in a low deadly tone, his hands wound tight around Jerome's neck. She hadn't heard Tyler come in and cried harder at the sight of him. Somehow he had found her.

He threw Jerome down, slamming his face against the carpeted floor continuously, while maintaining a relentless hold around his neck. Jerome clawed at Tyler's hands in an effort to get free, but Tyler wouldn't let up. It wasn't until Jerome's movements ceased that Tyler went for the gun he had tucked in the back of his waistband.

In a flash of an eye, Jerome heaved Tyler off of him, causing Tyler's gun to fly across the room. Tyler crashed hard into the corner of her desk.

Dallas screamed and crawled toward his gun, but Jerome was faster. He kicked it away and pulled his own gun from under his pant leg. She froze. A cold chill crept up her spine when he pointed the gun at her.

"This has been fun and all," Jerome said, his breathing labored as he wiped his bleeding nose with the back of his free hand. "But it ends here." He turned the gun on Tyler. "Which one of you wants to die first?"

*****

Still somewhat dazed from hitting his head against the edge of the desk, Tyler struggled to bring Jerome into focus through half opened lids. He had every intention of killing him when he walked in and saw him on top of Dallas.

When he and Quinn arrived, the first person they saw when they exited the elevator was Hank stumbling down the hall holding the back of his head. Quinn ran to him while Tyler went in search of Dallas. The fine hairs on the back of his neck rose as he walked up to Dallas's office door.

Dallas's tortured cry filtered through the large space as she begged for help. Tyler's heart lodged in his throat when he saw what was going on and he lost it.

"Please," Dallas sobbed, bringing Tyler back to the present. "Please don't shoot him. David already has the papers, and I'll do anything you want. Just don't hurt him."

Seething anger, fueled by an adrenaline rush rippled through Tyler's body. He wanted Jerome to die for putting her through all of this.

"Oh, that's very touching." Jerome mocked Dallas. "I'm thinking that if I go ahead and kill your boyfriend, then I can have my way with you without any interruptions. Or better yet, maybe I'll tie him up, and make him watch while I familiarize myself with your juicy body. First I'll finish what I started and rip off the rest of your clothes, and then I'll let my tongue explore your baby soft skin. And then, when I have you screaming my name and begging for more, I'm going to fu...."

"Grrr," Tyler growled and plowed into Jerome. His heart pounding, his head throbbing, he'd die before he allowed Jerome to put his hands on Dallas again.

They slammed hard into the wall then tumbled to the floor wrestling for the gun. Tyler punched him in the face then straddled him, hammering Jerome's gun carrying hand against the floor.

Jerome fought back, a relentless hold on his gun while he struggled beneath Tyler, both unwilling to give up. But Tyler's blood ran cold when, out of the corner of his eye, he saw Dallas go for his gun. "No!" he yelled when Jerome twisted his body and pointed his own gun at her.

The gun went off with a jolt, and Tyler tackled him again, not having a chance to see if Dallas was alright. He and Jerome, both their hands on the gun, rolled back and forth on the floor. Jerome shoved him against the wall, sending a sharp pain up his shoulder and to his neck, but Tyler wouldn't let go, he couldn't. He had to protect Dallas.

Suddenly, a shot went off and Tyler jerked back. His head connected with something sharp and intense heat permeated through his shoulder and across his back. Dallas screams could be heard in the background, but he couldn't move. Seconds later there was another shot and everything went black.

Chapter Twenty

Dallas sat in a chair next to Tyler's hospital bed, her head rested on the mattress as she caressed his hand. The last few hours had been a nightmare that she was glad they'd survived.

Tyler had saved her life. Had he not reacted as quick as he had she could've been the one lying in the morgue. She had watched in horror, as he and Jerome wrestled for control of Jerome's gun. It wasn't until she saw an opportunity to grab Tyler's gun, a few feet away that she found the courage to move. But moments before she reached the gun Tyler screamed "no" and she froze. His heart wrenching, agony filled command immobilized her with fear but saved her life. Jerome's gun had gone off and missed her by inches.

Jerome had quickly gotten the upper hand. He knocked Tyler into the wall, rolled on top of him, and then Dallas's heart stopped. The gun was pointed at Tyler's chest. A second later the gun fired. She screamed and on instinct dived for Tyler's gun, but never had a chance to use it. Everything happened so fast. When she looked up, Quinn had appeared out of nowhere and shot Jerome without batting an eye. That one shot sent Jerome straight to hell.

"How are you holding up?" Quinn asked, interrupting her thoughts as he and Harmony walked into the room.

"I'm doing alright," she stood and hugged Harmony. She hadn't seen her since they'd arrived at the hospital. The doctor had insisted on running some tests on her because of the blow to the head. "And are you okay?"

"I'm fine. You know how hard my head is. It's going to take a lot more than that to do any major damage." Dallas smiled and hugged her again.

"Were you able to reach Tyler's parents?" Dallas asked Quinn and reclaimed her seat next to Tyler.

He shook his head. "Nah, but I caught up with Skylar and she said she'll find them and they'll head down here. And before you ask, Hank is fine." Though Jerome had caught him off guard - attacking him from behind, Hank wasn't out long. By the time Quinn found him, he'd had David restrained in his office, and was on his way to Dallas's office.

Massaging Tyler's hand, she said to Quinn, "Thank you for what you did for Tyler tonight."

"Don't worry about it. I'd do anything for him. He's like a brother to me. Anyway," he shrugged, "I have no doubt you would've blown Jerome away had I not stepped in. Your training showed in how you held the gun. Considering the situation, you looked very much in control."

Dallas hadn't felt in control. She had never been so afraid in her life, but like Quinn, she too would've given up her life to save Tyler. *Even if it meant killing Jerome with my bare hands.*

****

Tyler opened his eyes slowly. He knew by the tubes attached to his hand and the beeping sounds coming from the machines that he was hooked up to, that he was in the hospital. He drew in a painful breath as he remembered what had landed him there.

In the next moment his heart rate increased and his eyes grew large with fear when he remembered Jerome's gun going off. Dallas. He tried to sit up, but was halted when a sharp pain in his shoulder rooted him in place. It was also at that moment he saw Dallas sitting next to him, her head resting on the bed and her hand covering his. He was surprised he hadn't noticed her the moment he'd awaken.

He must've made a sound because her head jerked up, and red rimmed eyes stared into his face.

Fully aware she jumped out of her seat. "You're awake. Oh, my God, you're awake! It's been hours. I thought you weren't ever going to wake up." She cried, tears streaming down her face. They fell faster than she could wipe them away.

"Shh, baby, don't cry," he whispered, his throat dry and voice raspy.

"I can't help it. I thought I had lost you."

Tyler held her hand. "You can't get rid of me that easy. I just got you back." She tried to laugh but it sounded more like a wounded cry.

"They said that you're going to be okay."

"Good to hear." He stared at her for a moment before saying, "What about you? Are you okay?"

She nodded.

"Baby, I don't think I've ever been that scared in my life. When Jerome aimed that gun at you, I thought … I never want to experience anything like that again," Tyler said, trying to fight the emotions welling up in his chest.

She swallowed. "Me either. I don't think I could've survived if…"

"Don't." He cupped her cheek and wiped her tears despite the pain roaring through his body. "We're here. We're safe."

They stared at one another until Dallas said, "I so want to hug you, but you're all bandaged up. Jerome shot you and the bullet just missed your heart and lung. It … exited through your back." Her sobs grew more intense with every word.

"It's okay."

"No, it's my fault. If I hadn't have gone to the office."

"Stop. Baby, it's not your fault. Come here." He held her hand, gently pulling her closer.

"I don't want to hurt you."

"Come on, it'll be worth it."

Quinn walked in shortly after Tyler gathered Dallas into his arms and his mouth covered hers.

"Damn, man. You're all beat up and still can't keep your hands off of her."

Dallas and Tyler pulled apart and laughed.

"I'll go and let the nurse know that you're awake," Dallas said, climbing off of the bed. "Quinn, please make sure he doesn't try to sneak out of here."

He saluted her and said, "Will do."

Moments later a nurse looking to be in her mid-fifties with salt and pepper colored hair and a friendly smile walked in with Dallas following close behind her.

"Welcome back Mr. Hollister. You had your wife pretty worried."

Tyler looked at his *wife* and lifted an eyebrow.

"What?" Dallas shrugged, amusement dancing around in her beautiful eyes.

Tyler laughed, but then sobered and mouthed, "I love you."

Two days later he was sitting up in bed watching a football game. He'd rather be at home, but he wasn't scheduled to be released until the next morning. He was just thankful to be alive. With all that had happened over the past few months, he decided that he wasn't letting another day go by without asking Dallas to marry him. He had almost lost her.

"What's up my brother?" Quinn asked. He walked in with a small paper bag under his jacket.

"Please tell me you snuck in some real food?"

"I snuck in some real food."

"And please tell me it's either a Chicago hot dog or pizza."

"It's either a Chicago hot dog or pizza." Quinn handed him the white bag.

Tyler snatched the bag and opened it. "Ah, man, you went to Hot Doug's. See this is why we're brothers. Good lookin' out."

"I'm glad you approve, but you have to eat fast. When it comes to your health, and following the hospital rules, that *wife* of yours doesn't play."

Tyler grinned. Dallas's take charge attitude was one of the many things he loved about her. Today was the first day she'd left his side. He had tried several times to get her to go back to the penthouse to get some rest, but she claimed she had to stay close to him. She insisted that there were too many cute nurses walking around. He knew she wasn't the jealous type, but he loved the attention.

He and Quinn ate and watched the game in silence, which was unusual. Tyler had a feeling something was bothering his friend when he had stopped by earlier, but he didn't say anything at the time. But during half-time, he had to ask.

"Is everything okay? You've seemed distracted from the moment you walked in."

Quinn walked over and stood in front of the window, his back toward Tyler. A few minutes past before he returned and reclaimed the chair near the bed.

"Something strange happened the night you were brought into emergency. And I can't shake it."

"Strange like what?"

"Do you remember me telling you about Alandra?"

Tyler remembered. She was the only woman to ever keep Quinn's attention for any long period of time. She died in Quinn's arms after being shot.

"Yeah, I remember. She was the one who worked for the CIA, right?" Quinn nodded. "What about her?"

He hesitated and sucked in a deep breath. "I think I saw her last night. In the ER working as a nurse."

Tyler stared at his friend. He was at a loss for words. It had taken Quinn years to get over her, and considering how he currently went through women, never settling down, Tyler wouldn't be surprised if he was still in love with Alandra.

Quinn slouched further down in his seat. "I know it sounds crazy, and I don't believe in ghosts, but I think it's her."

"Quinn."

"Granted this woman looked different, but despite the colored contacts, her hair being bone straight and dyed a reddish color, I would bet my life that it's her."

"Q, how could that be?"

His friend leaned forward and rubbed his hands down his face before standing. "I don't know. But don't worry, I'm not crazy. At least I don't think I am … it's just that there was something so familiar about this woman, and she seemed to have the same shocked reaction when she saw me." Shaking it off, he dug through his jacket pocket and handed Tyler the small Tiffany box. "Here."

Tyler wanted to hear more about this mysterious woman, but based on the way Quinn had shut down, the conversation was over.

"Thanks," Tyler said and grabbed the box.

"No problem. It was right where you said it would be." Quinn walked to the end of the bed and turned. "I can't believe you're going to finally take the plunge, but I'm happy for you. Dallas is a helluva woman."

Tyler nodded. "Thanks man. And thanks again for saving my life, and giving Dallas and I another chance."

"No sweat. Just don't screw it up. And this time, Ty, when you ask her to marry you, don't take no for an answer."

Chapter Twenty-One

Seven Months Later

"Are you sure you're ready to go back out there?"

"I think so," Dallas said, sitting on the side of the Jacuzzi tub in their master bedroom as Tyler wiped her forehead with a cold, wet towel.

"I don't know, baby. You don't look so good."

"Gee, thanks," she mumbled. "I want to know why they call it morning sickness when it's three in the afternoon."

"I'm not sure, but this is just the beginning, we still have eight months to go."

"Please don't remind me. I don't know how much more I can take. I'm so tired." She slumped against him. This seemed to be the norm for the past couple of weeks, and she was already tired of it.

Tyler tossed the towel on the vanity and scooped Dallas up into his arms. "I'm putting you to bed, Mrs. Hollister. I'm sure everyone will understand."

Dallas had temporarily forgotten they had a house full of people. They had invited everyone over to announce that they were pregnant, but she had spent most of the afternoon with her head over the toilet. Though she was thrilled, so far she had been sick from the moment her doctor told her the good news.

"Maybe I'll rest for a little while. But I want to spend some time with Simone before they fly out."

"Did I hear my name?" Simone asked, strolling into the room with seven-month-old Tim, Jr.

"I figured you'd be up here sooner or later. Why don't I take my nephew while you keep my beautiful wife company for awhile?"

"Sounds good to me." Once Tyler and the baby left the room, Simone sat on the edge of the bed. "So, how bad do you feel?"

"Like … like, I can't even find the words to describe how horrible I feel. One minute I'm suffering from hunger pains, then the next I'm gagging at every morsel of food Tyler puts in front of me. It's like a vicious cycle. Tell me how to make it go away," Dallas groaned.

Simone chuckled. "Girl, I only hope yours doesn't last as long as mine did. I was sick for thirteen weeks straight. Instead of gaining weight, I lost ten pounds. I'm not sure what happened, but eventually I was able to keep food down. So hang in there."

"I'm tryin'. If it weren't for Tyler being so sweet and attentive, I don't think I could do this."

"Yeah, I noticed him hovering around you for the past couple of hours. Tim was like that, and it nearly drove me crazy."

Dallas laughed but stopped when she felt like she had to make another trip to the bathroom. Curled up in a fetal position, she laid still hoping the feeling would pass.

"Ah, I hate seeing you like this," Simone said, rubbing Dallas's arm. "Can I get you anything? How about some water or juice? You want to make sure you don't get dehydrated."

"Okay."

"Be right back."

****

"I thought Mom, Dad and Skylar were supposed to be back in town first thing this morning," Tim said as he and Tyler wrestled with the large umbrella that they were attaching to one of the picnic tables. Though they had already set up ten tables, as more guests arrived, they added to that number.

"They were but when they arrived at the airport they were told their plane was going to be delayed,"

"Ah, man, I know Mom hates that, although I think they know about your baby surprise."

"Yeah, I figured as much. And I think we both know how they found out."

"Skylar," they said in unison and laughed.

Tyler stood back from the table and watched as a flurry of activity went on around them. With over ten acres of undeveloped land, there was still more than enough room outside for people to spread out and do whatever they wanted. Some guests sat out by the Olympic size swimming pool, while others danced on the makeshift dance floor near the DJ stand.

"I better check on the meat," Tyler said. He and Tim reached the deck within minutes of Harmony setting some covered platters near the grill before she reentered the house.

"So has Mom forgiven you for eloping, yet?" Tim asked, grabbing a beer out of the cooler near the patio door.

"I would hope so." Tyler raised the lid of his large Evedure grill, letting the sweet smell of barbecue fill the air. "It's been what, six months since we got married?" After the drama with David, he and Dallas had stolen away to Hawaii for some much needed rest and relaxation. To everyone's surprise, they returned as husband and wife.

"Yeah, but she was pretty disappointed. You were the last one. I think she had her heart set on a large wedding."

Tyler slid the steaks over and added some hamburgers and brats before closing the lid. "I guess, but that's not what my wife wanted." He loved saying wife. It seemed a long time coming, but was now a reality. "As long as I was marrying Dallas, I didn't care how we did it. I would've been perfectly fine going to the courthouse, which I did suggest."

"I feel you, man." Tim said and handed his brother a bottle of beer. "Weddings are definitely for the family. I would recommend to anyone, skip the big hoopla and put all your focus on the marriage, because that's where the real work is needed."

"I agree." Tyler tapped his bottle to his brother's in a toast before they both took a swig.

"So how's Chicago life?"

"It's cool. I've always loved the fast pace of Chicago. So I had no problem making that our main residence. The plan is to stay in the penthouse until the baby arrives. After that, we'll see."

"I'm still trippin' you're going to be a father. Especially considering how much of a player you were."

Tyler laughed. "Some days it trips me out too. But when the right woman comes along, you do things you thought you'd never do."

"I know that's right. What are you going to do about this Milwaukee house and all of the commuting back and forth?"

"Actually, I have a buyer for this place. We're supposed to finalize things next week. And as far as commuting, I drive up here about once a week, check on Mom, Dad and our properties and then head back home. Once the baby arrives though, I won't be making that many trips, especially since Dallas wants to open her own firm."

"Simone was telling me about that. All those years of trying to make partner, and then after making it, she's giving it up. I'm surprised."

"Yeah, she likes working with William, but now wants her own."

"What's up my brothas?" Quinn strolled up to them carrying a large grocery bag in one hand and a case of beer in the other. He placed the items down and greeted Tyler with a fist bump and Tim with a one arm hug. "Man, seems like I haven't seen you in like forever. How's it going?" he asked Tim.

"It's all good," Tim said before a frown covered his face. "But hold up. What about you?" He looked to each side of Quinn before he leaned back and stared at him. "I can't ever remember you showing up to anything we've had without a beautiful woman on your arm. What's up with that? Don't tell me you're losing your touch." Tim laughed and Tyler joined in when Quinn's brows furrowed and his lips smirked as if that was the most ridiculous thought in the world.

"Please. If anything, I have to beat them off. These women have been at me! Since I couldn't decide which one to bring, I figured I'd come by myself and just hang out."

They all laughed.

"Where are your women?"

"In the house. Is that the stuff Harmony asked you to pick up?" Tyler asked referring to the bag Quinn held.

"Yep. I'll take it to the kitchen. Who knew she could cook?" Quinn asked over his shoulder and made his way into the house.

Tim turned to Tyler. "So what's up with him?"

"What do you mean?"

"He looks tired, older."

Tyler sighed. "Yeah, he's got some things going on, but he'll be okay." At least Tyler hoped he would. Quinn hadn't been right since he ran into that emergency room nurse. He still believed the nurse was his beloved Alandra. He'd even gone back to the hospital to ask questions. He found out that the nurse's name was Velvet Agular, but she was always off duty whenever he'd visit.

****

Simone walked back into the master bedroom carrying two Popsicles and some bottled water. "Here, this might help."

Dallas sat up in bed. At least her headache had subsided, but she wished she could keep some food down. She was starving and hungrily grabbed for the Popsicle.

"Thanks. I can't believe I had forgotten about these."

"Well, I can't take credit for thinking of them. Tyler asked me to bring one up to you, and of course I had to grab one for myself." She laughed.

Dallas smiled at the memory of how the Popsicles came to be. "Once Tyler found out this was one of few things I could tolerate, he bought a few cases, *and* a freezer for the basement to hold them all."

Simone laughed. "I take it married life is going well."

Dallas exhaled a long sigh of contentment. She didn't know she could experience such happiness. A few days after her encounter with David and Jerome, Tyler had proposed. It took her the longest time to say "yes" because she couldn't stop crying. He was still in the hospital, but had enlisted the help of Quinn and Harmony to decorate the room, making it as romantic as a hospital room could be, music and all. He had even found a way to have food brought in. With several covered dishes on a white clothed table, she had no idea that when she removed the cover off the last dish, she'd find a light blue Tiffany box holding a five-carat marquise diamond ring. Once she did come to her senses, she insisted on them getting married right away. There was no argument from Tyler, by that next morning he had arranged for them to fly out the following weekend to the beautiful island of Hawaii.

"By the gleam in your eyes, I'd say things are going *very* well," Simone grinned.

Dallas blushed. "I'm sorry. I just never thought I'd ever be this happy. Simone, he's amazing. He's gentle, he cooks and cleans, he's attentive, and most importantly, I have no doubt he loves me. I've never felt this way before, especially not while I was with Mark."

"Speaking of Mark, what's up with him anyway?"

"Well, we're on speaking terms, and he and Tyler have called a truce," she smiled. "And most importantly, I don't blame him anymore for all my heartache. I've taken ownership of some things as well."

Simone leaned over and hugged her. "I am so happy for you. You've been through so much. It's about time some good has come your way." Simone reclaimed her seat.

Dallas placed her feet on the floor and reached for Simone's hands. "I can't imagine my life without you. Over the years we've been through some tripped out things, and our relationship has grown tremendously through everything. I love you so much."

"Aw, I love you too, sweetie. And you've been more than a friend to me. You're my sister, in more ways than one now." They shared a hug and held each other for a moment. Simone sat back in her seat and Dallas climbed back on the bed. "Oh, before I forget, Harmony said everything is under control down there so you don't have to hurry back."

"I'm glad. I was feeling a little guilty with her and Bianca doing everything."

"They're fine. And what are your thoughts about Harmony's new gig?"

"Shocked," Dallas chuckled. "What are the chances of her running into a modeling agent while filling out an application at Nordstrom? But seriously, I'm so happy for her. She has gotten so much work over the last few months and I think she's going to be okay living in New York."

"I think you're right, but speaking of shocked, I saw the article in the paper about David. I don't think 125 years in prison is enough for him. The thought of him taking millions of dollars from people breaks my heart."

"Girl, don't even get me started. It's hard enough as it is to encourage people to invest their hard earned cash and he goes and pulls some nonsense like that. Thank goodness William had contacted the SEC when he got suspicious that David was involved in something illegal."

"That surprised me, but it explained why the SEC started investigating the firm all of a sudden."

Dallas shook her head. "I'm glad this is all behind me. I get angry all over again when I think about the crap David put me through. For weeks I had nightmares about him and Jerome."

Simone frowned. "I didn't know that."

"I thought I told you. That was one of the reasons I started seeing a therapist. After about three months the dreams stopped, but I haven't stopped seeing the counselor yet. I still have a lot of baggage from my childhood to deal with."

Simone hugged her. "I'm so proud of you. You're finally taking care of yourself."

****

"I'm glad you're feeling better." Tyler kissed his wife's soft lips. They had closed the door to their last guest, and were now sitting in the family room.

"Yeah, me too. For a while there, I thought I would have to be holed up in our bedroom all day. But after the Popsicle I started feeling much better."

"Good. I would've hated for you to miss your own celebration."

"You mean *our* celebration." She touched her hand against his cheek, loving the smooth feel of his shaven skin.

"You're right, our celebration. We have a lot to celebrate, Mrs. Hollister. This past year has been wild. Sometimes I still can't believe you're back in my life and that we're married. I couldn't have planned this past year even if I tried."

"I know," Dallas sighed wistfully. "I love you so much."

Tyler gathered her in his arms and moved his mouth over hers. His lips sent shivers of desire flowing through her. "I love you too, and I plan to spend the rest of my life showing you." He stood and reached for her hand. "I'm thinking that since we're still newlyweds, we should probably go upstairs and do some newlywed stuff."

"Oh, really?" Dallas smiled at her handsome husband. "And what exactly do you have in mind?"

"Well, if you come with me, Mrs. Hollister, I'll show you." His eyebrows wiggled up and down suggestively.

Dallas laughed. "Lead the way, my love. Lead the way."

ABOUT THE AUTHOR

Sharon C. Cooper lives in Atlanta with her husband and enjoys reading, writing, and rainy days. She's a best-selling author who writes sweet and contemporary romance. Sharon is a Pro member of Romance Writers of America (RWA), a member of Georgia Romance Writers (GRW), and a member of the Page a Day Writers Group. To read more about Sharon, visit www.sharoncooper.net

Other Titles by Sharon C. Cooper:

Something New (A Sweet Romance - April 2012)
Best Woman for the Job (Short Story - Contemporary Romance - April 2012)
Blue Roses (Romantic Suspense - summer 2012)
Secret Rendezvous (Prequel to Rendezvous with Danger - fall 2012)
Rendezvous with Danger (Romantic Suspense – winter 2012)

Connect with Sharon Online:

Website: http://sharoncooper.net
Email: sharon@sharoncooper.net

Facebook: http://www.facebook.com/AuthorSharonCCooper21?ref=hl

Twitter: https://twitter.com/#!/Sharon_Cooper1

Subscribe to her blog: http://sharonccooper.wordpress.com/

Goodreads:
http://www.goodreads.com/author/show/5823574.Sharon_C_Cooper

If you enjoyed the story, please consider placing a review on Amazon.com or Barnesandnoble.com

Made in the USA
Middletown, DE
25 February 2020